The Heart of a Cowboy

Crossroads Creek Cowboys

Elsie Davis

Sweet Romance Publishing

Sweet Romance Publishing

Sweetromancepublishing.com

PO Box 778

Liberty, NC 27298

Proverbs 3: 5-6

Trust in the LORD with all your heart and lean not on your own understanding; in all your ways submit to him, and he will make your paths straight.

Chapter One

♥

"WHAT'S UP?" RUSTY ASKED, stepping inside the family's ranch home. His mother stood by the dining room table waiting for him. Pulling off his Stetson, he brushed the sweat from his forehead with his shirt sleeve, leaving a dirty-streaked patch. Then, after checking his boots for mud, Rusty moved farther inside and suddenly realized they weren't alone, the Christmas tree having blocked his view.

He took full stock of the people seated in the living room, all eyes trained on him. "You," he added, glaring at his older brother, "said Mother wanted to see me, not the whole family." He didn't appreciate the subterfuge any more than his family's overzealous care and concern for the past year and a half of his life.

His mother moved closer. "I do want to see you, but the others are a part of this meeting. It's past time for another discussion." She held herself stiff and upright, an imposing figure even at five and a half feet tall. But it was the firm tone of her voice that sent waves of warning down his back, putting him more on edge.

Rusty shook his head and huffed. When his family tag-teamed up on him, it never ended well. "I don't need this." Spinning around, he reached for the door, intent on making a hasty retreat.

"Stop right where you are, young man, and come have a seat," his mother ordered, effectively shackling him to where he stood.

If respect hadn't been ingrained in him since he was a child, he would have left anyway. But, instead, he moved back into the room and leaned against the oak table, refusing to sit.

"Sorry, Rusty." Clay had the good graces to look apologetic for his part in the deception.

"But if I had told you it was a family meeting, you wouldn't have shown up."

"Darn straight, I wouldn't have. Let's get this over with then, shall we? I finished mucking the stalls but still need to feed the horses, and they don't like to be kept waiting. Not to mention, I wouldn't want to be accused of slacking off or unable to handle even the simplest of chores. Oh, wait, I only get simple chores around here because my family treats me with kid gloves." The corner of his mouth curled up in distaste.

"Knock it off, Rusty," his sister stood and moved toward him. "This is exactly why the family feels the need for a meeting. Your attitude stinks. It's been a year since the operation, and yet you are still living in the past. For your sake and everyone around you, it's time things changed." As the middle child, but only girl, Rebecca had always been the bossy one in the family.

"Fine," he ground out. "Let's have it. I haven't let the chickens out of the pen like I did when I was twelve or stayed out past curfew like when I was sixteen. So, what am I in trouble for this time?" Rusty asked, unable to contain his sarcasm.

Clay stood, joining the others as they gathered around, closing in on him like they were rounding up a lost sheep...the family's black sheep, to be specific. "You're not in trouble. We just want to help you move forward. You're still brooding over something you can't change." His older brother had a way of calling him to task that sounded far too much like his father.

It wasn't a compliment.

His old man had died ten years ago, leaving a wake of deeply rooted anger. "Well, maybe, if you all stopped mollycoddling me, I wouldn't have this attitude," Rusty retorted.

"It's only right that as your family, we are concerned. Watching over you is done out of love. That's what you should focus on, not the limitations," his mother said, laying her hand on his arm with a surprisingly firm grip.

"And yet, that's exactly what you're doing. Focusing on my limitations." Rusty let out a deep breath, grabbing the back of the chair for support. He clenched the wood, his knuckles turning white as he tried to transfer his feelings onto the lifeless object. Anger at life. Anger at the situation. Anger at the senselessness of it all.

And guilt. Never forget the guilt.

What started out as a trip home, hoping to convince the local doctor to change the Cheyenne doctor's opinion, ended in Rusty moving home eighteen months ago. Referred to a cardiologist in Dallas, it was only after extensive testing he received the diagnosis that changed his life—forever.

Cardiomyopathy and a congenital heart defect.

And the news he would die without a heart transplant.

Gone were his rodeo days. And the heart transplant he received a year ago had saved his life. A new future was before him, but it was one he had yet to figure out, let alone live. Surely there were far better people who had deserved the donor heart, people who had more to give back to society than a washed-up rodeo cowboy.

"You're only twenty-eight. What is it you want to do with your new life? Not everyone gets a second chance the way you have," his sister said, zeroing in on the crux of the matter.

"If I knew, don't you think I'd be doing it?" he retorted. It's not like he hadn't asked himself the same question a hundred times since he woke up in the hospital knowing he had a new heart. The fear of his body rejecting the new organ, the rules, the medications...it was all there. That, and asking God, why him? Which was odd in itself considering he hadn't thought about his faith since he left home. But there was something about a near-death experience that had him, and it would seem, others, reaching out to the highest authority for answers.

Answers that didn't seem forthcoming.

"There might be some jobs in town looking to hire. Something you could handle...I mean...something not too strenuous," his mother corrected. "A new career. You know what I'm saying."

"Gee, maybe a washed-up bull-rider could wash dishes at the diner," he sneered. It wasn't fair to lash out at his family after everything they'd been through to support him. But they weren't making this adjustment any easier. Or maybe the truth more closely resembled the fact they were making his life too easy...and therefore, without meaning.

"Stop. This is what we're talking about," Rebecca chimed in, her arms folded across her chest, her frustration echoing his own.

They didn't understand. *Couldn't understand*. How did one pick up the pieces and move forward when you lost everything that defined who you were as a person? Gone were his bronc riding days. Gone were his roping days. Gone was the lifestyle he enjoyed because it gave him the satisfaction of knowing he was good at something. Something his father never thought him capable of, and the reason he left the ranch in the first place after his dad died.

It's not that he didn't want to figure out what came next in life; he did. But at every turn, his family reminded him of the doctor's orders not to overdo anything. Except by now, he could be doing more than the easy ranch jobs. His cardio rehab had gone well, but Clay wouldn't assign him the more strenuous tasks, taking them all on himself or doling them out to the ranch hands. Rusty was more like the gopher guy. The lowest hired hand on the ranch. "I've got to go feed the animals," he said, signaling the conversation was over. What else was there to say that hadn't been said already?

"Come to church with us, Rusty," his mother said, a hopeful expression on her face. "You used to like going to Sunday school. Maybe you could meet up with some old friends from high school, make some connections."

Rusty shook his head. "Sorry, Mother. Not my thing. Besides, I've made connections. Come Wednesday evening, there are loads of people who want to talk. It's the other six days of the week I avoid because I don't need people's pity." Six months ago, he started a program at the community center offering free food for dinner, like a soup kitchen, but different. More like an open-door dining service that welcomed everyone. The people in town rallied around the idea and it had become quite successful, but other than a few hours a week dedicated to bookwork, it occupied very little of his time. The idea wasn't even his to claim as it was more like a flash from his past.

"It's not the same thing and you know it. If you won't come with us, can you do me a favor? I need one of the kittens delivered to Laura Goodman in town. The kittens are old enough to go to new homes, and I'd like to find them all owners before Christmas. It's the one with the name "Faith" written on her collar. Laura is excited at having a new companion."

A horse or a dog was a companion, but a cat? *No way.* Margaret Mary Devoe was clearly a smooth operator and well versed in getting what she wanted. "Sure thing, Mother." He bit back the rest of his answer, figuring she would not appreciate more sarcasm about yet another easy job.

"Rusty, please come to church with us," his sister begged, trying to change his mind, something she used to be good at, but not anymore.

"I stopped going to church after I left home. Praying doesn't seem to make much difference most of the time." It hadn't made his father see him as a son to be proud of, and it certainly hadn't helped him out on the rodeo circuit. The rollercoaster ride on the road was never-ending with its peaks and valleys, and only a handful of cowboys made it big. Something that might have happened if his doctor hadn't pulled him from the circuit after his first mild heart attack and the discovery there was a hole in his heart.

Now he had a whole heart, but why did it feel so empty?

Chapter Two

♥

COURTNEY PUT THE VINTAGE Ford truck in reverse and backed out of the driveway. Loaded to the gill with everything she hadn't sent on ahead with the moving van, it reminded her of the Clampetts on the Beverly Hillbillies show. All she needed was a rocker strapped to the top and maybe a Christmas decoration or two.

Calling her mother with the itinerary was a priority, and Courtney pressed the speed dial on the Bluetooth screen. "Good morning," she said when her mother answered.

"Good morning, dear. Have you left yet?"

Courtney flipped the heat to high as the engine temperature gauge climbed, looking for added warmth. "Pulling out now. The snow has mostly melted off the roads from last night's snow storm. We only got two inches and they had the roads treated. Once I get out of Kansas and through Oklahoma, there shouldn't be any concerns about travel conditions. Based on the timing, we should pass through Dallas by lunch time and then be at your place by dinner." Of course, her mother would worry anyway until they arrived safely. It was a mother's prerogative, something Courtney did with Trevor as well. More so since Greg died. But then, her husband's death in a car accident while on a business trip changed a lot of things.

"Tell her about the mac and cheese, Mom," Trevor reminded her.

Courtney glanced at her eight-year-old son affectionately and nodded. He was growing up so fast and this past year had been rough, something no child should have to experience. And the reason she was more determined than ever to start over and build a new life for them. "And Trevor's requesting macaroni and cheese, of course."

His grin was all the answer she needed. There hadn't been many of those since his father died. Trevor's happiness was a priority and something Courtney could use a heaping dose of as well.

"Consider it done," her mother said. "I can't wait to see you both. There's so much we can do here together and just in time for the holidays. It'll be fun. Think of all the baking and crafting we can do. I'm looking forward to having my baby girl and my grandson home, even if the circumstances aren't good."

Total understatement. Her mother was one of those glass half full people, always trying to find the good in everything. Except Courtney was having a tough time figuring out how anything could be good about losing your husband after nine years of a happy marriage?

Courtney tried to squash the anguish bubbling up as she thought of Greg. They had been supremely happy together and blessed early on with Trevor. After that, life got busy. Unfortunately, there hadn't been time to add a little brother or sister to the family, something Courtney now deeply regretted.

"Sure thing, Mom." Moving in with her mother wasn't high on Courtney's list of things she wanted to do, but after selling the house and paying the bills, her account was depleted to the point of no return. *Broke being the operative word.*

Counting on the life insurance money had been a mistake. The company did everything it could to reject the claim, citing the need for an investigation. Greg's faith in God had been strong, and the love for his family undeniable. The very idea put forth by the insurance company that they needed to rule out suicide was deplorable. It was more a case of them grasping at straws to avoid paying.

"I'll keep you posted as we get closer. Love you," Courtney said, suddenly needing to hang up the phone. Taking a deep breath and exhaling slowly, she held the sadness threatening to engulf her at bay, not wanting to give in to her emotions in front of her son. Those were times best left as private moments.

"Okay, sweetheart. Give my love to Trevor."

"Will do." Courtney hung up the phone, gripping the worn leather steering wheel of the truck. Her husband's prized 1956 Ford pickup was the one thing she couldn't part with. Someday, it would be Trevor's. "Grandma says mac and cheese it is, and she sends her love, kiddo," Courtney said, reaching over to pat his leg.

"Good deal. How long are we stuck in the truck?" Trevor asked.

The eternal question asked by children worldwide when they started on a road trip and one they continued to ask until they arrived at their destination. It would be a long journey, but her goal was to take breaks along the way to stretch, hoping it would go better for her son. "The GPS shows Lafayette, Louisiana is a little over ten hours driving time from Wichita but then we have to account for stops. I figure Dallas will be a good place to find lunch and stretch our legs a bit. We'll be at your grandmother's for a late dinner, so not too bad." It was called leading by suggestion and her one hope at positivity.

"Easy for you to say, you're not the one sitting here with nothing to do. Long rides make me feel sick to my stomach."

So much for positivity. "I know. At least you don't have a time restriction on your video games. Maybe if you focus on that it will help." She shot him a grin and ran a hand through his hair affectionately, trying to sympathize with him.

Trevor went back to playing his video game, something that allowed Courtney to focus on her driving. It hadn't been her choice to sell her home and leave Wichita. Le Art Culinaire left her no choice when they gave her a temporary leave of absence from her position as an assistant chef. *Temporary* meaning 'you're fired.' It wasn't her fault she made mistakes because her head wasn't in the game. Okay, so maybe it was her fault...but she had good reason. Losing Greg had taken its toll, and she was having a difficult time adjusting.

Living with her mother wasn't a permanent solution, or at least Courtney hoped it wasn't.

When the insurance money came in, she'd have options currently unavailable.

Please, Lord, help the investigator understand the truth and be kind enough to see through this madness and release the funds. Prayer couldn't hurt, and it was her faith that had carried her forward as she dealt with the unexpected changes in her life. She would continue to trust in God, but it didn't keep her from questioning why Greg died in the first place.

Hours later, the sun was high in the sky and beating down on the dash. Courtney reached up to lower the visor, a white envelope falling into her lap. Clutching it in her hand, she remembered the contents and why she'd kept the letter.

A thank you from W.D.—her husband's heart recipient.

The agency had strict rules about the confidentiality of information. Their policy was to review any mail before sending it on to the recipient to maintain privacy. It was a slight connection with the past, one Courtney clung to, unable to throw the card away. Not a day went by that she didn't wonder how W.D. was faring. It was strange knowing someone in this country was alive with her husband's heart beating in their chest.

She started to push the envelope into the center console, stopping as the postmark caught her attention. *Crossroads Creek, Texas.* The place was a small town just north of Dallas. Courtney knew this because it was the same place where Greg was killed in the accident when he lost control of the vehicle. The car had careened over the side of the cliff at Farrier Overlook, rolling to the bottom.

Unfortunately, after he was airlifted to the hospital in Dallas, it was too late to save him. But Greg had been a firm advocate in the organ donor program, and he would be at peace knowing his heart had found a new home.

Lord, help me to understand.

Crossroads Creek. Fraught with grief, she hadn't made the connection between the postmark and Greg's accident. Suddenly, an idea hit her out of nowhere...or more than likely, perhaps God giving her a gentle nudge. Her pulse raced as she considered all aspects of what it would mean if she took a small detour.

Closure came in all sizes and shapes, and hers might very well be to visit the site where Greg lost his life. It was the most likely place to say goodbye to her husband, and Courtney wondered why she hadn't thought of it before. The town was only twenty minutes off the interstate. So if she didn't stay long, she'd be back on the road and headed for Dallas, maybe an hour behind her original plan.

"How about a side-trip, kiddo? There's a town near here I'd love to see, and I've heard so much about it. It will give us a good break to stretch our legs and gas up the truck, maybe even grab lunch depending on what we find." There was no way Courtney would tell her son it was where his father died or the real reason she wanted to go. Better to keep that information to herself and not push her son back into the cycle of sadness he dwelled in most of the time.

"Sounds good," Trevor said with a shrug. "As long as I don't lose service."

It was mind-boggling that her son understood the complexities of the internet and how it related to playtime on his tablet. And when a child was bored, it was at a parent's peril to come between a kid and the current video game they were engrossed in.

"Then it's settled." Courtney pulled over at the next rest area and reprogrammed her GPS for the added stop. They wouldn't stay long, maybe forty-five minutes tops, what with gassing up, a quick lunch, and an even quicker stop at Farrier Overlook. She pulled up her message app to send her mother a voice text update, preferring not to have to explain her decision, but letting her know she would be a little later than planned.

Courtney: We are planning an extra stop to stretch our legs and gas up. Should put us in Lafayette around eight instead.

Mom: Sounds good. Just be careful and keep me posted. Looking forward to your arrival. Safe travels.

Courtney got back on the interstate, and they rode in silence, the rule she'd implemented long ago in effect. They could talk, or Trevor could play games with his headset plugged in, but there were no gaming sounds in the truck to distract the driver. *Or drive her crazy.*

Hours passed, each mile marker taking her further away from her past life and toward an uncertain future. They'd crossed into Texas a while ago, the GPS showing only two miles until her exit.

"Take the next exit in 1.5 miles and then keep left at the fork," the English woman's voice ordered. Courtney followed the cues, trying to calm her nerves as trepidation settled in the pit of her stomach and started to grow. Was she doing the right thing? Hiding her emotions from her son had always been difficult at best. She gripped the steering wheel, her knuckles deathly white. A sign announced Crossroads

Creek was only two miles ahead. There was still time to turn and avoid the town altogether.

Courtney kept driving. She swallowed hard, tamping back the rush of emotions.

Smoke billowed from the hood of her truck.

Wait. What? She slowed down and pulled to the side of the road, anguish ripping through her. *How much more could one person handle?*

"What's going on, Mom? Why is the truck smoking?" Trevor asked the thousand-dollar question.

Or the hundred-dollar version, because no matter the value—it wouldn't be good. Courtney couldn't afford truck trouble right now. "I'm not sure." She glanced at the dash. "The gauge shows the engine is overheating. I can't imagine why. Your father kept this truck in mint condition."

"So what do we do?" her son asked.

She frowned, putting the truck in park, and turning off the engine. "I wish I knew. Hopefully, there's a garage in Crossroads Creek, and we can get a tow into town." More money she could ill afford. There was always her credit card, but after just paying it off, she was hesitant to charge anything. Especially without the means of repaying the money. "Sit tight while I make some calls and let me see what I can find out."

"Okay." Her son was more than satisfied with her answer and returned to playing his games.

Courtney climbed out of the truck and glanced around. There wasn't anything in sight other than fields and more fields. No houses. No barns. No people. Nothing. Boondocks was the word that came to mind. She tried to unlatch the hood, but the smoke was still pouring out. Burning her hand wasn't high on her priority list. Her one small salvation came from the realization it was steam, not smoke, and therefore no fire. She prayed the repair didn't require a new engine. But one thing was for sure, she wouldn't give up the truck. *Not for anything.*

She searched the internet for a garage in Crossroads Creek, only coming up with one. Prepared to call them, she paused as a truck pulled in behind hers. Her big-city fears kicked into high gear. She might be in the country, but it wasn't a place she was familiar with, and she had to think of Trevor. Keeping the phone handy, she walked toward the man headed her way.

Tall, good-looking, and decidedly a cowboy with his well-worn jeans, plaid shirt, Stetson, and dusty boots that had seen better days. She relaxed a little. Friendly was the word that came to mind when he smiled.

"Howdy, Ma'am. Having some trouble?" the man asked, glancing over at her truck and then back at her.

"Hi there. And yes, unfortunately the engine overheated. Smoke poured out from under the hood, but I'm pretty sure it was only steam and not fire." She wasn't an expert in engines, but common sense told her it was important information to give someone who knew their way around under the hood of a vehicle.

"Should have stuck with a Chevy," the man said, grinning.

Courtney bristled. "This Ford's good enough for me." Her chin rose a notch, although it's not like she knew the difference other than the name. It was Greg's and that was all that mattered.

"Let me take a look," the man said as he headed for the front of the truck and popped open the hood. Ten seconds later, he closed it. "Radiator is cracked. It spewed out all your fluid and caused the engine to overheat. You'll need a tow into town. Charlie's the only mechanic we've got, but he won't run the tow truck, seeing as it's Sunday. But you're in luck; I can tow you in. Name's Rusty Devoe," he said, reaching out to shake her hand.

"I don't know. I hate to put you to any trouble. Are you sure about the mechanic?" Courtney asked, trying to grasp the information and decide what to do.

"As sure as my name is Rusty." He winked. "Where were you headed?"

"My mom's place in Lafayette. My son and I are moving there." It's not like she needed to add the last part, her overloaded truck more than enough proof.

"I reckon you ought to give her a call. You won't be home for dinner," Rusty teased, his grin widening to the point it crinkled the corners of his eyes.

"What...oh, I hadn't thought of that." A truck repair and a hotel bill were more expenses she couldn't afford. "Yes, I'll call her. So I take it if your mechanic won't tow on a Sunday, there's no chance he'll work on the repair either?" she asked, knowing the answer before she asked.

Rusty chuckled. "Not a chance."

"Do you know where I can stay in town?" she asked.

"There's a nice bed and breakfast, but not much else. We're not exactly mainstream here," Rusty offered, stating the obvious.

"I see." A B&B sounded pricey, but it settled the issue of Rusty giving her a tow. *Free.* "I'd be forever grateful for your help getting the truck to town and me and my son to the inn." It's not like she had a choice but to trust the man, but then, there wasn't anything about him that made her worry she was making a mistake. Rather the opposite, she felt inexplicably drawn to his kindness, which was odd given her guarded nature.

"Good enough. Let me get the tow ropes." Rusty headed for his Chevy.

Courtney moved to the driver's side of her truck and pulled open the door. "Hey, kiddo. So the bad news is the radiator cracked. The good news is that Rusty," she said, pointing to the man, "is going to tow us to town and drop us off at a place where we can stay until the truck can be fixed tomorrow." So technically, none of it was good news, but some things you didn't share with your children.

Her son glanced at the man approaching, almost assessing him, but then shrugged. "Okay. Oh, wow. Look, Mom, he's got a cat, and it's loose. We've got to get it, so the cat doesn't go in the road."

Trevor bounded out of the vehicle. "Hey, Mister, your cat is out of the truck."

Rusty swung around and shook his head, dropping the tow ropes. "It's a kitten, and it's not mine. I'm just the delivery man. Guess I forgot to close the door." He moved quickly in the direction of the kitten, calling out to the little white furball hunkered down by the rear tire.

Trevor was the first one to catch up with the kitten. "Oh, she's so soft and pretty. I like her long fur and pink bow." He rubbed his face against the kitten's face. "She's purring."

Rusty reached for the kitten. "Thanks, kid. It will cause me a heap of trouble if I don't get Faith to Laura Goodman."

Trevor didn't budge, as though reluctant to give up his new friend. "That's a great name. How about I take care of her until you do? Trust me, I'm a good cat baby sitter."

"You've never had a cat, Trevor," Courtney corrected, wanting her son to be truthful.

"Maybe not, but I could be a good baby sitter, I mean cat sitter. I've always wanted a kitten. Do you have others, Rusty?" Trevor asked.

"Mr. Devoe, to you," Courtney interjected.

"Do you, Mr. Devoe?" Trevor repeated.

"Rusty's fine. Mr. Devoe sounds like my father. And yes, there are others. At the family ranch, that is. My mother is trying to find homes for them now that they are old enough." The scowl and tone of his voice as Rusty spoke of his father hinted they didn't have a good relationship.

"Can I have one?" Trevor asked, looking up at her, his eyes wide with hope.

"No. Maybe after we get settled and find a place of our own. Grandma's not big on pets, I'm afraid." It was a good way to put off the inevitable, as Greg had always promised Trevor a pet when he was old enough to take care of one. That day wasn't far off.

Trevor scuffed his feet on the dirt. "Shucks. I never get what I want."

"Tell you what, though. If it's okay with your mother, you could hang on to her until we get to the garage. Maybe you can keep the little minx out of trouble," Rusty offered.

"Can I, Mom?" Trevor asked, suddenly smiling again.

Her son's smile was enough of a reason to agree. "Sure thing."

Rusty finished hooking up the tow ropes. "Ready?" he asked.

"Ready. Just take it slow and make sure you signal well in advance when you're turning," Courtney instructed, trying to keep them on the same page.

Rusty quirked an eyebrow. "Promise me you won't hit my truck. She's special,' he said with a grin.

"As if. I wouldn't dream of hurting my Ford, so I'm guessing your Chevy is safe."

"Good. But in the race to the garage...notice who wins. Just saying," Rusty added, his increasing grin crinkling the corners of his eyes.

"What? You'll be tow...never mind." She shook her head and laughed. His teasing attitude was good for her wavering spirits right about now.

Chapter Three

❤

TEN MINUTES LATER, RUSTY pulled into a gas station and came to a stop by the side of the building. Courtney glanced around, not overly impressed. The run-down shop was in desperate need of a coat of paint. A rusted Gulf Oil sign hung on the side of the garage. Its bright orange logo was unmistakable even though the sign had seen better days. The gas pumps were cash only, as evidence by the handwritten notecards attached to the front with peeling and faded tape.

She slid out of the truck and met Rusty, Trevor not far behind and still clutching the kitten. "I thought we were just dropping my truck off."

Rusty pushed the door open and gestured for them to enter.

Chivalry was good, but why the place was unlocked was confusing as she could have sworn he said the place was closed. The wreath on the door was the only sign Christmas was weeks away. It didn't bode well if the guy who owned the garage turned out to be a Scrooge of sorts.

"He's here, just not working," Rusty said with a shrug of his shoulders.

A man who looked to be in his fifties or sixties came in from the side door that would lead to the garage. "Hey, Rusty. Glad you called when you did. I was just about to head over to the diner and grab some grub. Special is fried chicken, and I got a mean hankering for some of Beverly's greasy cooking." He chuckled, his grin revealing missing teeth and a gold crown in the front. "Reckon my stomach can wait a few minutes." The man was balding, but what thin, wiry hair he did have left was turning gray.

"Thanks for meeting us. This is Courtney Winters and her son, Trevor. And this here is Charlie, the owner of the garage."

Courtney shook the man's hand but made a mental note to check for grease after they left. "It's nice to meet you. I thought Rusty said you didn't work on Sundays."

The man's grin revealed a couple of missing teeth. "I don't. But talking ain't working, so here I am. Reckon the good Lord likes folks to be friendly every day."

So maybe not a Scrooge. Just someone not overly fond of decorating. Charlie had a point, just not one that would necessarily get her truck repaired.

"Trevor's been keeping an eye on the kitten I'm delivering to Laura Goodman. He's been a big help," Rusty said, nodding toward her son.

"Everybody helping everybody. That's the way this town rolls. Nice to meet you, ma'am. Rusty tells me you got radiator trouble. I looked up the part based on the information he gave me. 1956 Ford F-100 with a V8 engine. Classic. Is that the original bubble-wrapped windshield?" he asked, admiration in his voice as he glanced out the window.

"It is." Courtney glanced at Rusty with renewed interest. "For a man who prefers Chevy, you sure know a lot about my Ford considering I never told you the information." There was no way she would let that tidbit slip by without comment.

"Shop class. Guys learn trucks and engines." Rusty chuckled.

"It's also one of the most highly recognizable vintage Ford trucks because of the window and grill designs. There were only like six thousand made," Charlie added, his information surprising her.

"Now that's something I didn't know. It was my late husband's truck, and he got it from his father. It was meticulously cared for, which is why it's upsetting to have this happen." But all the more reason to make sure she hung on to the classic.

"Original parts do wear out," Charlie assured her.

"So, do you have a radiator on hand?" Courtney asked, hoping it was a simple fix.

Charlie shook his head. "*Ummm*, not a chance. The radiator for this truck would be special order only. Almost every part on her would be, especially if you're trying to maintain the original design. I called around and found a place that had one available. The radiator should be here in about a week."

"A week?" she exclaimed. "I can't stay here that long." A week of food and lodging expenses was out of the question. And any time someone used the word "special order," she could see the dollar signs racing higher.

"And you need to allow an extra day or so for me to do the repair. Sorry to have to deliver the bad news, but I reckon you don't have much choice, seeing as the truck isn't going anywhere without a new one." Charlie walked outside, leaving them to follow.

Just when Courtney thought things couldn't get worse, they did. Clearly, she had gotten the wrong message and should not have come to Crossroads Creek. But it's not like she had a crystal ball and could see God's plan for her life. But maybe this was still the better option, because the alternative—well that could have left her stranded on the side of the interstate.

Courtney didn't have to like it, but it's not as if she had a choice at this point. "You're right." She nodded and turned to Rusty, trying to maintain any small sense of positivity she could muster. "Thank you so much for towing my truck here. I don't suppose there's a way we could maneuver it into the garage so everything is locked up."

Charlie huffed and shook his head. "I'll have Rusty pull it around back where we can unhook the ropes. Ain't no one going to come around here and bother me, the garage, or anything I'm working on. Folks around town got better things to do."

"Well, okay then." Once again, her hands were tied when it came to directing the show. "Let me get a few of our personal belongings out of the cab. Rusty, is there any chance I could talk you into taking us to the bed and breakfast you mentioned?" Courtney asked, resigned to the inevitable." Not having a tow bill on top of everything else was a blessing. And it was the blessings she needed to stay focused on, no matter how large or small.

"Sure enough. Hope you don't mind if I drop the kitten off on the way. Otherwise, I'd have to do some backtracking," Rusty said, walking toward the vehicles.

"Of course, I don't mind." She grabbed their suitcases and loaded them into the back of Rusty's truck and then watched as he pulled the Ford around back. Then, pulling out her phone, she sent her mother a text.

Courtney: Truck broke down and was towed to a garage. There's a B&B in town we're going to stay at until the part arrives and the truck is fixed. I'll update you when I know more.

Mom: What? Are you both okay? Should I come to get you? Where are you?

Explaining to her mother why she detoured to Crossroads Creek wouldn't be easy. And on top of everything else she was dealing with at the moment, she didn't want to dive into it, a disagreement sure to ensue.

Courtney: We're fine staying here. I know you can't miss work. I'll text later. Going to get settled in and find some lunch.

Mom: Okay then, if you're sure you don't need me. Keep me posted.

It wasn't long before they were loaded up, Trevor and Faith sitting happily in the middle of the front seat as they headed toward the woman's house to drop off the kitten.

"Isn't Faith adorable, Mom?" her son asked, his non-stop chattering about the pros of having a kitten wearing thin.

"She certainly is." But not adorable enough to bring one to Lafayette and surprise her mother with an unwelcome guest.

As they drew closer to the populated area of town, Courtney admired the Christmas touches she spotted along the way. It reminded her of a country Christmas postcard she'd once received, the town warm and welcoming. She still had the postcard tucked away in a box somewhere, the image one that left an imprint on her heart. The town was in direct contrast to Charlie's place, a reminder that perhaps there was more to the man's story and she should not have judged him.

Rusty pulled into the driveway, and they all slid out of the truck. Trevor clutched the kitten in his arms as they headed up the heavily decorated path. Wreaths with a big red bow adorned every window. Icicle lights had been hung across the porch. Santa and his sleigh graced the front yard, although looking somewhat out of place without snow.

Laura met them on the porch. "I'm so excited to see you, Rusty, and that you've brought my newest family member. I've been waiting for Faith to be old enough to come live here," she said, reaching to take the kitten.

Trevor kissed his new furry friend and reluctantly handed her over to the woman.

"Who have we got here?" Laura asked, snuggling the kitten to her chest as she gazed at them, a questioning expression on her face.

"This is Trevor," Rusty said, putting his hand on top of her son's head. "He's been watching over Faith while I drove here. The little stinker got out of the truck, so you'll need to keep a close eye on the escape artist."

Laura beamed down at Trevor. "Thank you, young man. You've certainly done a good job, and I'm grateful."

"And this is Trevor's mother, Courtney Winters. Her truck broke down just outside of town, and I towed her to Charlie's place."

"That was sweet of you. Always were a good boy." Rusty hadn't been a boy in a long time, but Laura's opinion of him matched Courtney's own.

"We're headed to the B&B. Charlie said it'll be at least a week until the radiator arrives," Rusty added, clarifying why they were with him.

Laura shook her head. *Tsk. Tsk.* "Not going to happen. The B&B is full. Don't you remember Janice Edwin's daughter is getting married? She owns the place, and they hosted the entire event there. All the out-of-town guests are staying at the inn," she said by way of explanation to Courtney.

"I did forget. *Hmmm*, that's not good for Courtney and Trevor. I think the next nearest place is like thirty miles away. I can drive you," Rusty offered.

Laura shook her head. "Nonsense. The next nearest place is where she's standing. You can stay here—with me. I've got extra rooms, and it's just Faith and me now. I would love the company."

Staying with a stranger didn't sound like a good choice. Not in the slightest. "I would hate to be a bo..."

"Please...stay. Make an old woman happy," Laura insisted, her kindly face wreathed in a smile that echoed her offer.

"Laura's one of the sweetest people I know, if my opinion helps. If she says you're welcome to stay, she means it. And her place is spotlessly clean and safe, with lots of room for you and your son," Rusty said, vouching for Laura.

Put like that, Courtney found it hard to resist. *And then there was the money aspect.* The town seemed full of generous and kind people all too willing to help a stranger. It was as though God had provided her with another blessing to help her counter the negative and not giving Courtney more than she could handle.

"Okay, then. We will stay," she said, smiling. "Thank you so much."

"Then it's settled. Get your things and come on in. You're welcome to join us, Rusty," Laura said as they walked to the truck.

"No, thanks. I've got to get back to the ranch. Mother's got a to-do list a mile long." Rusty retrieved her suitcases and carried them to the porch.

"Tell your mother I said hello, and that I'm looking forward to our Sunday school meeting," Laura said, her comment putting Courtney more at ease.

"Will do. It was nice meeting you both." Rusty tipped his hat with a confidence born to a southern cowboy.

"You too, and thanks for everything," Courtney said, meaning every word. Rusty had been the kind of good Samaritan everyone needed around when trouble struck, a true blessing for sure.

"Wait," Trevor said, grabbing Rusty's arm as he started to turn away.

The tall cowboy turned back, a confused expression on his face.

"You forgot to tell Faith goodbye. You don't want to hurt her feelings."

Rusty seemed about to say something but then stopped. Instead, he leaned down to pet the kitten. "Goodbye, little one. Be good for Laura." And then he turned and left without so much as another word.

Talk about shocking...a cowboy with a heart...whether he wanted people to know it or not was another story.

Life had brought her to Crossroads Creek—even if only temporarily. It was a fitting name for where she found herself at this particular time in life—her own personal crossroads.

Chapter Four

♥

CAUGHT OFF GUARD WHEN Trevor reminded him to say goodbye to the kitten, Rusty had reacted on impulse. He had let the kitten out of its cage on the way to deliver it to Laura because it had cried pitifully, and he had given in to the feline pleas. What Rusty hadn't expected was the kitten to crawl in his lap and start purring. Or that he wouldn't be able to push the little furball away. Instead, he had found himself petting her. With no one around to see, what did it matter?

But a public display of affection toward a kitten was entirely out of character and not something he'd live down easily if word got out.

Rusty pulled into the ranch and parked, noting the rest of his family had returned from church. Which meant Sunday dinner was in full swing of preparations, and Rusty could disappear for a while without falling under the watchful eye of his family. It would be a good time to ride out and check fences, mending them as needed. He wasn't technically allowed to do the mending part according to his brother, but Rusty took great pleasure in doing the job anyway. The doctor had cleared him for all but the most strenuous of activities four months ago *and* staying in shape was high on his priority list. Going soft as a marshmallow didn't hold much appeal.

Following the sound of voices, he headed for the kitchen. As expected, his mother and sister were busy peeling potatoes and carrots, fully dressed for the roles in their festive Christmas aprons. By the look and smell of things, pot roast was on the menu. The meat would have been in the crock pot since this morning, but the vegetables going in the pot now would buy him at least an hour and a half. He would have plenty of time to ride out as long as his brother wasn't around to see him go.

"You're back," his mother said, looking up as he entered. "How did it go?"

"Interesting, to say the least. The kitten was eventually delivered safe," Rusty said, leaning against the counter, and grabbing one of the carrots to snack on.

"Interesting? How so?" His sister slapped his hand away as he reached for a second one.

"There was a slight detour involved." Slight being a huge understatement, but more than a little rewarding. It felt good not to have someone second-guess his every move and whether it would be too much for him to handle, and for someone not to look at him with pity in their eyes.

Both women stopped what they were doing to glance up at him.

"Like?" his mother prompted.

"A woman broke down on the side of the road just outside town, and I stopped to help." He would have stopped for anyone, so it was no big deal.

His mother nodded and smiled at him. "Any person of character would have stopped, especially any son of mine. Good job. Go on."

"She was passing through town, but the radiator on her truck had different plans. It cracked, and her engine overheated. I gave Courtney and her son a tow to Charlie's and then planned on taking her to the B&B. I stopped at Laura's place first to drop off the kitten. Long story short...the B&B is full, and Laura invited Courtney to stay with her until the truck is fixed, which could be a week or more." He recited the morning's events just enough to satisfy their curiosity.

Rebecca eyed him, her face scrunched with one of those corkscrew smiles of consternation as she tried to figure out what he wasn't saying. "Courtney, huh? Poor thing. Where was she headed? This isn't exactly passing through area."

Or so he thought. Rusty shrugged. "Lafayette. Her mom lives on the coast, and she's moving there."

"But that doesn't explain why," his mother countered.

"It wasn't like it was a get-to-know-you date or anything. It was a tow. But to satisfy your curious minds, she did say something about a late husband, so I'm guessing that's her motive." It was the last piece of information he should have given them. Talk about fuel for a fire.

"Is she pretty?" Rebecca asked.

Very pretty. "What's that got to do with anything?" he asked, pushing off from the counter. He knew exactly where she was headed with the question, and he'd had enough of this conversation. The women in his family had a one-track mind. *Marry off the Devoe brothers.*

"Well, is she?" his mother asked, seconding the request for an answer.

"Yes, stunning, in fact. Courtney's son is quite the charmer also," Rusty said, deciding to play a little of his own game, giving as good as they did. Although it was the truth, remembering how the boy was with the kitten and his attempts to convince his mother to let him get one.

Rebecca and his mother exchanged glances. "Interesting." His sister grinned.

Rusty paused by the door. "How so?"

"It's the first time you've shown interest in a woman since you've been home," Rebecca said, not pulling any punches.

At least they were honest with their intentions. But then, they didn't live with the daily reminders that Rusty did. "Don't even bother to go down that road. I'm not interested, and no woman who got one look at the scars on my chest would want me. Besides, a woman deserves more than a washed-up cowboy who could kick the bucket any day."

"I've asked you to stop saying that," his mother said, hands on her hips as she glared at him.

"And I've asked you to butt out of my personal life and let me do things my way. And that includes dating if and when I choose too again." *Which would be never.* No woman in her right mind would knowingly accept the challenges he faced in the future.

"Invite Courtney and her son to dinner," his mother said, a broad smile lighting her face.

She was clearly up to something. "You're not listening to me." Trying to reason with the Devoe women was pointless.

"I am, but I've raised you to be more aware of others and their plight. It must be very stressful for Courtney, and she knows no one in town. If we can help her, we should."

"Except your motives aren't as pure as you profess." Rusty understood their reasons weren't hurtful, but they were tiresome. After the surgery, he'd sworn off relationships, unwilling to give any woman a shell of the former man he had once been.

"Just think about it," his mother said, waving her hand in the air as if to dismiss the conversation.

"The answer is no." Rusty turned and left, his frustration building to a point he needed release. He headed for the back of the barn and to the woodpile. A short log-splitting session would soon cool him off enough to be able to ride out to the pasture. Until then, his horse wouldn't appreciate the tension, and mixed signals could prove disastrous. Horses were sensitive to people's emotions, and Thunder, was no exception.

Rusty swung the ax over his head, landing the mark every time with precision. Courtney would have been the type of woman who would have interested him in his rodeo days, but those days were over. It didn't mean he couldn't appreciate her beauty, her kindness, or her sense of humor. It's just that's where he drew the line. He wiped a bead of sweat from his brow before swinging the ax yet again.

"What are you doing?" his mother said from behind him. "You know the doctor said to take it easy. Do you want to end up back in the hospital?" she added, her tone scolding.

Rusty stopped swinging and turned to face her. "He meant no return to the rodeo, not to stop living. I keep telling you he cleared me for just about everything other than over-the-top activities...like bull riding. You all have to stop watching my every move and second guessing my choices. I mean it." Helping at the ranch as he regained strength had been good for him, but so far, being here had brought no joy. If he was going to put closure on the past, Rusty needed to figure out a way into his future. Something that wouldn't happen if his family kept holding him back.

"Except chopping wood is also quite strenuous and you know it. I don't think that's what the doctor had in mind," she huffed.

"Mother, please." He let out a deep sigh. "Let me be the judge of what is and isn't."

"Fine, I'll back off," she said, crossing her arms over her chest.

"Oh? Just like that, you agree. So what's the catch?" It was his mother, and there was no way she would reconsider this suddenly without a reason that suited her own purposes.

"There is one little thing. Ask Courtney to dinner. If you do, I'll back off and tell the rest of the family to do the same. But you also have to start putting together a plan for the future, one that we will stay out of unless you ask for help." His mother put forth her offer like she was negotiating a million-dollar contract in a boardroom. No room for anything but compliance.

Rusty shook his head, removed his hat, and ran a hand through his hair. "You don't give up, do you?"

"Do we have a deal?" she persisted, pushing him to make the choice she wanted him to make.

"Maybe," he hedged, trying to avoid making a promise he wouldn't keep.

"Maybe isn't good enough. Have a heart for the poor dears, Rusty." Her hand flew to her mouth, suddenly realizing what she'd said, a worried look on her face.

Talk about ramping up the guilt screws. "Fine, mother. I'll invite Courtney and her son. But if she says no, you still have to uphold your end of the bargain. And if she says yes, it doesn't mean a thing. I'm still not interested in any of your shenanigans, so don't even bother trying." It was easier to give in and put an end to this nonsense.

"No shenanigans. I promise." His mother nodded, taking him by the arm and leading him back to the house, and effectively ending his log-splitting session.

So much for escaping to mend fences. With any luck, Courtney would take the *'decline-his-offer'* possibility, which would be the end of this discussion. And then he needed to heed his mother's advice. It was time to move forward and spend less time stuck in the past, wondering what he could have done differently.

Besides not going to the doctors in the first place, that is.

His return home had become permanent, and his life changed forever. Which was ironic considering he had left home in the first place to prove to his family he could be successful in his own right. Rebecca was an attorney, and Clay had taken over the family ranch after his father died, and both well-respected members of the community.

And now, all Rusty had managed to prove was that he wasn't much good at anything. Which is precisely what his father had told him in an intense argument months before he died.

Chapter Five

♥

"WHAT WOULD YOU LIKE for breakfast, dear?" Laura asked as Courtney came down the stairs.

The older woman seemed pleasantly relaxed and at peace with her new kitten companion playing at her feet. The Christmas tree lights were twinkling, and the fresh aroma of pine and cinnamon clung to the air.

There was no way Courtney wanted to disturb Laura or put her out any more than she had already by staying here. "I was thinking of going to the diner I noticed in town. It would be easier for us to eat there and for me to decide my next move. My mother's offered to come to get me, and I'm trying to work out the logistics."

Laura frowned. "Oh, I was looking forward to you staying with me. Since my husband died, I've been a lonely old woman, and I don't get much company. That's why I wanted Faith," she said, scooping up the kitten onto her lap to pet her. "She's a Christmas present to myself."

Courtney could relate. "I didn't want to impose. You've been so kind already." Loneliness was a constant companion since Greg passed away, sneaking up on her when she least expected it.

"Nonsense. If there's no reason you have to leave right away, please stay. Make an old woman happy."

"You're not that old," Courtney said, shaking her head. However, the woman was wise in years, knowing how to turn on the guilt to get her way. And it wasn't like Courtney couldn't stay as there was nothing more pressing at her mom's other than figuring out what was next in her life. And then there was Trevor to consider. He would love more playtime with the kitten, the two having bonded last night.

Although on the downside, her son had also managed to ramp up his efforts to change her mind regarding his pet request. "Okay, we'll stay, if you're sure. But you need to let us help around here. No more treating us like guests."

Laura's kindly smile reached her eyes, filling them with genuine warmth. "You *are* a guest. As to helping, I'm okay with that too. It'll be just like when my daughter comes home, and we do things together."

Courtney was glad she had said yes. Telling her mother was another story, but she would deal with that later this morning when she called in the new plan of action. "Sounds like fun. Listen, I know I'm only here for a week or so, but do you know of anyone needing some part-time help? It would only be temporary, of course, but..." Initially, her thought had been to go to her mother's place and get a job to help pay for the truck repairs, but staying here, changed that. But it would be nice if she could make a few dollars to add to her dwindling savings account, especially as she still needed to buy Christmas gifts for Trevor and her mother.

"*Hmmm*. It's a small town, and I don't know of anything. You could ask down at the Golden Spoon. You said you wanted to go there this morning and that's the happening place in Crossroads Creek. If there's a job available, I'm sure Beverly Jenkins has heard about it." Laura chuckled. "She's the owner and that woman knows everything about everything."

"Sounds like a good idea to me. Thanks." Coming from a city where no one knew anyone and kept to themselves, it was a welcome thought. *Friendly neighbors.*

Laura set the kitten on the floor and it ran off to play. The older woman stood, using the arm of the chair to push herself up. "And while you're there, I'm going to pick up some food for the week."

"Oh, I should go with you and pay for the groceries. It's the least I can do." Courtney's funds were limited, but she wasn't looking to become a freeloader and take advantage of the situation.

"Nonsense. My daughter isn't expected to pay when she visits, and neither are you. I'm not strapped for money by any means, so stop fussing."

Laura's generosity was overwhelming and a blessing. "Thank you so much," Courtney said, hugging her. "I don't know how I'll ever repay you."

"You already are just by being here." Laura smiled and headed toward the kitchen, leaving Courtney standing there, utterly amazed at the turn of events. Kindness was everywhere in Crossroads Creek, and for the first time in a long time, she felt a sense of peace. Which was odd considering it was Crossroads Creek—the place where her husband had died.

Trevor came down the stairs like a bunny, bouncing from step to step. "I'm hungry."

"Me too. Mrs. Goodman has kindly invited us to stay with her for the week. We're going to stick around town and wait for the truck to be repaired, if that's okay with you?"

"Yay! That means I get to play with Faith," he said, scooping up the kitten and giving her a kiss on the head.

Courtney never doubted Trevor would be on board. "That you do. I thought we could go to the diner for breakfast. What do you say, kiddo?"

"Sounds good to me. I want a stack of pancakes this high." He gestured to indicate a pile way bigger than anything he could eat.

Courtney chuckled. "Maybe we could start with a kid stack, and then if you have room in that tummy of yours, we'll order another one." She knew he would be full, but it was easier than arguing about it and spoiling the outing.

"Good thinking because then maybe I could switch my order to waffles." Trevor grinned; her son always had a ready answer for everything.

"Let's go then." Courtney handed him his coat. "Zip up tight. It's a little cool out this time of the morning, and we're going to walk."

"Yes, ma'am." Trevor moved to grab his jacket from the coat tree.

Her son was a good kid and such a blessing to Courtney. *But growing up way too fast.* They headed outside, and hand-in-hand, headed toward the diner. Following the sidewalk and enjoying the sunshine as it warmed the chill off the morning air, she checked out the neighboring houses. Most were older cottages, but once they hit Main Street, the houses became much larger, and more Victorian in style. The residents of the town took pride in their yards, everything pristine, even in winter.

And then there were the Christmas decorations. Much like anywhere else in the country, there were inflatables in the yard, massive amounts of twinkling white and colored lights. An occasional Santa and his sleigh could be spotted on a rooftop, and wreaths hung on the doors. And every light post on Main Street sported a lantern and various Christmas decorations, proclaiming joy throughout the town. Christmas spirit was alive and well in Crossroads Creek.

Stopping at the Golden Spoon, they went inside, the overhead bells ringing in their arrival. Christmas music played from a jukebox in the corner. Seating was at a premium in the booths, the place filled with customers, and the low buzz of conversation and laughter sounded through the cozy diner. Courtney spotted a couple of stools at the counter and seized the opportunity to sit close to the register, hoping to meet the owner.

"Good morning. Haven't seen you two in town before. Welcome to Crossroads Creek." The server was a young woman with a bright smile, blue eyes, a shiny silver nose ring, and her long brown hair pulled back in a ponytail. Her name tag identified her as Christina, and therefore not the owner.

Courtney was sure in a town this size, the nose ring would have caused some raised eyebrows, but it certainly didn't seem to bother the beautiful girl. "Thank you. We were just passing through but had truck troubles."

"Yikes. Sorry to hear that. Charlie will get you all fixed up, I'm sure. Now, breakfast, that's our job. We've got a special that includes two eggs, your choice of meat, grits, toast, and juice, all for seven bucks. Can't go wrong with that deal," Christina offered, flipping her pad to the next page. "And for you, little man, we've got a huge stack of pancakes with strawberries if you like that sort of thing."

"*Mmmm*. I love strawberries," Trevor said, rubbing his tummy. "I'll have those. My mom already said I can have pancakes, so I don't need to ask again. Right, Mom?" he asked, turning his big, baby blues on her.

"Right, kiddo. And the special sounds good to me. With a coffee, please," Courtney added, more than ready for a heaping dose of caffeine to jumpstart the day. More specifically, her brain. Although Christina's cheerfulness went a long way to brightening the day of its own accord.

"Coming right up," the young girl said, turning away.

"Oh, hey, out of curiosity, is Beverly Jenkins in?" Courtney asked before the server moved off.

"Always. If the place is open, Bev's here." Christina grinned.

"Wonderful. Laura Goodman thought she would be a good person to ask about a job."

Courtney shifted on the stool as she jumped into the crux of what she needed...feet first.

"You're looking for work while you're in town?" Christina asked, a confused look on her face.

"If there's anything available. I'm not one to sit around and do nothing." She was also one who needed money, not that she would share that information with anyone. Courtney might not have much of her life left the way it once was, but she did have her pride.

"There's nothing I know of. I moved here about three years ago from Hallbrook, New Hampshire. Since I've been in Crossroads Creek, I know just as much about what's going on as Bev. It comes with the small-town-diner territory." Christina grinned. "But I'll double-check with Bev, just in case."

"Never mind, I trust you. You're a long way from home...if that's home, I mean," Courtney said, curious about the girl.

"My grandmother lives there. She has a place called Susie's Diner and I worked there a few years before striking out on my own. I wasn't a fan of the snow and cold," Christina said, pulling the order ticket from the pad.

"I'm from Kansas and feel the same way." Courtney was disappointed there weren't any jobs available but refused to focus on the negative.

Christina disappeared through the swinging doors that led to the kitchen area.

"Can you cook?" a man asked from behind her. Courtney spun around, only to come face to face with her rescuer.

Rusty.

Chapter Six

♥

RUSTY HAD INSTANTLY NOTICED when Courtney and her son walked into the Golden Spoon. And he couldn't help but overhear her odd request for employment, considering she was only here for a week.

"*Ummm*, yes," Courtney said, smiling. "Why do you ask?"

"Hi, Rusty. Mom and I are here for pancakes, and I'm *sooo* hungry. Hopefully, she doesn't have to fix *my* breakfast. She's a good cook and all, but I don't want to sit here alone. I don't know any of these people."

Trevor's comment was naïve and sweetly said, the humor not lost on Rusty. He ruffled the boy's hair. "I promise not to steal your mom away and make her fix your breakfast this morning.”

“Why did you want to know if I could cook?” Courtney asked again.

“There’s an event at the community center Wednesday evening. Unfortunately, Alfred, our normal cook, had to leave town in an emergency. Since you’ll still be here, you could help cover the position this week while I’m looking for someone else to fill the role.” Although after Trevor’s comment about not wanting his mother to fix breakfast, Rusty hoped he had not just made a colossal mistake.

“In that case, yes, I can cook. Technically though, I’m an assistant Chef, as we like to think of our food preparation as creativity not simple cooking. Or, I was an assistant Chef,” she corrected, a frown marring her lovely face.

Not a mistake by any means, then. Rusty nodded. “I would say that totally qualifies you for the job. Will you do it?”

“Sure. How hard can it be to cook for a small group of people, or kids, or whoever will be in attendance? It's not like this town is busting at the seams." Courtney grinned.

She was a take-charge person who faced whatever trouble was thrown her way—unlike him. Maybe he could learn a thing or two from the pretty lady while she was in town. "Great. I'll let the others know."

"Others?" Courtney asked, her brow furrowed in confusion.

"A handful of people from town help with the cooking...or creativity," he said, unable to resist the teasing remark. "They were a little worried we wouldn't find anyone on such short notice who could take the lead role. So Assistant Chef Courtney, you've been honorarily promoted to Chef for the week."

Courtney beamed, her smile transforming her face into one of joy. "Wonderful. I look forward to it. How much does it pay?"

Rusty paused, unsure how to answer. He hadn't thought this through well enough before tossing out the offer. The problem was, if Courtney was looking for a temporary job in a strange town after her truck broke down, it could only mean one thing. *Money issues*. He did a quick calculation of how much the repair would be. "How's three hundred sound?" It's not like he was rolling in the dough, but there was plenty enough to help her out.

Courtney's eyes grew wide in wonder. "For one night? That's more than I made in the city."

"It's also for the planning and preparation time that's involved," he added, not wanting to tip his hand there was anything amiss with the offer.

She nodded. "I'd say heck, yeah. With Christmas just around the corner and the truck repair expense, it will really help," she said, relief radiating in her voice.

The comment confirmed what Rusty suspected about money being tight, and that in itself was more than enough reason to agree with his mother about helping Courtney and her son. "Then it's a deal. Oh, and by the way, I mentioned to my mother about meeting you and Trevor. She's intent on having you over for dinner tonight. Interested?" It wasn't the most gracious of invitations, but then he wasn't necessarily pushing for her to accept.

"I'm sorry. I'm having dinner with Laura. She's been such a blessing to us, and I want to cook her a special meal. Tell your mother I said thanks for the sweet offer."

Rusty nodded, ignoring the slight disappointment that settled in his chest. "I'll tell her. Any chance you want to have breakfast with me since we're all here anyway? It would save me from eating alone." He was a certified loner now, but it didn't mean he couldn't have friends, and Courtney intrigued him in a way he couldn't resist. Plus, it would get him off the hook with his mother.

"Sure, why not." Courtney and Trevor slid off the stools. "We're going to move to a booth with Rusty, if that's okay?" she told Christina when she spotted her nearby.

"Of course." Christina followed, place settings in hand. "I didn't think you knew anyone in town," she said, looking back and forth between him and Courtney, curiosity firmly etched in her expression.

Which was precisely how gossip started in this town.

"I don't. Or not many, anyway. Rusty rescued me yesterday when my truck broke down," Courtney smiled at him sweetly as she slid in the booth after Trevor.

"Now I understand." Christina grinned. "I'll make sure your food gets delivered here." The server turned and walked away, but the look in her eyes said so much more.

The girl was positive she had interesting news to share—with anyone who would listen. *Which meant the whole town.* "Sorry. Everybody wants to know everything in Crossroads Creek, and you're a stranger in the area. Someone new for the gossip channels."

"Don't be sorry. I like the fact people are looking after one another. It's sort of sweet if you ask me."

"That's because you don't live here. Around this neck of the woods, we call it being a busybody." And Rusty had more than his fair share of attention over the past year.

Courtney laughed. "Busybody. Gossiper. Hen. You name it...most of it's sweet."

"Agree to disagree," Rusty countered. He'd lived here a long time and couldn't wait to leave when he had. Although, that was primarily thanks to his father's glaring disapproval.

"Mom, can I have some quarters? There's a pinball machine over there that looks super cool." Trevor held out his hand, pulling an assumptive close on his mother.

"Sure, but only two. Breakfast will be here shortly," Courtney said, digging the quarters out of her purse and dropping them into his outstretched hand. In the blink of an eye, the kid was gone.

"So what's an assistant chef from Kansas doing moving to Lafayette, the heart of the Louisiana's Cajun and Creole Country?"

Courtney glanced at her son playing pinball before turning back to him. "My husband passed away about a year ago, and I found us in a position of needing to start over. It's been a struggle...for both of us. So I sold the house, packed up, and I'm headed to my mother's to stay until I can get back on my feet. I'm not experienced in creole cooking, but I can learn. Besides, I read it is also called the *Happiest City in America*. Something I could use in my life right about now. But, unfortunately, I didn't get that far. Not yet anyway."

"I'm sorry. I can see where a change of pace would be good." Rusty had been right in many ways about Courtney, although in this case, he wished he hadn't been. He ached for her loss, understanding the difficulty she must be having to readjust. It made him think of the man whose heart he received in the transplant. More specifically, the man's widow. The agency was strict with their policy and wouldn't let him reach out to help her financially, but they had let slip the man had been married.

Maybe helping Courtney was the perfect way to give back to someone in need, someone in a similar position. Perhaps this would assuage the guilt Rusty felt toward the organ donor's widow. "Listen, I know you are busy tonight, but what about having dinner with us tomorrow night? You'll be here at least a week, and it might be a nice way to keep you and Trevor from getting bored." This time his invitation was sincere.

Courtney looked unsure of herself.

"Please. My mother's not one to take rejection easily. She'd probably send my sister to ask you again, figuring I made a mess of the request the first time." The volunteer program he started at the center was his way of giving back to others as he tried to figure out his new direction in life. A life that wouldn't be centered on his abilities and successes, but one based on helping others meet their needs and goals. The program was just the beginning. Helping Courtney would be another way to do the same thing.

"Okay. I'm sure Trevor will be excited. Thanks for inviting me. Everyone is so nice in this town. Be careful, or I may never leave." Her smile didn't quite reach her eyes, giving lie to the remark.

"Great. I'll let my mother know. Just be prepared; the family can be a bit much." It was only fair to deliver the warning.

Christina delivered their breakfast, and Trevor rejoined them, ending the chance for a deeper conversation. While they ate, Trevor did most of the talking, especially after he learned they would be visiting the ranch tomorrow evening. And the kid made no bones about why—the kittens, the horses, the cows, and all the other farm animals. Apparently, living in the city hadn't afforded much time to hang out on a cattle ranch.

When they finished, Rusty picked up the bill off the table and headed for the register to pay, Courtney close on his heels.

"I'll get mine and Trevor's breakfast," she said, pulling out her wallet.

Rusty shook his head. "That's not necessary."

"Oh, but it is," she said, placing a twenty on the counter. "Trust me. In fact, you should let me buy yours considering all you've done for us." She tossed another twenty down, emphasizing her point.

"You don't have to, but thanks," Rusty said as Christina rang up the order. It was a small concession, one that went against what had been ingrained in him since he was a child, but he would concede this one for the greater good.

They walked to the front entrance and stepped outside. "I'll see you tomorrow night then. You will have to pick us up, seeing as I don't know where you live or have a vehicle."

Rusty shook his head. "Oh, no. Did you forget you have work to do today? We need to meet this afternoon, say around one."

"But why?" Courtney asked, her brow drawn tight.

"I told you about the planning and preparation time for the job. That happens starting today."

"But surely we can do that Wednesday morning. I mean, how long can it take?" Courtney asked.

"*Ummm*, it's a project. Cooking for over two hundred people requires a lot of menu selection, food shopping, and then preparation."

Her mouth dropped open into a wide *O*. Two hundred?" she squeaked.

Rusty had intentionally not mentioned that one tiny piece of information, not wanting to scare her off. "Yes. It's a soup kitchen, and people from all over the area come in for fellowship."

"I see." Clearly, she didn't. "Well, okay then." Courtney didn't sound as sure of herself as she had earlier. "One it is then. Pick me up at Laura's place."

Courtney would have lots of help on Wednesday with the food preparation, and he had loads of confidence in her abilities. And as to the rest of the planning and details, Rusty intended to see to them personally by helping her.

And by the look of things...they both could use a friend.

Chapter Seven

♥

ENJOYING THE AFTERNOON SUN warming the porch, Courtney waited for Rusty. True to his word, the man pulled up in his truck sharply at one.

He got out and came around to meet her. "Where's Trevor?"

"Laura agreed to keep an eye on him. I think the lull of a kitten to play with was far greater than meal planning." To Trevor, just about anything would be better than work, but that was partly her fault. This past year she hadn't asked much of him in light of everything else he was dealing with.

Rusty pulled open the passenger door and stepped aside to let her pass. "Then let's get to it. I thought we should go by the center, and you can get an idea of what we already have for supplies, check out the kitchen facility and see what you have access to."

The woodsy scent of pine and musk wafted around her, reminding her of a warm fire on a cold night. "Sounds like a plan."

Rusty headed for the driver's side and slid in next to her. Putting the truck in reverse, he backed into the street. It was a short ride to the community center and once inside, it wasn't long before the enormity of what she'd agreed to do hit her.

Courtney withheld comment as she gazed around the kitchen, trying to assess the situation. The kitchen was way smaller than expected, had antiquated appliances, and the cookware was basic at best. When Rusty described the job, she'd been quick to point out there was nothing simple about cooking, but now, she wasn't so sure. An assistant chef without her tools took everything back to basics.

"Sorry, there's not a lot of extra money for fancy cookware and I'm sure this isn't what you're used to—but it's only for one night. And seeing as you're a chef, I imagine you can make anything work. Please tell me you haven't changed your mind." His boyish charm accompanied the comment as he sought to reconfirm her decision to accept.

"It will be fine. You're right. A professional can make do with what they have, so I look at this as a challenge." She grinned, more to prove it to them both that she meant every word. She hadn't always had high-dollar fancy named cookware, and the ones she had, were gifts. Christmas. Graduation from culinary school. Birthdays. And mostly from her mother.

"What a relief." His smile revealed crinkles at the corners of his eyes.

They were endearing, and like little telltale signs of genuine joy.

She moved to stand in front of the pantry after he opened the door to reveal the contents. Mentally she ticked off a list, relieved to find items that would come in handy. A variety of staple spices like parsley, sage, rosemary, thyme, and one of her favorites...paprika.

Although it wasn't the smoked variety, which always kicked up the taste buds into a full gear. Chicken stock. Pasta by the boxloads. And an overabundance of tomato sauce and tomato paste. There was also plenty of salt, pepper, sugar, and flour. "I'm glad to see your pantry contents are in better shape," she said, hoping to put him at ease. Rusty didn't need to worry...she would make this work.

"And I'm glad you approve. This is where all the cooking and food prep is done before the dishes are carried out to the tables in the main room. Follow me and I'll show you where the rest of the action happens."

The room was big, but not big enough in her estimation. Tables were set up, one after another and tightly squished together. Christmas decorations adorned every table and hung on the walls. There was even a tree in the corner, every branch weighted down with an ornament or draped in tinsel. The angel at the top was beautiful, the soft light casting her cream-colored dress and gold trimmings in an ethereal glow.

Returning her attention to the room, she frowned. At a quick glance, it would seem the seating would only hold a hundred or so people. "I thought you mentioned two hundred plus guests. The seating here doesn't compute."

"They sort of come in and go out, some early, some later, filling spaces that are vacated. Like a restaurant," he added, shooting her a teasing wink.

"I see. So it's not just the challenge of what to serve but figuring out what will keep hot the best and not dry out." A bit more complicated, but still doable at this scale.

"Exactly. So what do you think?"

She tapped her finger against her chin, a habit she had never been able to break when she was deep in thought and trying to solve a problem. Courtney reviewed some of the easier options. Spaghetti. Macaroni and cheese. Chicken soup. It was a soup kitchen, after all. Serving the same thing they normally received wasn't high on her priority list. "What did the previous chef serve?"

"Joe? A chef? I'm not sure he would like to hear his name linked with such a lofty title. He's a down-home country boy. But as to what he fixed...spaghetti, chicken or turkey soup, macaroni and cheese. The sauces on the spaghetti would be different though. Oh, and he liked to serve a salad and a dessert."

Courtney inwardly groaned. All the go-to foods she was thinking of. The same foods families had been serving for generations and that were tried and true favorites. "I see. I'd like to put together something different if you don't mind." Even if it was more complicated, she wanted to do it right.

"You're the boss." He grinned.

"Technically, you are since you're footing my bill," she teased. Rusty's smile slipped, but only barely. If she hadn't been paying attention, she wouldn't have even noticed the slight change.

Just as quickly, the smile was back in place. "Well, okay then, I give you full permission to make up your own menu. Just don't run the budget into bankruptcy." Rusty chuckled, the sound a little more forced than she liked.

Was there something he wasn't telling her? "Serving two hundred people makes it hard not to spend a lot of money no matter what is planned."

Rusty nodded. "So true. I trust your judgement."

"I'll need more time to come up with a menu."

Rusty glanced at his watch. "That works for me. I've got some errands to run, but I'll be back at one to show you around."

"Sounds good to me." Courtney grabbed his arm to get his full attention. "Thanks for letting me do this job. I promise I'll do it right," she said, hoping to reassure him.

"I've no doubt you will, so quit worrying." Rusty winked, settling any doubts she may have had in the back of her mind. He led her toward the truck. "Oh, and as for tomorrow, I'll pick you up and take you food shopping seeing as you don't have a vehicle. And then on Wednesday you'll be busy with preparations, and that's the part where I bow out of the operation. Trust me, the last thing you want is a cowboy whose handy-dandy skills in the kitchen are limited to opening a can and heating the contents. Joe and I had a deal, I stay out of his way during the cooking, but I show up for the serving."

No one could be that bad. Could they? If the last guy didn't want Rusty's help, perhaps there was more truth to the claim than she was willing to find out. "It sounds like a deal I should uphold," she teased.

Rusty glanced her way and nodded. "The good news is that we can drop Trevor off with my mother, if you're okay with that. I mentioned what we we're doing and she insisted Trevor come stay at the ranch with her. I think she's planning on doing some Christmas baking and would love the help. And then on Wednesday, he can hang out at the ranch with me. Then you won't have to worry about him at all."

This was a part she hadn't thought through. The offer was more than generous and there was no doubt Trevor would be over the moon, but her motherly reservations kicked in. It wasn't often she let Trevor out of her sight, other than to go to school, that is. "I don't want to trouble you." After Greg died, Trevor had become her lifeline to move forward.

"It's no trouble at all. Like I said, you're doing me a favor. And my mother will love it. I'm sure she will concoct all sorts of fun things for them to do together."

Put like that...how could she refuse? Trevor deserved fun and far be it for her to keep him from it. "Well then I guess it's settled. I know he'll love it...the problem is, he may never want to leave."

"No worries, a few chores will fix that."

The teasing glint in his eyes was proof he'd do no such thing as make Trevor work, but it wouldn't be the worst thing that happened considering how slack she had been with the responsibility side of his education this past year. It had been easier for her to simply pick up his toys and his room. "Absolutely."

Rusty's brow lines deepened as he contemplated her answer. "You know I was just teasing. Right?"

"Yes. No. Maybe. But honestly, something small wouldn't hurt. Maybe he could help your mother in the house considering the generosity of the invitation."

"Let's worry about that later," he added, clearly unconvinced.

Rusty dropped her back off at Laura's place and she waved goodbye to him as he pulled away. He was a kind and generous man and hit high marks when in the attractive department. The idea of shopping with a man other than Greg seemed a bit odd, but she wouldn't dwell on it.

"I'm back," she called out to Laura and Trevor, but there was no answer. "Anyone here?" Walking into the kitchen, Courtney spotted the note propped up on the table.

Took the kitten to get her shots. Should be back by three.

Laura

Courtney took a deep breath and then exhaled. She wasn't used to having to trust so many people with her son, but she did trust her own instincts. These were good people trying to help a stranger in a bad predicament.

Glancing at her watch, she noted it was two-thirty. With thirty minutes to herself, it was the perfect opportunity to figure out the meal plan. Courtney pulled open various cupboard doors in search of Laura's cookbooks. The third door was a goldmine. Cookbooks lined eight shelves, all neatly organized. *A chef's dream.*

Book after book she poured through the pages, all while sipping a cup of tea. But the job wasn't as easy as she would have liked. It was rare to have a few moments to herself and when she did, she typically found herself going over the past and trying to figure out the future.

She hadn't told Trevor that his grandparents had offered for them to live in their house. Courtney wanted her independence more than anything and living with Greg's parents or even her own mother didn't rank high in her opinion. They all wanted to take care of everything, but Courtney had other ideas. At least with her mother, it would be easy to move out when the time came. Greg's parents, not so much. Not to mention, rural North Dakota wasn't exactly brimming with job opportunities for her as a chef. At least in Louisiana, there would be plenty of jobs.

When Courtney had left home, ready to take on the world, it had been a rude awakening. She'd gone from one caretaker situation to another. Life with her mother after her father had passed away had been difficult, but the two managed to work through issues. But at eighteen, she headed for college and the freedom that came with moving away from home.

How quickly everything changed when her first boyfriend duped her and stole all her savings that had been meant for a car. And it wasn't long after that she'd met Greg while coming out of the bank. It was love at first sight, and even her trepidations after her first boyfriend had flown out the window. In hindsight, perhaps their quick marriage had been reckless. Together they survived the challenges of a new relationship and had been extremely happy. Greg had taken care of her in a different way, care born of true love. But Greg wasn't around anymore and it was time she stood on her own two feet.

Courtney said a prayer, hoping for the strength to be strong for both herself and Trevor. She let out a deep cleansing breath and focused on the calm that washed over her as the unsettled feeling in the pit of her stomach eased slightly.

Turning her gaze back to the cookbooks, she made notes, trying to find the perfect menu.

It wasn't long before she heard Laura and Trevor come through the front door. "I'm in the kitchen," she called out, eager to see her son.

A hug from Trevor always brightened her day.

Chapter Eight

♥

It had taken most of the night for Courtney to figure out what to serve, but by morning she had a full menu. One she was totally satisfied with, and one, that she hoped Rusty would approve. He had said it was up to her, but she still wanted his input. "You almost ready to go Trevor? Rusty should be here any time."

Her son jumped off the sofa and slid on his jacket. "I've been ready. I still can't believe I get to go to a real ranch and see the other kittens."

"Well, just remember your manners, young man. You need to thank Mrs. Devoe for the invitation and you mind her. Rusty says his mother wants to do some baking so I'm sure the two of you will make some fabulous Christmas cookies or some other special treats. And I for one, can't wait to taste them." Courtney slid on her own jacket and checked her appearance in the hallway mirror. She might not have designs on Rusty, but it didn't hurt to look her best.

"I'm sure they won't be as good as yours, Mom," Trevor said, her son pulling out all the sweetness stops.

"You're right...they'll be better." Courtney ruffled her son's hair when he grinned. "Just make sure you save me one or two."

A horn sounded out front. "He's here. Enjoy the rest of your morning, Laura. I'll see you after the shopping is finished and the groceries are put away at the community center." Shopping for this many people would be a feat, but one she was ready to tackle.

"Take your time, dear. That Rusty is a sweet boy." The twinkle in the woman's eyes gave away her intent.

"He's not a boy." The rest of her comment Courtney wouldn't touch.

Laura grinned. "I'm glad you noticed," she said, waltzing out of the room with the kitten tucked safely in her arms.

It was no use arguing with some people, and Laura was one of them. Courtney had a feeling the woman was hearing wedding bells, but there was a lot going on in Courtney's life that the good people in this town didn't know. *Nor would they understand.*

She and Trevor headed out the door and made their way to the truck where Rusty had come around to open the doors. "Good morning," she said, climbing in after Trevor.

"And good morning to you. Any luck with the menu?" Rusty asked, pulling the zipper of his jacket up a little higher. Without the sun, the chill from the previous evening hadn't faded away.

She nodded. "Somewhere around two a.m., I figured it out."

"Ouch." One eyebrow quirked up, a trick she had never been able to master.

"You can say that again, so you better agree with my selections, mister." She was clearly joking considering Rusty was footing the bill

"Sounds like a challenge," he teased, shooting her a wink. "My mother is thrilled you're coming over, Trevor. And I did tell her to make sure she took you out to the barn to see the kittens."

Trevor's smile was instantaneous. "Thanks, Rusty. Do you have other animals? Like horses, pigs, cows, and chickens?" he asked, his youthful awe causing Courtney to smile.

"All of the above, I'm afraid. They're a lot of work and the pig pen forever stinks. It's not as glamorous as you think." Rusty gazed up at her, as if remembering their conversation about giving Trevor a chore or two. He shook his head, as if reading her mind.

There would be no stall mucking for Trevor on today's agenda.

"I wonder if Charlotte will be with the pigs. That would be so cool," Trevor exclaimed.

"Charlotte?" Rusty questioned as he backed out of the driveway.

Courtney grinned. Of course, he didn't know Charlotte. It's not like he had kids of his own or had been around his nephews much.

"You know, Charlotte from Charlotte's Web. Only I know Fern doesn't live with you, and your pig probably isn't called Wilbur," Trevor explained, his voice taking on a serious note. "That's just in the movies. But Charlotte, now she could be at your ranch. Mom told me there are writing spiders everywhere, one just has to look."

"Technically they are yellow garden spiders and writing spider is simply a nickname for artistic arachnid," Courtney explained for Rusty's sake.

"You always said use my imagination—so I am." Her son frowned up at her.

Trevor was right. Who was she to rain on his fun? "Good point. Maybe Mrs. Devoe can help you look for her." She glanced at Rusty, a silent look of understanding passing between them.

"*Look for her*?" Rusty questioned. "That's not a problem. It's more a matter of showing you where to find the little eight-legged artist.

Wilhelmina loves her friend Charlotte and they talk at night. No matter how many times I take down the web, Charlotte rebuilds and each time it seems she leaves a message in them."

"Really?" Trevor asked, his face aglow in wonder.

"Really," Rusty confirmed, his tone serious and matter of fact.

"What does the web say? Is it different every time?" Trevor asked.

"Well, now, that's where the problem starts. Spiders and pigs have their own language and this Charlotte is definitely speaking in spider. I can't understand a word she writes. Maybe you could figure it out for me?"

The fact Rusty would play along impromptu, endeared him to Courtney more. The man was as real, thoughtful, and as kind as anyone she knew. Maybe better. And he was good with Trevor, her son's adoration shining through as he held on to every word Rusty uttered.

"That would be so cool. Do you hear that, Mom? I'm going to try and decode Charlotte's message for Rusty."

It's not like she wasn't sitting in the same truck. Courtney grinned. "I heard. That will certainly keep you busy and out of trouble."

They pulled onto a side street and Rusty drove up the long driveway. The ranch house stood stately in its charm. White-washed and well kept, much the same as the barns she spotted in the distance. The front porch and every window was covered in Christmas decorations. Garland, wreaths, and bows. All masterfully arranged to make the home picture perfect in its tranquil Christmas setting. All they needed now was snow, but that was something people in this area didn't see often.

An older woman, Rusty's mother she presumed, rose from one of the rocking chairs and came toward them.

"It's so nice to meet you, my dear. I'm Margaret Devoe. All my friends call me Mary so feel free to do the same. Come in, come in. My son has told us so much about you," his mother said, holding out her hand.

Courtney felt instantly at ease in the woman's presence. She wasn't very tall, leaving Courtney to think Rusty's height must have come from his father. But his good looks and charm were certainly his mother's doing. "It's a pleasure to meet you, also. And this is my son, Trevor. He's been pretty excited ever since you issued the invitation. Thank you so much for your kindness."

Trevor stepped forward boldly and held out his hand. "Hi, Mrs. Devoe. It's a pleasure to meet you and thank you for the invitation," Trevor said, mirroring Courtney's words. "Did I say that right, Mom," he asked, glancing up at her.

Courtney laughed. "You did splendid."

"It's nice to meet you as well, young man. I've got a fun day planned—just the two of us. Can you all come in for a cup of coffee or tea?" his mother asked again.

Rusty shook his head. "We've got to get the shopping done and Courtney will be here tonight for dinner. You can plague her with your nonsense then," he teased, answering for them both.

His mother's smile slipped slightly, reminding her of when Rusty did the same thing. "Fine. And it's not nonsense." Mary turned toward Courtney and reached for her hands. "I'm so sorry you are having truck troubles, dear. But folks here in Crossroads Creek love new faces when people come through here. The town has always believed that a stranger is a friend we've never met. Now that we've met, we need to see how to keep you from leaving." His mother chuckled, giving her hands a squeeze before releasing them.

"Unfortunately, that can't happen. Trevor and I are moving to my mother's place in Lafayette. But it's a beautiful sentiment that you would welcome me otherwise." There was no reason to be rude in answer to the woman's kindness. Courtney just wasn't going to put any ideas into her head or encourage the woman in any way. *Much the same way she had to tamp down Laura's enthusiasm.*

"See you both tonight. Trevor, you behave and mind Mrs. Devoe." She hugged her son.

"Yes, ma'am. Now can we go see the kittens?" he asked, turning to Mary, her son more than ready for his mother to disappear so he could get on with the fun.

Rusty chuckled as they got back in the truck. "That went well. You do know that was my mother trying her hand at matchmaking? I told you they could be a bit over the top."

"Yes, but you and I know the truth, so it's harmless fun on her part. I'm thrilled she asked to watch him and since we both know what she's up to, it won't matter. Neither of us will be taken by surprise." Courtney wasn't sure if her words were to reassure him, or herself, but either way, she wanted to draw the line in the proverbial sand. Or dirt, in the case of the ranch.

Rusty nodded. "True. So what did you come up with for a menu?" he asked, smoothly changing the subject.

"My creative genius kicked in late last night, and I know just what I want to fix and what you should do going forward to mix things up a bit. You know, after I leave town," she said, grinning over at him.

Rusty quirked up his eyebrow, a dead give-away as to his thoughts. The man didn't like change. "And what's that? Simple is still my mode of operation."

"It is simple if done right. Theme nights are always a big hit with a large crowd, and for tomorrow night, I decided on "Pie" night." The idea had come to her out of nowhere, and she'd latched on to it. Now she held her breath, waiting for Rusty to approve. It was too late to start the planning over, but she wouldn't tell him that just yet. That piece of information could wait until she needed ammunition to convince him.

Rusty frowned. "You do realize people are coming for dinner, not just dessert?"

"I'm well aware. Pie also includes Shepard's Pie and Chicken Pot Pie. I can add a fresh garden salad and of course, Apple pie and ice cream for dessert."

"Apple is the pie of choice in America," he teased, shooting her a wink. "It sounds like a lot of work. Are you sure it's doable in the time frame you have available?"

They pulled into the parking lot of the Super Save grocery store. The place was packed judging by the number of cars filling three-quarters of the available spaces.

"Absolutely. It's called an assembly line. Oh, and it also includes pre-made flaky dough we can roll out for the pies. Normally, I wouldn't consider premade, but this is a different circumstance. And as you already mentioned, time is limited for preparation." It's not like anyone back in Wichita would know, or care for that matter. And neither did she. Desperate times called for desperate measure. *And a little prayer*. At least that's what her mother always told her.

Rusty circled back around the parking lot and pulled in one of the empty spots. "If you think it's doable, I'm totally on board. Everyone will love the change in menu. What did you mean by theme night?"

"So next week and each week after, pick a theme and find easy recipes. Like Italian night.

Mexican night. BBQ night. That sort of thing," she explained.

"I see. Sounds difficult unless I can convince you to stick around." Rusty chuckled.

"Tempting, but not possible." Courtney knew he was just teasing.

Minutes later, they were inside the grocery store, each with a cart. "Let's get the non-cold food first," Courtney suggested, heading for the produce aisle. "We need potatoes, fresh vegetables for the salads, salad greens, and apples for the pie, of course."

She parked near the apple display. "These are Granny Smith and they make delicious apple pie," she said, starting to fill a bag with the shiny, green and tasty looking apples, checking for bad spots first.

Rusty stood next to her, but hadn't joined in. "How do you know how many to buy?" he asked. "It's not like this is a small family dinner."

She stopped counting, making a mental note so she wouldn't lose track. "Use simple math. A pie is eight servings. You said over two hundred people will come through for a meal. So add ten percent for overage which is two hundred and twenty people. Now divide by eight and you get," she paused, trying to do a mental calculation, "seventeen and a half pies. So we'll make eighteen. Whatever is needed for one pie is multiplied by eighteen. Follow me?" she asked, tossing him an apple.

Rusty grinned. "Sure thing. Why don't you just tell me how much to get of everything?"

"It's simple math for creative cooking," she said tossing him another apple. "Now start filling a bag, mister."

"Throw me one more and be amazed," he said, totally confusing her.

Courtney couldn't resist finding out what he was up to and tossed him another apple.

Rusty caught it, tossed it back into the air, and proceeded to do the same with the others. One by one, he caught an apple and juggled it back up, keeping her on edge.

Each time, she held her breath, waiting for one to drop to the floor and splatter. Courtney glanced around, hoping no one who worked there saw him. But she also couldn't hold back the laugh that escaped as he executed the moves, much to her delight. "Where did you learn that?" she asked.

One by one the apples fell into his hands and he stopped juggling. Like a pro. "The rodeo. Need to have something to do for fun when you can't afford much else and you're sitting around waiting on your next bull ride and not trying to overthink that you're about to climb on the back of a two-thousand-pound animal—willingly." He shot her a wink.

"You're a bull rider?" This was something she hadn't seen coming. A totally dangerous career and one that took courage, strength, and an element of crazy...at least in her opinion.

"*Was* a bull rider. Retired now." Rusty's voice had grown tense, his easy smile nowhere in existence.

"Did the young guys drive you out?" she teased, trying to lighten his mood.

"You could say that," he said, putting the apples in a bag. "How many more should we get?"

It was a not-so-smooth change in subject but she knew well enough to let the subject drop.

"Roughly one hundred and fifty. It might be easier to grab the bags of Red Delicious. They have about ten apples each, so fifteen bags," she said, putting the paper bag of Granny Smith apples she'd handled into her cart for Trevor.

"Sounds like a plan," he said. "I should probably keep these," he said, his grin firmly back in place as he glanced down at the apples in his hands, "seeing as I played with them. No customer would appreciate taking these home." He chuckled.

"That's what I was thinking and why I'm keeping these for Trevor," she said gesturing to her cart.

They loaded up with the necessary bags of apples and then moved on to the vegetables, systematically picking out what was needed until their carts were overflowing. By the time they picked up the French vanilla ice cream, they were on their fifth and sixth carts. And having long since returned to an easy camaraderie, the subject of the rodeo was a closed one—not that she stopped wondering about his reaction.

The checkout process was equally demanding and time consuming as they tried to keep all the cold food products together, especially the ice cream. It wouldn't do to have it melt before they returned to the community center.

When the bill was tallied, Courtney went into a state of shock when she saw the total of the bill flash up on the digital screen. Just short of a thousand dollars.

"Wow, I had no idea how quickly this would add up. Perhaps I should have stuck with your simple cooking plan because I'm sure the menu was more budget friendly." She worried he would be upset with the expense.

Rusty shook his head. "Don't worry about it. The donations we receive cover almost all of the costs, and with a meal like this, the donations are sure to go higher. People will love this meal, if you can pull it all off, that is."

"Well, okay then. And by the way, I can pull it off." Or at least she hoped she could. He did say there would be others to help her, and even though she'd never done anything like this, she would give it her best shot. Being in charge of an event like this would certainly stand her resume in good stead. And she needed all the help she could get after being let go from her last job.

They loaded the groceries into the back of the truck and headed for the community center.

"I think this is an amazing program you have organized." She steered the conversation to a subject Rusty was comfortable with. "But I'm curious how a retired cowboy decides to go all in with something like this?" Courtney asked, hoping to understand what made him tick.

Rusty shrugged. "That's easy. At one point I was a hungry, down-on-my-luck cowboy, and I found a place much like the community center just outside of Cheyenne that offered free meals to anyone in town. It's open to everyone, not just people who need a meal. Once I started winning, I didn't need the program, but I kept going back there to eat."

Interesting and confusing. "But that doesn't make sense. Why make the program for everyone? It seems counterproductive to me."

"It's the people who don't need the food that keep the funding strong. This way lets them meet and mingle with the others who do. They see the reality of good people who need help, make friends, offer guidance, and best of all in some cases, even provide jobs. It's awe-inspiring to say the least."

She could hear the pride in his voice, and rightly so. Put the way he said, it was an amazing program that went well beyond supplying food to the needy. *It gave people access to a better life.* "Wow. I hadn't thought of that. There is way more to you than a retired rodeo rider, and I must say, it's endearing."

"You are putting way too much emphasis on the program. It's the only thing good I do, and the truth is, I started it because I was bored."

His comment startled her. It was almost as if he didn't want her to like him. But why should that be a problem? They were just friends. Unless it was simply his way to remind her he wasn't looking for a relationship.

But then, he knew she wasn't either—*so why the warning?*

Chapter Nine

♥

AFTER DROPPING THE GROCERIES off at the community center, Rusty had gone back to the ranch to check on things with Trevor and his mother. The two were knee-deep in baking cookies and he'd made himself scarce, using the time to knock out a few chores before the designated time to pick Courtney up.

Arriving at Laura's place, Rusty was pleased to see Courtney sitting on the porch. The fact his pulse raced a little faster when he spotted her wasn't something he wanted to give much thought to, unsure what it could possibly mean. The warmth of her smile was a definite attraction and one he needed to resist. So maybe the truth was closer to the fact he knew what the racing of his heart meant, but also knew that it was his cue to leave well enough alone.

More complications in his life was something he didn't need.

Rusty slid out of the truck and met her on the passenger side. "Good evening. I feel a little out of place seeing as you changed and I didn't," he said with a shake of his head. Her outfit was still jeans and boots, much like this afternoon, but now with the addition of a crème-colored pea coat, stylish came to mind and all but shouted city girl. Even her hair had been neatly pinned up, silver hoops dangling from her ears.

Very beautiful indeed.

"It's not like I'm dressed up or anything," she teased, shooting him a playful smile. "I could go back inside and change if it would make you feel better."

Rusty shook his head. "Not on your life. You look great."

Courtney's shy smile was more than a little endearing. "Thank you," she said, her cheeks flushing a light pink.

Driving through town, it wasn't long before he pulled up to the ranch house. The minute they slid out of the truck, the front door opened, and there was a flurry of activity on the porch. It would seem the welcome committee was in full force. His mother, his brother, his sister and her kids, and of course, Trevor, were all there. A true family affair, and the only one missing was his brother-in-law.

They were making way too much of Courtney coming to dinner, but he was used to his family and shouldn't be shocked. It was Courtney he was worried about. "I promise they won't bite. Well, maybe just a little, but I think you'll do alright," he said, keeping his voice low enough the words wouldn't carry on the slight breeze to anyone else.

"It'll be fine, trust me. I've learned to handle my in-laws, and if I can do that, I can handle anything." Courtney laughed.

Rusty made the introductions and it wasn't long before Trevor and his two nephews were off and running in the front yard with a game of tag, having already bonded and become good friends.

"We are so happy you could join us," Rebecca said, stepping forward to hug Courtney. "It's not often I have a woman my age that I can talk to. I live in a testosterone-filled world with the exception of my mother. And after dealing with boys being boys, and then dealing with men who act like boys, I'm ready for a change of pace."

Rusty took offense at being labeled as a man who acted like a boy, but then, truth be told, he probably had been that guy since he'd been home. And to be grouped with his brother and her husband, well that wasn't such a bad thing, was it?

"What a sweet thing to say. Thanks for the dinner invitation, I'm really looking forward to getting to know everyone. Your kindness barometer is clearly overflowing the way you have taken us under your wing. And thank you, Mary, for letting Trevor visit today. Shopping has never been his thing. He had such a great time at the barn, making cookies, and playing outside."

Mary nodded, her sweet smile reaching her eyes in sincerity. "No problem, deary. He's a good boy and minds well. Better than my own did if my memory serves me correct."

"It wouldn't take much for that, Mother," his brother said, playfully giving Rusty a shoulder push as if the two were comrades in arms.

Maybe once upon a time, but it hadn't stayed that way. "For sure," Rusty said, not looking to go down memory lane.

"You and Rusty had such a hard time staying out of trouble." His mother laughed.

"And here I thought Clay was always such a good boy." The truth was, once upon a time his brother liked to get into mischief with him. And then one day, he simply stopped. Rusty remembered it well as it had been the day after his brother's thirteenth birthday. It was as if he had grown up overnight and put away his childhood. Rusty hated the loss of his closest friend and big brother, and after that it seemed they drifted apart.

"Clearly old age is rattling your brain. Either that or the jarring you took on the back of a bull," Clay said, grinning.

"Or both," his sister quipped, joining in to tease him.

His mother led everyone inside, where they made their way toward the dining room.

"Rusty, could you set the table? It would be a big help," his mother added, knowing the last half of her comment wouldn't brook any opposition.

She had always had the gift when it came to getting her way. "Sure thing. Not like I have a choice unless I want to be sent to my room without any dinner," he teased, shooting Courtney a wink.

"I've got to run down and feed the cows before dinner, and while I'm there check on Fertile Myrtle. She's about to give birth to twins, and I want to be able to call the vet as soon as she shows signs of trouble," Clay said, making a beeline for the back door, neatly escaping from the cluster of women.

For once, Rusty didn't mind not having to do the chore, preferring to stay right where he was at.

"I wouldn't mind setting the table," Courtney offered.

"You are our guest. Perhaps you could sit on the stool and talk to us. We'd love to know more about you," his mother said, gesturing to the barstool nearby.

"I'd much rather be doing something productive. It makes me feel useful, and less like a freeloader," Courtney said, impressing Rusty that she was standing up to his mother.

Few did.

But then, Courtney was a strong woman. Or so she seemed on the outside. Inside, he didn't know her well enough to make that assessment. Perhaps by the end of the week he would have her all figured out. But for what, was the question.

"Well in that case, if you want to stir the sauce, that would be great. Sometimes it wants to stick to the bottom of the pan and it's never good when you get a little blackened flavor on the bottom of your sauce that doesn't come from a spice jar." His mother grinned. "And maybe you could fill everyone's water glass?"

"I'd love to," Courtney said, moving to the stove. "If you heat the pan before adding anything to it, everything sticks less. It's a physical transition that takes place on the stainless steel."

"Really? That's a great tip. And all the more reason we hope to see more of you while you're here. Just think of what I could learn. Perhaps some of your cooking knowledge will rub off on Rusty." Mary chuckled.

Rusty headed back into the dining room to set the table. The sound of laughter and raised voices came from the kitchen, Courtney obviously holding her own.

Another set of loud voices caught his attention, as the kids came barreling into the house and into the living room. At ages eight, ten, and eleven, they were definitely on the rambunctious side. They raced up towards him, Trevor stopping short in front of Rusty.

"Jordan said you used to be in the rodeo. That's awesome! And he said you used to ride bulls. How cool is that? I've never even seen a bull up close. Do you have any here? Can we go down to the barn? I want to see your horse. Will you show me what you do?" Trevor asked, firing off a non-stop list of questions.

"Slow down, Trevor. And yes, I used to be in the rodeo, but I'm not anymore." At some point, he would accept the change in his life, but so far it hadn't happened. Which made it all the more difficult to discuss. "I don't have any bulls here. I do have my horse. And dinner is almost ready, so we can't head for the barn as there's not enough time." *Thank goodness.* Rusty didn't want to encourage Trevor's enthusiasm, but unfortunately, there was nothing to be done about his nephews going on and on about his career as a bull rider.

"What about after dinner? Please..." Trevor's voice had a slight whine, but it was the dejected look on his face that tugged at Rusty's heart.

"Uncle Rusty was the best. He could ride those bulls and stay on for eight seconds and he's won lots of buckles. You gotta show Trevor how you ride, Uncle Rusty," Lee said, his eyes shining bright with admiration.

Buckles that he kept tucked away in a drawer. The last thing he wanted was reminders of the past. "Maybe some other time. You boys should go wash up for dinner."

The kids filed out of the room, the peace a welcome change after the whirlwind of emotion.

"What was that all about?" Courtney asked, as she came into the room, a serving tray in hand. She placed it on the table and then turned to look at him, waiting for an answer.

Rusty shrugged. "Nothing. Just the boys coming in from outside. I've sent them to get washed for dinner." *And to put an end to the rodeo chatter.*

"Good idea," Courtney said, her smile warming him with her praise.

It wasn't long before his mother rang the dinner bell that hung just outside the back door, alerting Clay it was time for dinner. The others all took their places at the table.

"Mom, did you know Rusty used to ride in the rodeo?" Trevor asked, his eyes wide with wonder.

Apparently the conversation had been ended, but not forgotten.

"I did. It came up today in conversation." Courtney looked at Rusty, a question in her eyes.

Trevor stopped eating, a thoughtful look on his face. "Rusty, I know you said we couldn't go look cause it was dinner time. But you said we might go to the barn after dinner. I want to see the kittens again. And I want to see your horse. *Please.* I bet he's the coolest horse ever," Trevor said, turning on his boyish charm yet again.

Everyone gazed in Rusty's direction, waiting for his answer. Talk about pressure. "I'm sure we can manage to see the kittens and the horse," Rusty relented, unable to totally disappoint the kid.

"Do you think you could teach me to rope and ride?" Trevor asked, on a roll and not sensing

Rusty's reluctance to talk about anything remotely associated with the rodeo.

But Trevor's roll just hit a pothole.

Rusty shook his head. "I don't rope anymore and I don't know the first thing about teaching a kid to ride. The rodeo is a part of my past and that's where it will stay."

Trevor's crestfallen look rattled Rusty, and the kid remained silent, making it all that much worse.

"Sorry. You're only eight which is a little young. It's a dangerous sport." And before he turned nine, the kid would be in Lafayette. *Problem solved.*

"But you taught us to ride Uncle Rusty," Jordan said.

His nephew didn't understand Rusty's reluctance and outed the truth, as though it were one of his proudest moments. "That's because you practically live here on the ranch and begged me every time I came to visit." Secretly, it had been one of his fondest memories associated with the ranch, something he'd done on one of his few trips home.

"And you learned to ride when you were seven, rope when you were eight, and ride young bulls by the age of ten," his mother said, correcting him. "I think Trevor is the perfect age to start learning."

It's as if they were all conspiring against him. "Again, I lived on a ranch and grew up around horses. Trevor's never visited a ranch until today. And don't forget, he'll be gone soon," Rusty said, determined not to give in to the pressure from his family.

Rebecca frowned. "Mom, quit pushing him," his sister chimed in, rallying to his defense. "You know he's not supposed to do strenuous work. The last thing he needs to be doing is teaching somebody how to ride a bull."

Although, judging by the tone of her voice it could be she was trying to manipulate him, but one thing was for sure...her comment irritated the heck out of Rusty.

"No one starts off on a bull, not even close. But he could teach the kid to ride a horse, don't you think? Rusty *can* ride and teaching a kid can be done from the saddle," his brother said, grinning at Rusty. His brother and sister were on the same side...the wrong one.

"True," his sister said, nodding.

"For that matter, while Courtney is in town, he could teach her also. Riding a horse is a thrill everyone should experience in their life. Whether it gets into their blood and they stick with it, is up to them," his mother added.

Definitely a con to get what they wanted—their matchmaking attempt way too obvious.

"I'm all for learning to ride," Courtney said, adding to the pressure. "But if Rusty's got medical issues and shouldn't be dealing with the stress of teaching us to ride, I think we shouldn't push him into something. Exactly what kind of medical issue are we dealing with?"

It was the sympathy and concern in her voice that agitated him the most. He'd had enough sympathy from everyone in town and especially his family. "It's nothing. I'm fine now and my family needs to stay out of it. I prefer not to discuss my health. And yes, I have the ability to teach Trevor to ride a horse, and you, if you're truly interested.

"In fact, tomorrow would be a great day to start his lessons. Since Courtney's got to be at the Community Center all day prepping for tomorrow's event, and I need to be as far away from the kitchen as possible. I can certainly keep Trevor with me and we can hang out here to stay out of the way." The words tumbled out before he could stop them, mostly because he didn't want to be thought of as less of a man in Courtney's eyes. Old-fashion pride had him speaking up, and whether he wanted to give lessons or not, became a moot point.

"Really? You mean it?" Trevor asked, his smile suddenly back in place.

"That's no fair. Why can't we ride with him?" Lee asked, crossing his arms over his chest and adding a pout for good measure.

"Because you've got school tomorrow, and Trevor doesn't because he's moving to Louisiana. It's a different situation, and your education comes first, young man," Rebecca said, calming her younger son.

"Yes ma'am," his nephew's crestfallen look sending an entirely different response.

"Are you sure? Courtney asked, doubt lacing her words in contrast to her previous proclamation.

"It will be fine—trust me. If there's one thing I know how to do, it's how to ride a horse. And if Trevor's not ready I'll put an end to the lesson."

"But I don't want you to feel pressured," Courtney offered.

Too late. "It's fine. The others are right…I'm an expert rider so I should be able to teach."

"Well that settles it then," Courtney said. "I guess you can have a lesson tomorrow, Trevor."

"Yay!" Her son jumped to his feet to race around to the opposite end of the table and give his mother a hug.

It was easier to give into the riding lessons than to pursue the subject of his health. A subject Rusty wasn't keen on discussing—with anyone. *Least of all Courtney.*

By the time dinner was over, Trevor was more than ready to go and see the kittens and meet Rusty's horse. Of course, the kid also had an agenda which he made no bones about. He wanted to be introduced to the mare he would be riding tomorrow.

"Can we all go to the barn, Uncle Rusty?" Jordan asked, after the table was cleared.

"Of course. The womenfolk can take care of the rest of the cleaning up," Rusty said, shooting his brother a grin.

"Don't even start with that women stuff." Rebecca tossed a towel at him. "Your Uncle is just teasing. There's no such thing as men's and women's chores. Which is exactly why your Uncle Rusty had to set the table before dinner. Almost all work can be done with the right resources, whether they are household chores or ranch chores. Trust me, growing up, I had to do both."

"Which is why you became an attorney." Rusty chuckled, his tension easing now that he was fully committed to teaching both Trevor and Courtney how to ride, the prospect quickly gaining favor.

"You're not helping. I'm trying to teach the kids a valuable lesson," his sister persisted.

"Okay, enough of the lecture. The boys already know all that, *and* they knew I was teasing."

"Just be sure it stays that way," Rebecca said, glaring at him.

Rusty and Clay headed for the barn with the boys, more than ready to escape. "We won't be gone long," he said to Courtney. "Will you be okay on your own? Or would you rather come with us?" he asked, shooting her a wink. "Maybe meet your horse," he added.

"I think I'll stay right here. Trevor's getting attached to those kittens and if I'm there, it increases the odds I'll give in to his pleas. That would not bode well. For my mother, myself, or Trevor." Courtney chuckled. "And by the way, you don't have to teach me. I was just teasing."

"I wasn't. You're not afraid, are you?" he asked, not wanting her to back out now that she had agreed.

"Maybe. Let's just table that part of the discussion for now."

"Don't say I didn't offer to spring you from the women in the kitchen. Or more like, don't say I didn't warn you to run," he added in hushed tones before heading out the back door.

"Consider myself warned," Courtney called out after him.

She was as feisty as she was sweet, a combination he rather liked.

A lot.

Chapter Ten

♥

Courtney and Mary watched through the back door as the three boys and two men headed toward the barn. Lined up in a straight row they looked like a force to be reckoned with. "I had a lovely time this evening. Thank you again for inviting us," Courtney said, just as Rebecca joined them.

Mary put an arm around her waist and drew her close for a semi-hug. "You're welcome, dear. It was just as much fun for us. A change in pace is always nice and it's not often Rusty brings a woman home."

"You can say that again," Rebecca said. She pulled her sweater jacket around tighter. "In fact, you're the first. Sure is chilly outside tonight. Not sure I'd want to be out in the barn closed in with the scent of manure, sweat, and hay. Sounds like a recipe for allergies." Rebecca laughed.

Who was Courtney to dash the women's fun? Fanciful notions of a happily-ever-after wouldn't happen, but the pair would find that out soon enough. You couldn't make two people fall in love, especially when one of the two, had already had one great love in her life. Something they didn't know and something she had no intention of explaining. "Me either."

"You know, I haven't seen Rusty smile this much since he's been back home. You're good for him," his mother said. "Trust me, a mother sees and understands these things. Too bad I couldn't convince you to stick around. The town could use someone who could cook as well as you do, so your talents wouldn't go to waste. I promise."

Perhaps Mary did need reigning in a bit. Although, she wasn't the first to comment about Courtney sticking around beyond the end of the week. Rusty had jokingly said the same thing.

"In Crossroads Creek, Mother? I'm sure Courtney would be overqualified, but that being said, it sure would be nice to have her and her cooking around."

Mary nodded. "True. I just know she'd be good for Rusty." The two women talked as if she weren't standing there.

It was time to put an end to the discussion. "That's very sweet of you both, but I'm already committed to moving in with my mother. It's time I moved forward with the next stage of my life. My husband passed away a little over a year ago, and it's been a difficult time to say the least. I'm sure you can understand my need to regroup." It wasn't easy vocalizing her thoughts and feelings, but it was more than necessary to stop these two in their matchmaking efforts.

"We understand, dear." His mother nodded. "Rusty's medical issues brought him home eighteen months ago, and we keep pushing him to move forward with his life now that he's mostly better. Sometimes, life knocks you down a little harder than expected, but hope is always just around the corner. A person needs to open themselves up to possibilities. Likewise, perhaps your possibilities could be right here in Crossroads Creek."

They had gone full circle back to Rusty's medical condition. His family was quite protective of him, even if they didn't see it. She understood some of the animosity Rusty exhibited in regard to their interference in his life. It was a lot like her in-laws and even her own mother. *They all thought they knew best.*

Rusty had been obvious in his desire not to discuss his medical history for reasons of his own, something Courtney could respect. She, too, kept the book on her life closed. *For the most part.* Trevor, on the other hand, was the lucky recipient of riding lessons in Rusty's quest to change the subject at dinner earlier.

It was a wonderful opportunity, one that wouldn't come around again anytime soon. *If ever.* Truth be told, she too was looking forward to the opportunity to ride. It wasn't something she had ever done as a child, but neither would she push Rusty to honor the offer.

After the kitchen was cleaned and spotless, she moved back to the doorway, gazing out at the beautiful starlit sky. "It's breathtaking how clear it is out here in the country. I can see forever," she said, awed by the wonderous heavenly sights.

"The absence of city lights makes everything brighter, clearer. You should ask Rusty to point out some of the constellations in the sky. He was always better in science class than I was," Rebecca said, without a hint of jealousy.

The easy camaraderie between the brothers and sisters wasn't something she'd ever experienced as an only child. And family fun...that was a thing of the past with Greg gone. Courtney truly enjoyed spending time with Rusty's family, but it also made her realize what she was missing—and by extension, what Trevor was missing.

The Devoe family wasn't at all like her stuffy in-laws with their upright attitudes in life. Which was exactly why she refused to move in with them at their urging. It would be all too easy for them to take over her life, something she wouldn't let happen. She'd vowed to move forward and be strong for Trevor, and she couldn't do that under someone's wing of favor.

Unfortunately, it also meant tonight was just a tease for something she couldn't have. *Would never have.* Even Trevor seemed to be in his element playing with the other kids. The Devoe family had welcomed them both without reservation. An odd feeling of warmth settled in the region of her heart, one she embraced.

This was the most relaxed she'd been since Greg's death. And it was all due to Rusty and his family. And Laura. Well, okay. So Crossroads Creek itself. Every inch of the town was in full splendor of Christmas and elicited a depth of emotion she hadn't expected.

Last year, she almost hadn't put up a tree. For Trevor, she'd gone through the motions, but the result was the same. The Christmas spirit was noticeably missing in both her and her son. This year, the timing of her move was lucky and that she wouldn't have to fake the Christmas joy. Her mother, Laura, and the Devoe family had more than enough to cover her shortage.

"So when do you think your truck will be fixed?" Rebecca asked.

"Charlie said the part would be in by this weekend and then he'd need half a day to drop in the new radiator." Too long in Courtney's mind. She felt at loose ends, living in a stranger's house, her belongings in a storage unit in Lafayette, and the rest on the truck at the garage. She was truly living out of a suitcase.

Not exactly the life she had pictured for herself a short year ago.

"Well, then, you need to come back to dinner another night later in the week. Maybe we can plan something fun with the boys," she offered.

"There's always the skate rink," his mother chimed in, not to be left out of the planning stages.

"That sounds like fun, but neither Trevor nor I skate." It would seem there was a lot of adventure and experiences available here. Trevor would be in his element and hate to leave. What kid wouldn't want what the ranch offered?

"There's always a first. Look," she said, pointing outside. "There's all our guys."

Trevor ran ahead and jumped up on the porch, racing inside the house.

"Whoa, slow down, young man," Courtney admonished.

"Yes, ma'am. But you should have come with us. Hope followed me around the barn and chased a ball. And then I met Rusty's horse, Thunder. He is all black, like the horse in Black Beauty. And he's so big. Way bigger than me. And then there was my horse. She has this huge white mark on her head, but the rest of her is brown. *Hmmm*...I think Rusty called it Bald. Which makes no sense cause she has lots of hair. Her name is Angel. I like angels, don't I, Mom?" Trevor asked.

"Not so fast, I can't keep up with you." Courtney laughed, ruffling her son's hair. His love of life reminded her so much of Greg, it was hard not to embrace the connection.

"A sentiment I second," Rusty said, grinning as he joined the group.

"So who's Hope?" Courtney asked, regretting it the minute she circled back to the comment. *Chasing a ball could only mean one thing.*

"My favorite kitten and she's all white. Isn't that cool? Please, Mom, can we take her to grandma's house? She needs a home and I can take care of her. I promise," he added, the last spoken like a solemn vow.

Courtney would love to give in, but it wasn't in the cards. Not just yet. "You probably could take care of her, but the timing isn't right. I'm so sorry, Trevor."

Her son's bottom lip jutted out, his shoulders slouched in defeat.

"You should count your blessings and not focus on what you can't have," Courtney admonished.

"Okay," he mumbled. "So can I really ride Angel tomorrow?"

"Absolutely. If Rusty says it's okay and he's right there to teach you, I don't see why not,"

Courtney said, grateful for the olive branch that would pull her son back out from his funk.

"Promise?"

"I promise. Wild horses couldn't change my mind," she said with a grin, trying to tease her son out of the blue mood he'd fallen into.

"Angel isn't wild," Trevor added innocently. "She's the tamest horse I've ever met."

"The only horse you've ever met. And the wild horses thing, that's just an expression that means nothing will change my mind. Tomorrow you can ride, but only as long as you listen to everything Rusty says and mind him. Do we have a deal?" Courtney asked.

"I will." Trevor nodded, his good mood fully returned.

"Let's go play a video game," Jordan said.

"You've got fifteen minutes, guys. School night," Rebecca reminded them.

"Okay," they responded in unison before running out of the room.

"It's a bit chilly out, but there's not a cloud in the sky. Do you want to take a walk?" Rusty asked.

"We were just talking about that very thing. A walk sounds lovely and it would give us all a chance to enjoy the fresh air. Just let me get my jacket," Courtney said, excited at the prospect.

"Oh no. Not me. I see the sky all the time. I'll keep an eye on the boys," Rebecca said, waving her hand as she left the room. "Enjoy."

"I've had a long day and I'm worn out. I think I'll stay put," Mary said, rejecting the offer. Suddenly, the refusal to join the walk fell into place. It was clear what they were up to, but there was no turning back on her response. They had definitely scored a point on this round, but she was onto their methods.

Rusty helped her into her jacket. "Shall we?" He gestured toward the back door.

Suddenly shy, Courtney stepped back. "Lead away. You know where to go." It was easier to follow him into the darkness than to let him see how much her nerves had gone into overdrive. Luckily, the pitch-black night would help keep her secret. "Can I ask you something?" It was easier to lead the conversation and let him lead the walk.

"You can ask, just not sure I'll answer," he teased, taking her by the hand as they passed through a gate to the pasture.

"Fair enough. You mentioned you were in the rodeo and when we talked, you said something about younger guys taking over. I got the impression it was a natural transition. Now, I'm not so sure. Several times your family has mentioned about your medical condition, but you are very hush hush about it all. I'm not prying into your medical history, but I'm curious about something else entirely. From what I gather, you've been working on the ranch for the past year and a half. The thing is, I sense you resent being here, and I wonder why you stay." Maybe it was the night sky, or the fact he was still holding her hand, but something gave her the courage to ask what had been uppermost in her mind.

"It's that obvious, huh? This is my brother's ranch. My father had him slated to run things from the beginning and I was basically unnecessary. Clay was the golden boy, while I was the problem child. My father never thought I did anything right and that I wasn't excelling. It's why I left the ranch in the first place. But as to being back…he's still my brother and I help out as much as I'm allowed. The *ummm*, medical condition required down time, and then surgery. And afterward, R&R was on the menu. This was where I grew up, and it was all I had left. So, I stayed."

"But why continue to stay if it doesn't make you happy?" she asked as they reached the end of the lane and turned back toward the house.

"I'm still trying to figure out what to do after the rodeo life," Rusty said, surprising her with the truth.

They had a lot in common on that score as it was the same problem she was experiencing. Figuring out what to do with her life, only her circumstances were different.

Courtney had a feeling there was far more to his story than he let on. It was almost as if he was adopting a carefree, live each day as it came lifestyle, something that didn't impress her. People needed plans and goals. A focus. But then his lifestyle was in complete odds with the image of the man she knew, the one who delivered kittens to old ladies, helped stranded motorists on the side of the road, put together an entire soup kitchen program, and offered to give riding lessons when it clearly wasn't his first choice of activity.

Or second or even third, for that matter.

The question was...who was the real Rusty Devoe?

Not that it mattered. She was leaving in a few days, but for some reason...it did matter. She felt compelled to help him, even though it made no sense. "We should get going," Courtney said, when they arrived back at the porch. It was getting late and she didn't want to wake Laura by arriving past her bedtime.

"Okay. I'll meet you out front. That will give me a chance to start the truck and get it warmed up."

"Great. And Rusty...thanks for tonight. Truly," Courtney said, moved by yet another act of thoughtful kindness.

"You're welcome. Truly." He gazed down at her for what seemed an eternity, the silence of the night between them. But then he turned, stepped off the porch, and disappeared around the house and into the dark of the night.

Rusty was definitely one of the good guys, but how to help him see his way clear of whatever was holding him back, she didn't have a clue.

Especially given he wasn't an open book.

Chapter Eleven

❤

Arriving at Laura's house sharply at eight a. m., Rusty pulled into the driveway and waited a few moments, expecting Courtney and Trevor to appear any minute as was their norm. Several minutes ticked by and he decided to check on them. Rusty knocked and it wasn't long before the door opened and Laura stood there.

"Good morning, Rusty," she said, a bright smile on her face.

The older woman hadn't been quite herself the past couple of years since her husband's passing, and people around town not only noticed, but were worried. Loneliness was a hard void to fill, something he knew all too well. With plenty of time spent on the road as a rodeo cowboy, he was more than qualified as an expert on the subject. Talk about a lonely job, that is, unless you were into the parties and rodeo bunnies—which he was not. "Good morning, Laura. Did I get the time wrong for picking Courtney up?" he asked glancing down at his watch.

She shook her head. "Oh no, they're almost ready. I think all the excitement yesterday wore Trevor out and he was a bit difficult to get up and moving this morning."

"I see. Well, that's good then considering he's spending the day with me at the ranch. Perhaps he'll be easier to keep up with if I don't have to worry about him running off anywhere." His experience with kids added up to zero, so why he offered to give the kid lessons was beyond all rationale. Except he wasn't thinking rationally at dinner when he made the offer. He was think-ing about changing the subject of his medical history.

"I heard you were giving Trevor riding lessons. I can tell he needs some extra male influence in his life, most likely because he's lost without his father. This is a really good thing you're doing, Rusty."

Laura would do well to keep her praise on reserve mode until he got through the day. There was no telling what would happen between now and then. "Well, it's the least I could do since Courtney is helping me out by filling in the position of glorified cook tonight."

"You two seem to be getting quite close. Perhaps there's a special connection happening between you?" Laura made no bones about wanting information—matchmaking information.

A subject he needed to stay clear of. "We're just friends. She's passing through town, and although, yes, there's a connection between us, it's called friendship. I don't even know what I'm doing with my life, so I'm not exactly in a place to offer a woman anything." And of course, he had already decided there would never be a place for a relationship of that nature in his life again. Between his medical condition and scarred body, the vow he made to himself not long after he got out of the hospital hadn't changed. If anything, the sense it was the right decision had grown stronger with each passing day.

"Hogwash. Connection is what it takes. It's where it all starts. And if it's fate, you can't avoid it, young man. Don't go thinking you know more than God," she admonished.

"Yes, ma'am." It was easier to agree at this point than to argue, especially since he noticed a flurry of activity out of the corner of his eye as Courtney approached. She was already having to deal with his family and their matchmaking efforts, and she wouldn't appreciate Laura jumping in the mix.

"Sorry I'm running late. Trevor will be down in a minute," Courtney said, a broad smile on her face. Dressed in jeans and a light blue blouse, she reminded him of fresh country sunshine. Her blond curls bounced prettily around her face as she scurried around the room picking up toys.

"It's all good. Laura was explaining to me that Trevor is a bit tired this morning. I reckon that's a good thing, especially when it comes to riding lessons."

Courtney stopped in her tracks and gazed at him. "So you're really going to do that still?"

"I did promise—and I keep my promises." Not that he wouldn't jump at the chance to get out of it, but a deal was a deal. No matter what the circumstances, honor was important to him.

Trevor bounded down the staircase. "Hey, Rusty! Are we headed to the ranch right now? I can't wait to see Hope and Angel." The boy didn't slow down one iota as he pulled on his jacket and zipped it up.

Rusty remembered having the same level of enthusiasm about the ranch at Trevor's age. It only took a few years after that to realize his father didn't share the joy. His old man thought of the ranch as a job, nothing more...nothing less. And not one he enjoyed. "We just need to drop your mother off at the Community Center and then we'll head to the ranch. But fair warning, we've got a couple of chores to do while it warms up this morning before the lessons."

Courtney shot him a surprised glance but didn't say a word.

Trevor nodded. "Okay. I promised mom I would do whatever you asked me to do today and that I would be a good boy. I'm gonna be on my best behavior."

Rusty laughed, noting the promise had been delivered with such a serious expression for a young boy. "Thanks for making it easy for me today," he said, shooting Courtney a grin. "I figured you were right and a couple of chores would build character. I also figured it would free up the time needed to focus on Trevor."

Courtney smiled. "I'm all for it."

On that note, they all headed for the truck. It wasn't long before they crossed town and pulled up to the Community Center.

"Trevor, we need to go inside for a minute so I can introduce your mom to everybody."

"Okay, but just a minute," Trevor said, dead serious. The kid was keeping his eye on the prize so to speak, which bode well for today's adventure.

"Thank you, Rusty. I do appreciate you doing this. I'm nervous enough as it is without having to suffer through introductions on my own," Courtney said, sliding out of the truck.

He hadn't seen this side of her before—the not-so-confident side. Courtney always exuded a strong personality, as though she were a force to be reckoned with. Maybe the past year had made her stronger, but this other side, was endearing. It elicited a need for him to protect and lend support.

Rusty took her by the hand and led her inside. "You'll be fine. I promise," he said, hoping to reassure her. The minute her hand was in his, the connection he knew existed intensified. The feeling of belonging was not something he expected. It was a feeling he couldn't explain, but he was loath to let her hand drop even after they entered the building.

And since she hadn't pulled away, he kept her hand right where it was—firmly locked in his own, and only dropping it as they moved into the kitchen.

Most of the others were already there, ready and waiting to begin the meal preparations. "Hey, everyone. I wanted to introduce you to

Courtney Winters, and her son, Trevor. Courtney has graciously agreed to help us out this week, seeing as Alfred had to leave town on an emergency. She's an assistant chef from Wichita and we are quite lucky to have her, even if it's only for today. Wait till you see what she has in store. If you all would simply follow her lead, and at some point introduce yourself, that would be great. Courtney has some great ideas on how to ramp up the menu and still get it ready by six o'clock when the doors open."

Several of the volunteers murmured and nodded, the general sense in the room one of relief that they wouldn't be called to step up and take charge of the kitchen.

Courtney stepped forward to address the staff. Flipping her hair back from her face, a move he recognized as nerves, Rusty sent her a smile when she looked in his direction.

"Good morning, everyone. Thanks for the warm welcome and I look forward to working with you. I thought about doing a theme night and came up with the idea of "pie night" for this evening's event. So today we're going to serve

Shepherd's pie, Chicken pot pie, and Apple pie, as our featured dishes. I thought I would pick up some ready-made flaky crust dough for us to use. Mind you, I wouldn't normally go this route, but given the circumstances, I feel it's called for. And if we put everything together assembly-line style, we could turn out massive amounts of casseroles and Apple pies in short order. So if anyone has any questions before we get started I'm happy to answer them."

Tommy raised his hand at the back of the group. "Who's going to be doing what?"

"Good question, and one I have an answer for. There will be assigned stations. I'll make a list of what we need done and leave it up to everyone to volunteer for the section or sections they prefer. And if you're open to anything, then you can just let me assign what might be leftover."

Murmurs rippled through the group, but everyone seemed more than satisfied with Courtney's answer. The room fell silent, and they turned expectantly back to Courtney.

"Well, if there are no other questions...then let's get to it," she said, taking charge.

Rusty and Trevor were soon back in the truck and on their way to the ranch, and he felt confident Courtney had everything under control. Trevor was nonstop talkative about Angel and making sure Rusty knew just how good he would be at riding. The kid had no clue what was in store, because for Rusty...riding horses was far more complex than simply climbing onto a horse's back and riding off into the sunset.

When Trevor wasn't talking about Angel, he was talking about Hope. But on that score, Rusty was pretty certain that no matter how many times the kid asked his mother for the kitten, the answer would not change.

They pulled into the ranch and Rusty felt as though his ear had already been talked off. He was used to doing chores alone and this was a whole different scenario. Not a bad one by any means, just different. As a loner, he hadn't spent much time around kids other than his nephews on the rare occasion he had come home for a visit.

Trevor bounded out of the truck and raced around to his side. "So what do we do first? Put on a saddle?"

Rusty shook his head. How quickly kids forgot the parts they didn't want to remember. "No. Remember I told you we need to do chores first. I have responsibilities I can't ignore, and one of those is feeding the horses. They expect their morning meal at the same time every day or they can get ornery. I'll start to explain horses and what makes them unique, what they need from us as their human owners. Angel has a lot of needs, and you need to understand more of her personality and quirks in order to be able to ride her. Angel must like you and trust you."

"But she already met me. And loves me. I did feed her a carrot last night. Doesn't that count?" Trevor asked hopefully, some of his exuberance waning.

"She smelled you and you passed the first test, which does count. But there's more to it than feeding her one carrot on the first meeting. You need to trust me on this."

Trevor nodded. "So what kind of chores?"

Rusty was willing to test the kids tolerance of all things horses. Starting with the worst chore for any kid. "The first thing anyone needs to learn is how to muck a stall."

"What's mucking? I'm not sure what that is," Trevor asked, a questioning expression on his freckle-specked face.

"Mucking is another word for cleaning. Horses eat, and they for the lack of a better word, poop a lot of manure. And pee. Lots and lots of pee." Rusty was trying to think in terms that an eight-year-old boy would understand and find funny.

"I have to clean poop?" Trevor asked, his face scrunched up into a frown.

Okay, so maybe funny in a joke and not when they had to work with it. "Yes. It's something I do every day. And if you want to ride, you get to muck out Angel's stall. We lead them out to a feeding area and clean while they are outside so it doesn't scare them."

"Please tell me I don't have to pick it up with my hands and that you have a shovel or something. That would be gross." The kids sense of humor had returned and Rusty wouldn't mess with his head.

"Yes. We have something called a pitchfork to do the dirty work. You simply have to operate the tool," he said, shooting Trevor a grin. "A pitchfork is designed with three tines, which are like metal fingers. It makes it easy for you to scoop up the manure and dirty hay, and then we toss it into a wheelbarrow. After we have a full load, it's hauled out to the manure pile and dumped. That pile is used for compost and making fertilizer...so it doesn't go to waste."

"Sounds like a lot of work. So if the manure makes fertilizer, what's the fertilizer used for?"

"It makes the plants grow big and strong," Rusty explained. He hadn't realized this would turn into a science lesson.

"Plants? Like flowers?" Trevor asked, suddenly stopping.

"Like flowers, yes, but on a cattle ranch we use it to fertilize the ground so it helps the pasture grass grow better. Although some of it does go in our vegetable garden."

Trevor shook his head. "No way. The plants here grow because of horse poop? No one would believe me if I told them."

"It's true." Rusty grinned. "But it doesn't affect the food we get from the plants, so don't worry."

"I don't know. Still sounds like a lot of work just to throw it on plants for food. And it sounds disgusting."

"It is work, but if riding horses becomes a part of who you are, then it's well worth it. To me, there's no greater sense of purpose and peace than riding the land and communing with Mother Nature." He loved the rodeo, but it was the countryside rides that captured his love of horses in the first place. *The sense of oneness with the world.* Something he hadn't experienced in a while—and perhaps something he needed to focus on. Maybe that's where he would find the answers he was searching for in life.

They started walking toward the barn again.

"But you love riding bulls, right?" Trevor asked.

The kid had no way of knowing it wasn't a subject Rusty cared to discuss. "I did. And yes, it was a huge thrill. But riding bulls comes with its own set of issues. *Dangerous issues.* It takes a lot of practice and experience to master bull riding."

"I wanna be just like you when I grow up," Trevor said, beaming at him.

The boy had a great attitude, but it wouldn't be Rusty teaching him to ride a bull. And in Lafayette, there would be few and far between chances anyway.

Rusty pulled open the barn door and the two entered, the familiar smell of horse sweat, hay, and manure assailing his senses. *This is where he belonged.* And even though his career as a rodeo cowboy was over, he couldn't imagine doing anything with his life that didn't involve horses. Figuring out what that looked like, well, that was another story entirely.

The thought of Courtney on a horse riding beside him through the countryside flashed through his mind, but he quickly pushed the image away.

Trevor ran ahead to where the kittens were located, dropping to his knees to scoop up Hope and nuzzle his face against hers. "She's purring, Rusty. She recognizes me and she loves me as much as I love her. My mom has just gotta let me have this kitten," Trevor said, a slight whine in his voice. Something that always happened when it came to trying to get his way.

Trevor had as much of a chance convincing his mother to let him have that kitten, as Rusty had of a riding a bull again. *None.*

"Well, she says it's not a good time to get a kitten. You need to listen to her because mothers know best." It was an interesting thought, given his mother and some of her ideas, Rusty clearly didn't think were for the best. But he had no intentions of getting into a philosophical discussion with an eight-year-old on the subject. "You should just enjoy the time you do have with Hope. Make the most of it, and then you'll have those memories to take with you when you leave."

Trevor's pitiful expression tugged at his heartstrings. The boy had been through a lot and Rusty would have a hard time saying no to him. But it was Courtney's decision, and he would abide by it.

"But I really want her," Trevor whined.

Rusty shook his head. "You can't always have everything you want. It's a part of growing up and life."

Trevor's face fell, a mask of indifference echoed in his eyes. The boy had retreated to a place Rusty couldn't follow, and it took him off guard to see the change.

"You mean like wanting my dad to come back?" Trevor asked.

Rusty drew up short. This wasn't something he had seen coming. And he was the last person who should be answering a child's questions about his father, or about life and death for that matter, given his own history with his father. "Your mom said your dad's in heaven. That means he can't physically be here with you on earth, but I'm positive he's always with you. In here," Rusty said, tapping his heart to emphasize the point. He had no idea where the words were coming from, but he was thankful they were there.

Trevor scuffed his feet on the ground, kicking up hay. "I guess. I just miss him. A lot," he said, his voice vibrating with a level of anguish that hit Rusty square in the gut.

It made him want to reach out and protect the child and hug Trevor. Rusty resisted the urge, unsure of how the gesture would be received. He couldn't replace the child's father. Laura's words came back to mind about Trevor needing a male influence in his life. Perhaps she was more right than either of them had realized.

"My dad died, too. But it was a long time ago. I can tell you from experience it'll hurt less in time." Rusty originally thought it would be a quick process, but as it turned out, it had taken him far longer than he could have ever expected. The only logical conclusion was that his father wasn't there to give him what he wanted which was a seal of approval. That was the hardest part of letting him go. "But I know something that will help turn your blues to a more positive way of thinking right about now," Rusty said, coming to a decision.

Trevor scrunched up his face. "Mucking stalls is supposed to cheer me up?"

"Tell you what, right after the horses eat and we finish the stalls, we'll go for a ride. No extra lessons on care and horses until after the ride. Or during the ride," he corrected. Rusty was about to break all the rules he had just created about learning how to ride. Maybe they both needed some fun right about now, but the horses care came first—no matter what.

Trevor's face lit up like a beacon. "You mean it?"

And just like that they were back on track. "I do. I'll explain things along the way as we go, so you must pay close attention and really focus." Angel was one of the friendliest, sweet-tempered mares, and Trevor would be fine riding her. Rusty would stick close, and on the upside, it would also give him an opportunity to observe the kid to see where his talent for riding fell.

"I will, I promise."

Forty-five minutes later, the immediate chores were done, and all without complaint.

"That's it, kiddo. Time to ride."

"Yes, sir," Trevor followed him to the tack room.

"We'll start with Thunder's saddle so you can watch what I do. Then, we can work together on saddling Angel to reinforce what you learned. Deal?" He said, grabbing Thunder's saddle and heading for the pen.

"Deal."

Trevor was an avid listener—and learner. Rusty explained about blind spots, approaching from the left, and what to expect once in the saddle. The basics to make Trevor's first ride a success.

"Alright then. It's time to ride," Rusty said, knowing this was the moment the kid had been waiting for. Some of the enthusiasm was rubbing off on him, as he remembered the rush of adrenaline he'd experienced as a boy learning to ride. "Just remember all the tips I told you and stay close to me so I can teach you more as we take a slow walk down the pasture lane."

"Yes, sir," Trevor beamed as Rusty lifted him up into the saddle.

"Put the fronts of your foot in the stirrup and drop your heel slightly. This will keep your foot from slipping through."

"Yes, sir." Trevor sat straight up and did what he was told, not a lick of fear present.

Rusty adjusted the stirrups to fit Trevor's leg length, and then rechecked the cinch strap and bridle, making sure everything was just right. "Keep a light touch on the reins, and remember the horse knows the signals, so it's you who needs to learn them. If you need to keep one hand on the saddle horn for balance," he added, touching the raised knob for emphasis, "then it's okay. As a beginning rider it's important you feel comfortable and safe. To turn, gently move the reins against the horse's neck on the opposite side of the direction you want to go. It's called a rein signal. When the strap touches a horse's neck, they know what to do because they are well trained. And you say *whoa* to stop." It was a lot of information at once, but he could repeat it as they moseyed through the pasture.

"Yes, sir."

Rusty took the extra lead attached to Angel in hand, and mounted Thunder. He led Angel forward to get things moving, letting Trevor experience the thrill of his first ride while Rusty ultimately had control of the horse.

By the time they reached the end of the pasture, Rusty was convinced the kid was a natural. And best of all, Trevor paid attention, followed instructions, and the results showed. For lesson number two, Rusty would need to go back to the basics and show the kid a lot more about horses and understanding them, but this was an excellent start.

Realizing what he was thinking, gave Rusty pause. Lesson two meant he intended to continue teaching Trevor, and this wasn't a one-off occurrence. It was totally unexpected, but the truth was, Rusty sort of enjoyed showing Trevor the ropes.

"I can't wait to show my mom. Do you think she could come out and watch me tomorrow?" Trevor asked.

"I don't know. That's something we'll have to check with her and her schedule. She did sort of agree to a riding lesson." And Rusty relished the idea of teaching Courtney and spending more time with her.

"Does this mean you will give me another lesson?"

Rusty nodded. "Sure thing. You did a good job today, son."

Trevor looked up at him, a frown marring his face. Just as quickly, the frown vanished. Rusty realized his mistake in calling him son, but the word had just slipped out. Lucky for him, Trevor didn't make a big deal of it.

"Since I did really good today, can't you please teach me to ride a bull? I wanna be able to tell the kids at school that I rode a bull. That'll mean I'm big and strong. And everyone will like me. They'll think it's really cool. Please," Trevor said, turning his baby blues on Rusty and hoping for a yes.

Talk about turning up the pressure, but Rusty wasn't one to be coerced. Not by his family and not by a young boy. "Riding bulls for other people is never the answer. If you ride bulls, it comes from your heart. It has to be something that's a part of you. You ride for yourself and the challenge. And as to me teaching you, I just don't think that's a good idea. You've got a lot to learn between today and something like that happening. It's a dangerous sport and requires intensive training. You'll be leaving soon, so there's not much point."

Trevor's crestfallen face caused knots to form in Rusty's stomach...proof he wasn't immune to the boy. "But I'll think about a roping lesson if you continue to do well and stay focused on learning the basics of riding," he relented. It didn't mean he would do it, only that he would consider showing the kid the ropes.

As to bull riding, the sport had been his life. But learning to ride for himself and teaching someone were two different things. How could he leave the rodeo way of life behind if he did not let go of it entirely? Luckily, none of it mattered. It was just like he'd told Trevor...the kid was a long way from being ready for a bull.

They unsaddled the horses and Rusty explained the process of grooming the horse after a ride, showing Trevor how to brush them and use a curry comb, something horses loved if used correctly. He handed Trevor an apple treat to give his horse as a reward for being patient with the process. Trevor held out his hand, palm flat, just the way Rusty had taught him. Angel nibbled it off the boy's hand with the delicacy of an oversized pet whose mouth was bigger than Trevor's hand.

"We should head back to the house and check in with my mother," Rusty said when they finished and led the horses back to their stalls.

"But wait, we were supposed to look for Charlotte. Remember?" Trevor asked, suddenly remembering the spider, the pig, and Rusty's promise.

He had forgotten, but the reminder spurred him in the direction of the pig pens. "I hadn't, but since we're here, it's a good time to see if we can spot her. Look over there," he said, pointing to the far back right-side corner. "That's where I normally see the spider."

"I don't see any web. Where else does she go?" Trevor asked, gazing around the pen, still hoping to find the writing spider.

"I'm not sure. Let's look around in the other corners and up in the rafters. You never know what we'll find." Rusty led the way, making a great show of searching for Charlotte and any sign of a web.

Trevor climbed up on the stall rails to get a better view. "I don't see her. Maybe something happened to Charlotte," he said, the sadness in his words making it obvious he thought the spider had come to a tragic ending.

Perhaps his line of thinking was directly attributed to the loss of his father. Rusty wasn't an expert in kids, but it would make sense. "Or maybe she's tucked in a hole or a split in the rafter to keep warm. We can check again tomorrow when you come back." Assuming Courtney didn't nix the idea.

Trevor's smile slid back into place. "Thanks, Rusty. You're the best." The kid jumped down and headed for the door that led out of the barn.

"You're welcome, kiddo." They headed for the house, side by side. Spending time with Trevor came easy, the boy making him feel wanted. *Useful.* Something Rusty hadn't felt since coming home. The fact was, Trevor didn't know about Rusty's heart condition and didn't see him as a medical project.

Coming home had been the right thing to do at the time, but he was ready for something more. The trick was tapping into the level of satisfaction he had experienced today, which meant figuring out *why* it was different.

Chapter Twelve

♥

STEPPING BACK FROM THE counter, Courtney glanced around the kitchen, satisfied with the efforts of the team. They were more than ready to kick the night off, and if the comments of the others were anything to go by—the evening would be a huge success.

A menu change was always a good idea, and staple foods that appealed to almost everyone was another check in the win column. She couldn't help but fast forward her thinking process toward the future. There was a lot riding on this evening, something she hadn't thought of when she first agreed to take over the responsibilities of planning and preparing for the event.

If all went well tonight, the bonus of a reference from Rusty on her resume might make finding a job in Lafayette a lot easier. The community center was only a temporary, one-off job, but it was unique in that it catered to such a large group of people.

It wasn't the first time she considered breaking down in Crossroads Creek to be a blessing in an odd sort of way. And so far, her troubles hadn't multiplied. In fact, they were kept simple.

This was truly a lesson in faith and trusting in God's plan for her life. She could have broken down anywhere, but instead, she had landed here—a small town filled with kind people who welcomed her into their midst. Especially Rusty, who saw fit to introduce her to his family and offer her the job. She wasn't likely to forget his part in all this, giving him full credit for turning a bad situation into an acceptable one. *More than acceptable considering the fun she and Trevor shared with his family.*

The only thing she needed to be careful of was letting Trevor get too attached to the kitten,

Laura, and mostly, Rusty. The latter being the hardest to negate or would be after Trevor's riding lesson today. The bond between the two might rise to a level not soon forgotten, especially as her son might be searching for a replacement father figure in his life. Something else out of her control.

It was like having a friendship partner, something she hadn't thought she would ever experience again, and the thought made her more than a little nervous. The emotional pull of sharing dinner with his family drew her in, but it wasn't right. It wasn't fair to Greg, which is why she had to nix any developing feelings she had for Rusty.

Of course, Greg's parents hadn't let go of their son yet, and spoke almost as if their son were just away on a business trip. It made it more than a little difficult for Courtney to move forward with life when they constantly brought his name up. Things like wondering what he would say about her decision to move home. Or questioning her judgement for staying in

Crossroads Creek. And most of all, raising her son on her own. *Heaven forbid.*

It's not like Courtney could change the past, but the future was different. It was hers and hers alone. And then there was her own mother she had to deal with. She too, hadn't liked Courtney's decision to stick around town. But unbeknownst to anyone else, there was an added benefit to staying in Crossroads Creek, and not just the truck repair money she would earn tonight.

The extra days would give Courtney time to ask around town about W.D. *The organ donor recipient for her husband's heart.* The idea had come to her out of the blue, and since then, it was never far away. With each new person she met, Courtney held her breath, waiting to hear their name and wondering if this might be the moment. The reality, of course, kept her grounded. She might never meet the person. Crossroads Creek was small, but by no means a ghost town. Instead of hundreds of residents to sift through, the welcome sign announced there were close to four-thousand residents.

The thought had crossed her mind about Rusty and the medical condition he didn't want to discuss, but luckily, he was R.D. not W.D. The trick in asking around town was figuring out what to tell people without raising suspicions.

"Hey, Rusty," one of the staff called out, ending Courtney's trip down personal introspection lane.

She spun around just as he reached her side, her pulse racing at his sudden appearance.

"Hey, everyone. How's it going?" Rusty asked, his gaze settling on her for the answer.

"These ladies and gentlemen are quite the hard workers. We finished in record time. They even had time to sample the food by way of getting their own dinner before the evening begins and they miss out. It would seem that has happened on more than one occasion." Courtney frowned. Without the people's support, the whole event wouldn't be possible.

"Good thinking. Perhaps I should do the same before I get started."

Courtney nodded. It was a discussion she would have with him later. "Help yourself. We are going to start carrying the first round of dishes out to the tables and warmers, so fill a plate. You can be the official taste tester, but you have to tell me the truth." It's not that she was worried about her cooking, but more so, things like ready-made crust, low-fat milk, salted butter substitutes, and, of course, cooking sherry versus real dry sherry. Little things that made a big difference.

"Of course," Rusty said, scooping moderate portions of both pot pie and hamburger pie onto his plate.

The man had clearly worked up a hunger, as he had more than enough to feed two people. Hopefully, not everyone ate the way he did, or she would have sorely under planned how much food to serve, not having considered a cowboy-sized appetite. Courtney watched him as he took a bite. "Well?" she prompted when he didn't say anything.

"This is really good Shepard's pie. I was savoring the flavor," he said, spooning in another bite.

She breathed a sigh of relief. Rusty had her worried there for a minute. "Thank goodness."

"Like you were truly worried. You are a chef, unless you fudged on your credentials," he teased.

Courtney shook her head. "Assistant chef. Past tense. Big difference."

"You're an amazing cook no matter what title you carry, so quit worrying."

"Thank you."

Rusty finished the Shepard's pie in record time and started in on the Chicken pot pie. "Oh," he said, his eyebrows going up in surprise. "This is different and delicious. Is that cheese I'm tasting?"

"It is. When I was younger I remember going to a restaurant that served it this way. The recipe, or the idea for the recipe stuck with me. I had to concoct my own version, but it works. It's one of my favorites, but I haven't had the occasion to make it lately."

"Why is that? Doesn't an assistant chef help plan the menu? You seem to excel at that as well as cooking."

More compliments. Courtney needed to be careful not to let his remarks make her head swell. Pride always cometh before the fall. "The place I worked for was more of an upper-end social restaurant geared toward nouvelle cuisine."

Rusty grimaced. *"No view cuisine*? What's that—or do I want to know?"

"It's a type of fine dining that creates light, delicate dishes that focus more on presentation and flavor. It's combining healthy food and art all in one."

"Sounds like you leave hungry," he teased.

Said the man who could put away a monster-size plate of food. "You're not the first to think it, and you won't be the last. But nouvelle cuisine is more about the well-rounded dining experience." Truth was, Courtney always left hungry when she ate at Le Art Culinaire, unless, that is, she ate double portions. Which would be more like six portions for Rusty.

He rinsed off his dishes and turned to face her. "All done. What do you need me to do?"

"It looks like the others have taken everything out to the dining room. We still have a few minutes before the doors open. You could help me serve, while most of the others clear tables and seat newcomers, if that's okay with you?"

"Organized chaos. And with the added bonus of working alongside you, I'm in." Rusty grinned, following her into the other room. "Thanks for doing this. I mean it. This is so much more than I had hoped for at the last minute."

"The program means a lot to you, doesn't it?" she asked, sensing his sincerity.

"Absolutely. It's a way of giving back to the community that gives me a sense of worth. Helping them to see and understand that I'm not just a retired rodeo cowboy living off my brother's coattails. Or that I'm like my father. He wasn't a popular man in town, to say the least."

There was a wealth of meaning in his comments. Not the least of which was the reflection of anger, shame, and hurt. "I'm sorry. You're not your father and I don't think anyone would begin to think that. As to living off your brother, that's between you and your family. I know you have some medical issues going on that you don't want to discuss, and that's fine, I'm not trying to pry. But you need to realize your medical issues don't define who you are as a person. Only you can do that."

Rusty pulled back, as though shocked at her words. "Enough on this subject," he said, gesturing toward the door. "Our guests have started to arrive."

Moments later, the first person stood in line, with several others lined up behind the woman. The event had officially begun. "Good evening, welcome to Pie night," Courtney said, noting the elderly woman's wrinkled skin and bright red lips did nothing to detract from her smile or her aging beauty.

"Good evening, dearie. Pie night sounds like a winner." She reached out to pat Courtney's arm. "Thank you so much for doing this."

"You're welcome. It's a lot of work to put together, but what fun. What would you like for dinner tonight? Shepard's pie, Chicken pot pie, or both?"

The woman held out her plate. "Both look delicious and I'm not one to pass up delicious."

"Save room for Courtney's apple pie, Mary Lou," Rusty chimed in, adding a helping of pot pie to her plate.

"Yummy. In that case, make these small portions, please," Mary Lou said, shifting her gaze to the dessert table for a peak. Moving off to find a seat, the woman stopped to talk to a few people along the way.

"She's a regular. Such a dear old lady who lost her husband a few years back. Comes every week for the company, I reckon," Rusty explained.

"I remember you saying this was way more than a free meal to a lot of people. I'm beginning to understand. Talk about a great concept."

"It's way more to the entire community—which is why I vowed to keep it running."

"So you're going to stay in Crossroads Creek then?"

"I don't know. It all depends on where life leads me. But I would hope someone would take over the responsibility if I did leave. After all, it's a...never mind, no sense worrying about what hasn't happened yet. Isn't there something in the Bible about not worrying?" he asked, changing the subject with a wide-eyed grin that left her reeling.

"There is. You seem to remember way more about what you learned in church than you let on," she teased.

Rusty shook his head. "Don't tell anyone. Let that be our little secret or I'll never hear the end of my family trying to get me back to church."

"What's so awful about church? You could meet sweet people there, if you gave it a chance." Not that she was one to talk. She hadn't been back to church since Greg died. Something she kept planning to rectify but simply hadn't happened. Perhaps to avoid the sympathetic looks and prying questions that brought up bitter-sweet memories of life with Greg.

Rusty frowned. "Sweet, nosy people who spend too much time worrying about a retired cowboy."

Something else they agreed on, not that she'd tell Rusty. It wouldn't do to give him more fodder for living in the past. They both needed to move forward by the sound of things. "I'd say you're lucky to have caring people around you, no matter where you meet them. The world needs more sweet, nosy with good intentioned people to care." *Now if she could only heed her own advice.*

"Says you."

Not really. It was a good place for a change in subject lest she be considered a hypocrite if he learned the truth about her. Courtney turned her attention to the line of people to be served, the buzz of excitement and conversation at high levels in the community center. A few times Courtney glanced around, taking stock of the smiling faces. A few kept to themselves, but most folks chatted with one another, making the rounds like it was social hour.

A soup kitchen wasn't a good way to describe this event at all. It was more like...a soul kitchen.

As the line waned, Rusty turned to her. "I gave Trevor his riding lesson today. He's a natural and paid attention. I was impressed."

"Oh, I was meaning to ask you how it went, but things got busy. I'm glad it went well, but then I didn't expect otherwise. He was over the moon about riding horses today, and I had a hard time getting him to go to bed last night."

Rusty winced. "Well, he did well enough that I sort of committed to another lesson tomorrow, but only if you agree. I wasn't sure what your schedule looked like."

She appreciated his concern for her, but he needn't have worried. Courtney wanted to see Trevor's smiling face once again, and free riding lessons was the deal of a lifetime. "Seeing as I'm just passing through town, I'd say my schedule is pretty wide open. If you're offering another lesson, I'd be a fool to pass it up. If it's free, that is? It is, right? My finances are fairly tight at this point with the move and all." Her explanation sounded reasonable. It probably wasn't fair to let him give lessons for free, but it's not like she had a choice. It was either that or refuse the lessons...something she wouldn't take away from her son.

Rusty nodded. "It's free. And it's only riding lessons. He wants me to teach him about the bulls, but he's not ready. Not by a long shot. Although, I did mention roping once he master's the riding basics."

"I totally agree. I'm not sure I'm ready for him to be on the back of a bull. Thank goodness you use the voice of reason in your decisions and haven't let Trevor wrap you around his little finger. The kids quite good at it with his charming smile and winning ways." Courtney laughed.

"Now *that* is something we can agree on." The corners of Rusty's eyes crinkled as he grinned back at her.

United they stand, came to mind. Apparently, Trevor was trying to work his magic on

Rusty. The question remained, who would win? Her son could be quite convincing.

"That's the last of the line," John said, coming to stand by the serving table.

Courtney glanced around, noticing for the first time the place was almost empty. "Perfect. Thank you so much for everything you did to help make this a success." The tall, young man had been of great help in picking up the slack in just about every area of the process today. It had come as no surprise he wanted to attend culinary school in the hopes of running his own restaurant one day. *Much like her.*

"You're welcome. It was an awesome experience. I've locked the front doors, and all that's left is cleanup," he said, putting another chair on top of the table after wiping it clean.

Courtney let out a deep breath. "Thank you. What was the general response to tonight's meal?" she asked, more than a little curious. Stuck behind the serving table she hadn't been able to get a good read on the situation. To her face, people had been enthusiastically generous in their compliments, but it was the not-to-her-face remarks that were more important.

"All good. Well, all except this one guy who had a problem," John added, his smile only slipping a little with the news.

"Make that two people then," Rusty chimed in.

"And what was wrong?" Courtney asked in concern, determined to know the truth, no matter whether good or bad.

John shrugged, unable to hold back a grin. "The guy didn't like mixed vegetables in the Shepard's pie and had to pick them out. Said it needed chipotle and jalapenos to be a Texas Shepard's pie. Man grumbled something about you not being from the south."

"You rat. I can live with that, although, it sounds like he's been watching Rachel Ray's cooking show on TV." Courtney chuckled. "Guess I can't please everyone. What about the other?" she asked, turning to Rusty, equally determined to hear any negative reviews.

"Well, this man's sentiment was one I heard often when people stopped to say goodbye. It's not as easy to brush off as the Texas versus traditional debate," Rusty said, his voice totally serious.

"So what's the fatal flaw? Don't keep me hanging." Courtney held her breath, waiting to find out the worst, especially since it sounded like a complaint by many folks, not just one more.

"It was the one piece of pie limit on dessert." Rusty shot her a wink.

Picking up a napkin on the table, she tossed it at him. "You had me worried there for a minute."

"There was never any reason you should worry. You're a professional. Tonight was a huge success. My biggest problem will be figuring out an encore for next week after you're gone. Unless, that is, I can talk you into staying," he asked, hope lacing his voice.

Rusty was dead serious—but it wasn't in the cards for her and Trevor.

On the upside, the success of the evening had given her so much more than she could have thought possible. While she served, a thought had taken hold—one that wouldn't rest. Especially not after the turnout tonight and the success.

Instead of getting a job in Lafayette, for the first time, Courtney began to think about opening her own business. Be her own boss. If she could handle this event for over two hundred people, she could easily run a deli. It would be the perfect scenario for a single mother trying to make a living, raise her son, and enjoy the fruits of her labor.

Of course, all of her grand ideas depended on one thing.

The insurance money.

Chapter Thirteen

♥

THE NEXT SEVERAL DAYS passed by like the wind for Rusty. It was as though Courtney and Trevor had blown into his life, but when the winds of time moved forward, they'd roll out of town just as quickly. The idea of not seeing Courtney every day didn't sit well.

And then there was Trevor. His star protégé. *His only protégé.*

The kid was a natural on a horse, his confidence growing rapidly with each lesson. And every day, Trevor continued to ask about roping lessons and riding bulls. Rusty's answer was always the same. *When you're ready for the roping and not a chance on the bull riding.* A gentle no, but still a no.

But this morning, somewhere in the wee hours between dark and the dawning of a new day, something changed. As slivers of sunlight streamed across the sky like rays of hope, an image of Trevor came to mind, his enthusiasm endless. The image was closely followed by one of himself at that age. Longing to ride and experience the thrill. It was in those years his love for riding had been fostered. How could he deny a child the same experience? Especially when he had the knowledge to teach the kid.

The end result was a new decision...one of compromise. There still wouldn't be any bull-riding lessons—as that was something Rusty wasn't sure he could handle mentally or emotionally. It was too close to the past and the part of his life he'd left behind.

But Trevor was ready for a roping lesson, and perhaps, a trip to the local rodeo to watch bull riding in action. He'd have to talk to Courtney first, unwilling to commit to either one without her permission.

Trevor's enthusiasm was a huge catalyst to the change in Rusty's decision. Horses were partners, and their trust was critical when it came to working together successfully. Angel and Trevor had developed that bond and the idea of the kid leaving without a chance to experience a potentially life-changing opportunity, didn't sit well. What if this was Trevor's moment to shine? What if God had brought them both to this point for a reason?

And maybe, this was about more than Trevor wanting roping lessons or going to a rodeo. Perhaps this was about the boy having a male figure in his life. Not to replace his father, as Rusty had no misgivings that he could ever be that person. But Trevor could use someone to look up to—someone to learn from.

An idea slowly took root, and then suddenly sprouted. Roping and riding lessons for kids. *Why not?*

He might not be thrilled with the changes in his life because of his medical condition but teaching children about horses would be a way for him to connect with the past. And to move forward. It was a capital idea...but one that needed lots of capital. *Something he didn't have.*

For now, Trevor would serve as his first student, and the challenge for Rusty would be to discover if he had the talent and patience to work with kids on a continual basis. *Something he'd never done.*

Another thought emerged, one that settled deep in the recesses of this brain and wouldn't let go. What if this was the direction God wanted him to go all along? A better plan than to fade into the sunset as a washed-up cowboy in a few years when he couldn't compete any longer.

This was something that would combine his passion for the rodeo with an even more rewarding purpose...teaching children the same respect and joy for the profession. Wouldn't that be a worthwhile gift to offer others in return for the magnitude of the gift he received? *Something to give him back a feeling of worthiness.*

The guilt toward the widow of the man whose heart beat in his chest would never go away, but perhaps there were ways to alleviate the intensity of the emotion. Rusty had written the woman a thankyou note but privacy laws kept him from contacting her directly.

An image of Courtney came to mind. She, too, had lost her husband. And by the looks of things, she was on her own struggling to make ends meet. What if the other woman was in the same situation? He shoved the plaguing reminder of a situation he had no control over out of his head.

Courtney and Trevor were due to arrive any minute. They had become daily guests at the ranch, and his mother had gone to pick them up this morning while he did chores. Coming out of the barn, Rusty spotted the dusty cloud billowing in the air behind his mother's car as she made her way down the driveway to the house.

As soon as his mother parked, Trevor jumped out from the back seat and started running toward him, waving his arm in the air. "Are you ready to ride, Rusty?" Trevor asked, beaming up at him.

The kid had a way of wrapping Rusty around his little finger with that boyish grin. "Just about. Let me go grab a few snacks and a couple of drinks."

Courtney emerged from the car and waved. She had been a little skittish with her first riding lesson, but Rusty held out hope she would gain the confidence and soon come to enjoy riding. Although time wasn't necessarily something they had. Which was precisely the reason he planned to expedite the process before she left town. "I was thinking we could get your mom on a horse again, and this time go outside the pen." Rusty grinned, knowing Trevor's not-so-subtle plea to his mother would more than likely be all it took to make it happen.

"Sounds like a good idea to me. Then I can really show her how good I'm doing," Trevor added.

"Yes, you can. But don't turn into a showoff or it will come back to bite you in the behind."

"That doesn't sound like anything I want," Trevor said, frowning.

Rusty ruffled his hair. "Good. Keep it that way."

Courtney approached, her smile warming him. "Hey there. Thanks for giving Trevor another lesson. Your mom had to hurry inside and get lunch started. It was nice of her to pick us up, but I'm starting to feel like such a burden to you all."

"Never that. My mother was running an errand, so it all worked out well. And we enjoy having you both around. You two certainly manage to add a spark around the ranch, especially with my sister coming round more with the boys. They have plans, you know," he said, shooting her a conspiratorial wink.

"So what's Trevor going to learn today? Maybe I could help your mother in the kitchen," Courtney offered.

"Not so fast. We want you to join us today. You know, have another lesson. I thought you should get back on Misty and ride again—this time up to Lookout point for some hot soup and fresh baked bread. It's my version of a warm carrot to entice you to say yes." Rusty chuckled.

"Say yes, Mom. Pleasssseee. I want to show you how good I'm doing." Trevor laid the request on thick, just as Rusty expected him to.

Courtney looked up at Trevor and then at Rusty. "Tell me you didn't bake it, Mr. Can-Opener-Is-More-My-Style," she teased, her tinkling of laughter reaching her eyes as they danced in merriment.

"You're safe. My mother made it." He shot her a wink. "It was her suggestion we go for the ride, and I sort of agreed. I think she's fixing the thermos with our soup as we speak."

"Assuming I would go," Courtney said, not missing another of his mother's subtle pushes.

"Absolutely. And who can resist a fifteen-hundred-pound softie like Misty?" Rusty added for good measure.

Courtney absently ran a hand through her hair several times as she thought over her options. "Fine. But we go slow. I'm a little nervous in case she takes off and throws me."

"Not Misty. But that being said, I do want you to have the confidence that even if she did take charge of the ride, ultimately, you're in control and have the final say so as to whether you go with her or not. But again, I wouldn't put you on a horse you couldn't handle. What you're asking about would be out of character. Besides, I'll be right there with you and can help."

Courtney frowned. "I don't understand. If she takes charge of the ride, how can I make the decision whether to go with her or not? Wouldn't that require us to be separated? Do I make her stop and get off? Because walking back doesn't sound like much fun either. Although, I guess given the alternative..."

Trevor took his mother's hand and fell in step between the two of them as they headed for the house. "Rusty told me all about it, Mom. It sounds scary, but all you have to do is throw yourself off the horse and roll on the ground. Oh, and he said look for a soft place."

Courtney gasped. "What? Quit pulling my leg. That's not even remotely funny."

Rusty shook his head. "So that sounds way worse than it is the way he explained it. Perhaps I need to work on what I say and don't say. I mean, it's true, but the reality is...it should never happen. Especially not here and not with me." He needed to dial back Trevor's comment if he wanted Courtney back on a horse.

"I want no part of throwing myself off a horse. Perhaps I should stay put and help your mother, after all," Courtney said, shaking her head.

"I've only ever had to do it once...trust me, it's not common," Rusty said, trying to reassure her.

"Were you hurt?"

"No. Nothing more than my pride. The mare had a case of barn disease and I was testing her with a rope lead, back before I knew any better. She wanted the barn, I wanted the pasture. The mare gave in, but not graciously. She took off running and there was no stopping her. It was either let her decide when to stop and possibly pitch me somewhere I didn't want to go, or I take control and roll off. So I dug deep for courage and then it was over. Honestly,

I shouldn't have used the rope mouth bit on her in the first place, so technically it was an amateur mistake on my part and entirely my fault."

"Come on, Mom. You gotta come with us," Trevor pleaded.

"Trust me, Misty and Angel are docile mares and it won't be an issue. They are well trained and I'll be close by." He had a lot to learn when it came to teaching others about riding, the first of which was *not* to scare them.

Courtney let out a heavy sigh. "Okay, then. I'm trusting you."

His mother met them at the door. "Here's a saddlebag with lunch and hot coffee. You three have fun. And don't rush back on my account. I've got lots to keep me busy that doesn't involve riding a horse much nowadays."

Rusty reached for the pack. "Thanks, Mom."

"I get coffee?" Trevor asked in wide-eyed wonder.

Rusty wasn't allowed to have coffee until he was twelve, so there was little chance the kid would experience it today.

"No. There's hot chocolate for you, young man," Rusty's mother answered, wrapping her arm around Trevor's shoulders to hug him.

"*Aww* shucks. I wanted to be like a grownup." Trevor kicked at the ground, a slight pout to his lips that echoed his words.

The three of them laughed.

"But the grownups don't have miniature marshmallows. I packed them special just for you and added a few extras."

"Growing up will happen soon enough. Enjoy your youth while you can," Rusty said, hoping to tease him back into a good mood.

Trevor shrugged. "That's what my mom says all the time, but it sure seems like grownups have all the fun. Other than the marshmallows," he added.

"I don't know. Most grownups work during the day, not ride horses for fun." It was a gentle reminder, but one that needed saying. It also reinforced the kid's need for a male role model. Courtney was an amazing mother, but sometimes, it would seem Trevor responded quicker to his own subtle urgings for a change in the boy's line of thinking. Not that Rusty under-stood kids, but he had been a boy once upon a time.

"But you do. I want to be just like you when I grow up. Ride horses whenever I want and work on a ranch. Maybe even ride bulls if you show me how," Trevor added.

They had come full circle as Rusty loaded the food and drinks into the saddle bags that he had strapped on earlier when he readied the horses.

"Trevor, you need to quit pestering Rusty about bull-riding lessons. He's the expert and you need to respect his decision," Courtney said, coming to his rescue.

She was right, but only partly.

Rusty was an expert at bull riding, but that's where the truth fell by the wayside. The reason he wouldn't say yes was entirely about himself and nothing to do with Trevor—something he admitted after his family had called him out on the subject. At eight, bull-riding lessons started on the back of a goat, and Rusty wasn't worried about Trevor's ability. This was about Rusty opening himself up to the past he had to walk away from. "Don't forget, you have a roping lesson coming up. Maybe after we get back from our lunch ride, if there's still time I can show you the ropes," he said with a grin.

"Yes!" Trevor beamed. "Oh, the ropes...I get it. Did you get the joke, Mom?"

"I did. And I'm pretty sure around a cowboy it's a joke that never gets old," she teased.

"That's true." Rusty held out his hands to let Trevor use his interlocked palms as a stepping stool. The kid hoisted himself up and into the saddle.

"Good job," Rusty said after Trevor settled into place and picked up the reins, holding them in the grip Rusty had taught him.

He turned his attention to Courtney, letting her use the stirrup, but making sure he was right there beside her in case she needed help. She pulled herself up and into the saddle in one try, impressing Rusty with her ability. "Nice work. You remembered that well."

Courtney smiled. "Let's just hope that's not all I remember."

"You'll be fine." Rusty mounted Thunder and soon the three of them were ready to go. "You can lead, Trevor, but stay on the path along the fence line. And stay within range where I can offer you tips when necessary." It was also for the boy's own safety, but it wasn't something Rusty need to share. Letting the kid have a sense of accomplishment and pride was important.

"Yes, sir." Trevor beamed, giving Angel a gentle nudge forward.

Trevor was at the age when he wanted to start testing his wings of independence and it wouldn't bode well to clip them—or at least let him know they were being clipped. Something he would do well to remember if he was able to move forward with the riding school plan.

"Look, Mom, I'm riding on my own," Trevor called out, swinging around in his saddle to see her.

"Yes, dear. That's awesome. Maybe I can learn a thing or two from you," she added.

"Good idea. I'll make sure to teach you everything Rusty taught me. Just hold your reins loosely, and even if you're nervous, try not to show it. The horse can sense your mood." Trevor recited some of the information Rusty had shared, proving he paid attention, and that it had sunk in.

"Thank you for the tip, Trevor. I'll try to keep that in mind."

Her son moved further forward, leaving the two of them to catch up.

"He's a good kid. Listens well," Rusty said as they rode side by side.

"He is. It's been hard on him this past year and I can't thank you enough for what you're doing. I haven't seen Trevor this happy in so long, especially with a genuine smile. One I can feel right down to the toes."

Rusty laughed. "Glad to hear it. There's something I wanted to run by you, to see what you think. I value your opinion, especially as it's one of the only non-biased ones I can find around here at the moment." He urged Thunder closer to make it easier to have this discussion.

Courtney glanced up at him. "Let's hear it."

"This whole thing with Trevor, the lesson thing, has me thinking. You know how I told you I was looking to find what I wanted to do with my life now that I retired from the rodeo?"

She nodded. "Yes, of course."

Rusty wasn't used to opening himself up to others for their opinion, but this was different. It was Courtney, and he trusted her. "It was something you said, but it makes sense. If I teach kids to rope and ride, it's giving back a part of what I know to the next generation. Making a difference. What do you think? I mean, I know it's a little early to get carried away as Trevor is only my first student and I need to keep working with him to see how it all plays out and if I have what it takes to teach children."

"I think it's an awesome idea. But you didn't mention bull riding. Why not?" She watched him closely, almost a little too close.

Rusty didn't miss the fact she was letting Misty manage the trail without much guidance. He hadn't been prepared for the introspection portion of where the conversation might go.

"That's a whole different level. One I'm not certain I would want to take on."

"Why not? You're an expert in the area as well, and you would be exactly the kind of teacher a child needs if they get the fever. It's a dangerous sport and children need to learn from the best. Which makes you perfect for the job based on what your sister and mother have told me. They followed your career closely and I hear you were quite good."

Were being the operative word. It was news to him his family had taken any interest in his rodeo days, much less to follow him on the circuit. But it didn't change the here and now. "You mean more like—those who can't do...teach." Rusty frowned. "I'll think about it." It was easier than saying no and trying to justify it. "But what do you think otherwise? I mean, if Trevor keeps doing well, then I could take on other students. Maybe open a school."

"Except Trevor and I have to leave when the truck is fixed. Lafayette isn't exactly a weekly lesson driving distance away. You will need to look for another willing test student. That shouldn't be too hard to find." Misty whinnied. "See, even my horse agrees."

"Since when did you become an expert in horse language?" It was easier to laugh off her comment than to dwell on the rest of what she said. The truth was, everything in his life was fleeting and subject to change. *Just like his heart.*

Some of the joy of the afternoon fled. The problem was if he started something he couldn't finish, what good would he be to anyone? Maybe the answer wasn't teaching and that he should just stick with laborer duties at the ranch. Simple things he could handle. "Yeah, it was a dumb idea. Never mind."

"I didn't say that. It's a great idea. Look, maybe I can find a way to get Trevor back here sometimes. Especially if you're still doing the lessons for free. It just won't be a lot. Maybe every other weekend."

Her olive branch sounded more like a custody schedule, but it was better than he had a minute ago. Not to mention, the idea of her coming back to Texas sent his pulse racing knowing it meant he would see her again. "Now that's a plan that works for me. It's settled then, Trevor is my first official student. I reckon it's the beginning of the planning process for a school. Just don't tell anyone in my family. It's still a long shot to pull everything together, including making sure I'm the right guy for the job. And then there's the fact I would need to find the monetary resources for such an undertaking. And I don't want my family pressuring me."

"My lips are sealed," Courtney said, sliding a fingertip over her lips. "And, oh by the way, you have two students. I count." She grinned.

"That you do. And you are doing well. Perhaps I should distract you more often," he teased.

Rusty couldn't help the rush of exhilaration at the sudden possible change in direction of his life, an excitement he hadn't felt in a long time. Maybe there was more to this plan, especially if his passion about it equaled his passion for the rodeo. A new and rewarding direction in his life would be like winning the lottery. Something he never expected, but now that his brain was in high gear, it would be difficult to shut the thought process off.

Tonight, after Courtney and Trevor left, he would sit down and pencil out a plan of action. He needed to begin by doing his research to come up with a cost feasibility report, discover what other schools charged, and what would be needed for a quality program. If he did this, it would need to be done right.

More than ever...this seemed like a gift from God. What else could explain the sudden appearance of Courtney...just when he needed her the most. He hadn't been on the right track buried in resentment, but now, everything was changing.

Although, his growing feelings for her weren't anything he wanted to dwell on, but he did want her to see there was more to him than a useless cowboy hanging out on his family's ranch and wallowing away his life.

They may not have a future, but it didn't stop him from wanting her friendship...and her respect.

Chapter Fourteen

♥

Courtney watched her son in amazement as he showed her everything he had learned. Turning right. Turning left. Stopping. Backing up. He looked far more comfortable on a horse than she did, or at least that's the way it appeared.

They rode another thirty minutes before Rusty caught up to Trevor and called their ride to a halt for lunch.

Courtney slid off the horse to the ground and started to rub her legs, easing the stiff ache of a non-rider. She felt more comfortable than she had before, proof that practice really was effective. "That was fun," she said, smiling at Rusty as he joined her.

"Good, I'm glad you are enjoying yourself." He took the reins from her and tied them to a tree, Trevor following his lead and doing the same with Angel.

"Did I do better today?" her son asked, seeking approval from Rusty.

"You certainly did. Which confirms my decision to give you a roping lesson and that my confidence in your skills isn't misplaced. I just need you to understand that at first, you might find it boring. But the key to a good roper is to start with the basics and then practice. It's the same with anything you do in life if you want to do it well," Rusty said.

By the sounds of things, Rusty envisioned a dull afternoon for Trevor. But then, he didn't know her son as well as she did. All the signs were there...Trevor was eating up the attention and thought Rusty hung the moon.

"Cool. How boring can it be? I mean riding a horse and throwing a rope sounds easy enough." Trevor shrugged, trying to be tougher than his adorable face made possible.

"Maybe so. But it's the mechanics that count and for that, you need to learn to throw the rope...from the ground. No riding."

Trevor frowned. "But—"

"And no buts. It's my way or no way...take your pick," Rusty said, not budging on his plan of action.

The man had a stubborn streak that would stand him in good stead teaching kids. Children had a knack for getting what they wanted, but if an adult couldn't be swayed by their tactics, they were usually rewarded for holding their position. *At least in the long run.*

"Your way," her son mumbled, clearly not a fan but still totally on board.

Rusty pulled the saddle bag off his horse. They walked to a clearing, and all around her were open fields and a mountain range in the distance. The vastness between here and the distant peaks could easily give a person a sense of freedom if one dared to dream of riding the land.

She helped Rusty spread out the blanket, barely getting it laid out before Trevor sat down, cross legged, claiming his corner. "I'm hungry," he said.

"I bet you are. Riding works up an appetite," Rusty said, sitting beside her son and pulling two thermoses, sandwiches, and protein bars out of the bag.

"That explains why I feel like I could eat all three of those sandwiches." Courtney laughed.

"Most likely, but you only get one," he teased, handing her a sandwich. "It's plenty big though as my mother believes in hearty meals. This is ham, turkey, roast beef, and cheese. She does this weird thing where she puts mustard on the meat side and mayonnaise on the cheese side, so I hope you enjoy it."

Courtney gazed at him, her eyes wide with surprise. "Sounds delicious. And not so weird...since I do the same thing."

Rusty's eyebrows shot up. "*Aha*...my mother will think it's fate. Be careful who you tell," he added with a chuckle, and then handed the smallest sandwich to Trevor.

"Thank you," her son said, unwrapping the sandwich and taking a giant-sized bite. "*Mmmm*."

Rusty chuckled. "Enjoying that much?"

Trevor nodded, taking another bite to prove it. Stuffing one's face wasn't something she'd taught him to do, but Courtney opted to let it slide this time.

Rusty poured the cups of coffee and chocolate and handed them out.

Normally she liked a little creamer in her coffee, but out on the range, unless she planned to go find the nearest cow and milk it, it would seem creamer was out of the question. She took a sip, savoring the chicory flavor. "This is good. Perfect for a cold afternoon." One could gain a new appreciation for anything when the setting was right.

Conversation lulled as tummies were filled, the chocolate covered protein bar serving as a perfect dessert. One that would also fortify them with the added calories for the ride back to the ranch.

"Can I go ride a bit more while you two finish eating? I want Mom to see me when she isn't busy trying to stay on her own horse," he teased.

Rusty knew Trevor's limitations, and since he was in charge of the riding lessons, she kept silent to let him answer.

"It's fine by me, but you need to stay close enough that you can see us and we can see you," Rusty said, his voice firm in the directive. "Angel needs to be able to hear my commands if necessary. Safety above all...comes first."

"Okay. But then when can I go ride alone?" Trevor asked, desperately trying to move into big-boy status.

Something Courtney wasn't ready for, not by a long shot. She wanted to keep Trevor young and by her side. Maybe it was wrong to hold on so tightly, but after losing Greg, he was the mainstream of her life. *And her joy*.

"When I think you're ready," Rusty answered noncommittally.

Trevor looked about to say something, but clearly thought better of it as he turned away

and walked to his horse. Rusty stood and followed. Her son untied the reins, moving to the
left side of the horse. Rusty put out one hand
to steady Angel, but otherwise remained silent,
letting Trevor try to get on the horse.

With one foot in the stirrup, Trevor hopped
on his right leg, trying to push off and gain
upward momentum. Angel moved slightly, and
Courtney was relieved Rusty was there to over-
see the process. Her son was forced to pull his
left foot back out of the stirrup and start over.

"You want a hand?" Rusty asked when Trevor
failed a second time.

"Yes, please," her son answered, the words
almost forced.

Trevor had an independent streak as wide as
her own and Courtney was positive he would
see this as a major setback. She turned her
head, hoping to catch Rusty's response better,
as she herself was extremely interested in the
answer.

"It takes time to learn how to mount up for
a ride without assistance because it requires
strong leg muscles to make it happen. Mount-

ing and dismounting is only part of the equation of knowing when you're ready to ride out
alone. If you come out of the saddle, it's a good
idea if you can get back in it. Trust me, I'll
know when you're ready."

To an eight-year-old, especially one small for
his age, Rusty's answer was perfect. Giving
Trevor an attainable goal, but one that would
require practice. And the rule would eliminate
any possible moodiness with the decision. *It
was actually quite genius.*

Rusty formed his hands into a cradle to help
lift her son up onto the saddle. After making sure he was settled into place and holding
the reins correctly, Rusty nodded and her son
nudged the horse forward. Rusty came back
to stand next to her, keeping a close eye on
Trevor.

"You are good with kids and I think you'll
make an excellent instructor," Courtney said.

Rusty turned to look at her. "And you're a
good cook. Maybe you should open up your
own place. Have you ever even considered it?
Crossroads Creek could use someone with your

talents," he added, shooting her a grin before returning his gaze to Trevor.

It was as if he'd read her mind. "It's interesting you should mention that, as I've been thinking the same thing. In fact, I was toying with whether to run it by you or not."

"I'd love to hear what you're thinking. I've got to keep an eye on Trevor, but I'm all ears." He shot her a grin. "Trevor totally understood my position about riding alone after I explained it to him. It won't be long and he'll have it figured out, but until then, I can't be too careful."

The look of pride on his face revealed how much it meant helping Trevor, but it was a two-way street. In return, Trevor needed what Rusty could give him as a male role model. "Like I said, you're a natural-born teacher and would make an excellent instructor," Courtney added.

"Let's hope the bank agrees with you. So tell me what you have in mind for a restaurant."

"I'm thinking more along the lines of a deli. We know I can cook. But helping you out this week has shown me I can also manage people and a large number of guests successfully. A deli would require a lot of instant fixes, but also lots of specials prepared ahead of time for each day. And a deli would never see the numbers of people who showed up at the community center, so I totally think I could pull it off." Just saying the words out loud made them seem real, the excitement growing within her as she pictured the grand opening of her own business.

"What a great idea. It makes perfect sense. And I wasn't joking when I mentioned you sticking around town. A deli would give the locals at Crossroads Creek a second choice of where to eat. And don't forget, Trevor loves it here."

"You just don't want to lose your student," she quipped.

"I don't want to lose either of my students," he said, his voice dropping to a low, husky tone filled with a wealth of meaning.

Her pulse raced as little butterflies settled in the pit of her stomach. *Rusty didn't want her to leave town.* Was it for her cooking...or something else entirely?

She wished things could be different between them. It's not that she didn't think of him often, or even consider some of the what ifs, because she had. But the answer never changed. Greg would always come between them. And rightfully so. "I can't do any of this without the insurance money, and by the looks of things they are doing everything they can not to pay out. It's ridiculous, but until then, I can't make any final decisions about where to go or what to do with my life." It was the safest answer she knew, and one grounded in truth, even if it ignored the emotion of his comment.

Rusty took her hand, his warmth seeping through her skin. "I understand, trust me. Better than you think. Both of us are in limbo, waiting on someone else who controls the purse strings to decide our lives. It doesn't seem right, but that's exactly what we are dealing with. In the meantime, I like having you around. My life hasn't had this much excitement lately and you've brought a lot of joy my way. I'm hoping it's something we can continue." Rusty leaned in closer, his face mere inches from hers.

Courtney tensed, the sudden undercurrent between them confusing. She swallowed hard, wanting him to kiss her, but not wanting him to kiss her either. She couldn't move, her brain racing for some sort of coherent thought.

The sounds of a xylophone crashed into the moment, startling Courtney as she realized it was her cell phone. She shook her head and grabbed the device, pressing a button to silence the blaring tone and answer. Guilt washed over her as she realized the impact of Rusty having almost kissed her. She glanced at Trevor, hoping he hadn't witnessed the exchange. "Hello," she said, focusing on the call and not recognizing the number. *Talk about saved by the bell.*

"Hey there. This is Charlie from the garage."

"Hi Charlie." She said the greeting for Rusty's sake. "Are you calling with good news and my truck's fixed?" she asked hopefully. Judging by what just occurred between her and the man sitting next to her, she couldn't get out of Crossroads Creek fast enough.

"Not exactly. More like a case of the delays. The guy called and said the carrier lost the package. They are having to send out a new one. But he is expediting the shipment, so I fully expect it by Friday."

Courtney shook her head and drew in a deep breath, trying to focus. "Friday? Oh, dear. I hadn't planned on five more days. Are you certain it can't arrive any sooner?" She'd already imposed on Laura for an entire week and adding another five days didn't seem like the right thing to do. *Talk about overstaying your welcome.*

And she didn't want to think about the impact of five more days around Rusty.

"Sorry. That's the way things roll around here. Slow and slower."

It wasn't Charlie's fault and complaining would get her nowhere. "Okay. Keep me posted if anything changes."

"Will do," Charlie said before hanging up.

Calling her mother to come to get her seemed like her only choice at this point. She glanced over at Rusty who was watching Trevor. It gave her a chance to observe his side profile. A strong jawline, handsome face, his cowboy hat tipped forward comfortably. The man was a walking cologne ad, as the scent he wore wafted toward her. A scent that made her think of rugged men—like a cowboy. *Fitting.*

"Trouble?" he asked, turning to face her, catching her off guard.

Her face suffused with heat. It was as though he had sensed her watching him. "You could say that. The carrier lost the part and the replacement won't be in until next Friday. And that's with rush shipping."

"Sorry. I know that's not what you wanted to hear, but these things happen. Usually for a reason." Rusty reached out to grab her hand again, reminding her of what they shared moments ago.

She pulled her hand back, not looking to venture down that path a second time. "Well I'm all out of reasons why this would be a good delay?"

"Maybe not for you, but I see one for me." Rusty grinned, not at all put off by her withdrawal.

Courtney frowned. "What's that?" she asked, knowing it was better to tackle any issues between them head on.

"If you stay, you can cover another Wednesday shift at the community center. It pays well." His grin deepened, crinkling the corners of his eyes.

Rusty had a point. A good point that was the most irresistible green carrot she could have imagined. Money. Something she desperately needed. But the situation was complicated because of what almost happened. And that problem existed because she liked Rusty. A lot. Her admiration for him had gone up exponentially when he revealed his plan for a school. A bright future for a handsome retired cowboy who delivered kittens to old ladies. What was there not to like?

His wanting to kiss her was another matter entirely. She didn't see him as the type to play foot loose with her, which only left one other reason—he was interested in a relationship. Something she couldn't give.

Not with him. Not with anybody.

But what if God was showing her other options for a future? Or pushing her out of her comfort zone and trying to convince her to live again? Even if one day she might be ready, the fear of failure in life and relationships, and the fear of losing her independence, would always hold her back.

Rusty hadn't said a word as he waited for her answer, his gaze on Trevor.

She could do this. Courtney swallowed hard, forcing herself to speak. "I'll stay and take care of Wednesday night."

Rusty glanced her way, a happy smile on his face.

"On one condition," she added quickly.

"What's that?"

"No more of what just happened. *U mmm*, you know before the call. I like you...a lot. More than I should, but I'm not looking for a relationship and I don't do casual anything. I loved my husband and I'm not sure I can ever love anyone else, so there's no reason to even try. Does that make sense?" she said, hurrying through her answer, trying to lay it all on the line.

Rusty nodded even though his smile had waned. "It's a deal. We can be friends with no expectations. I'm not sorry I tried to kiss you as you are a beautiful woman, but I am sorry if it made you uncomfortable."

"It's okay, honestly. It was flattering to say the least, but I did want to set the record straight."

"Consider me warned," he teased, his smile firmly back in place. Perhaps a little too firmly. "Trevor, bring it in," he called out. "Time to pack our bag and head back to the ranch." He offered Courtney a hand to help her to her feet.

"Thank you," she said, letting him pull her up.

"No, the thanks all go to you. You saved me from having to scramble Monday morning trying to figure out what to do about Wednesday's dinner."

Courtney smiled. "I'm glad to help. Not to mention, the money is good." So good, she was willing to risk sticking around town and Rusty, and not call her mother to pick them up.

There was no reason she and Rusty couldn't be friends.

Men and women did it all the time. Didn't they?

Chapter Fifteen

♥

Rusty hadn't planned on giving in to his mother's invitation to church this morning, but he had. He hadn't stepped inside the place in over ten years.

"I'm so glad you decided to join us today," his mother said, stopping at the large double wooden doors and giving him a hug. "It does my heart good."

He chuckled. "Maybe it will do something for mine also." Judging by her pursed lips, she didn't appreciate the comment. "Sorry, it was just a joke." *Agreeing to the visit was as much for himself as his mother, but he wasn't about to let on to that fact.*

Since he had been home, Rusty felt unsettled. But now, things were different. More specifically, the time he spent with Courtney. He was realistic enough to admit she was a large part of the equation, but that's where the understanding stopped. Rusty knew he cared about her, but she had made her point all too clear regarding the *almost kiss.* It was the easiest way to refer to the momentary concession of his feelings. And the result...Courtney wasn't interested—not by a long shot.

He might have been gathering his courage to tell her about his medical condition, needing to see her response. Wanting to know if there was any hope for the two of them. And the fact he had even been willing to say anything at all, was proof of how much he cared. Courtney was different than anyone he'd ever met.

But now, having agreed to her terms, there was no turning back.

Maybe he was secretly hoping going to church would reward him with answers about the direction of his life. Or maybe it was simply his mother's insistence that got him through the front door, but Rusty was okay admitting that perhaps a part of him was looking for something different. Something better. Although what it could possibly be, he wasn't sure.

As they entered the sanctuary, a young boy waved, catching his attention. Courtney and Trevor. The kid motioned for him to join them.

Rusty glanced at his mother. "Do you mind if I sit with Courtney and her son? Trevor's hard to resist when he beckons." He grinned, knowing his mother would be beside herself with glee with his request. "I see Rebecca over there waiting for you with the boys."

"By all means, go. Poor girl shouldn't sit alone not knowing anyone in town," his mother added, a fresh smile lighting her face.

Which was precisely the reaction he expected. But then, his mother didn't know Courtney had already rejected him, and Rusty had no intentions of being the one to dash his mother's happily-ever-after dream. *She would find out soon enough.* There was nothing she wanted more than for her children to be happy—that, and more grandchildren. "Laying it on thick still, I see. I'll let it slide seeing as we're in church, but remember, you promised."

"Yes, I did. Now go." His mother gave him a gentle shove in their direction.

Rusty scooted past a few churchgoers seated at the beginning of the row and sat next to Trevor. "Hey there. Thanks for the invite. Beats sitting with my mother and sister." He chuckled.

Courtney's smile was like a ray of sunshine in the church. "You're welcome. I didn't expect to see you here, so this is a pleasant surprise."

"Rusty is my friend. Course he's gonna sit with me." Trevor's innocent comment had them sharing a secret smile over his head.

"That's true, young man. Friends sit together." And he and Courtney were friends so it made perfect sense. *Not that anyone in town would believe otherwise.*

The praise team started to play and sing. The room fell silent as the harmonized voices filled the sanctuary with vibrant music, their love for God clear. Rusty listened, letting the peace and wonder settle around him. As others joined in and sang, it was Courtney's sweet voice that caught his attention. His heart responded to the melodic tones that almost seemed to call to him.

He had felt this inexplicable draw to her on several occasions, but nothing as strong as this morning. It was a good thing she had already warned him off, because after this, he would have been hard pressed to stay away.

All too soon, the music ended and Rusty felt a sense of loss. He wanted to take Courtney's hand and hold her close, but he knew better. The pastor stepped up to the pulpit and began to deliver a message. As he listened, Rusty couldn't help but feel it was directed at him. A message of hope. When life knocks you down, you get back up knowing each and every day offered hope for a brighter tomorrow.

It was almost as if his mother had told the pastor he was coming and what he needed to hear. But that was nonsensical considering he had only relented to come an hour before church started. When the pastor finished, the people all stood and filed out into the foyer.

Rusty, Trevor, and Courtney joined in the mass exodus. He paused and searched for his mother and sister.

Steve Jenkins, one of his teachers from high school came up to him, a welcoming smile on his face. "Great to see you, Rusty," Mr. Jenkins said, clapping him on the back. "Haven't had much opportunity to chat with you since you been home. Always seems to be something going on. Any chance I can get you and your girlfriend to lend a hand at the beverage table? My wife, Mary Ellen, normally handles it, but she wasn't feeling well this morning and stayed home."

The man was as much a talker as he was a teacher, and clearly it spilled over into the rest of his life. "I reckon I can help. But *ummm*, Courtney isn't my girlfriend," he added, shooting her a glance knowing she wouldn't be happy with Mr. Jenkins' comment.

"Rusty's *my* friend," Trevor announced proudly. "And my horse-riding teacher."

Mr. Jenkins shot Courtney a wink, his grin wide as he nodded. "I see. Well the help would still be appreciated."

"Count me in. Courtney?" Rusty asked, glancing at her, curious if she would go along with him or turn tail and run.

"Sure. Why not? It's not like I know anyone in town and need to mingle," she teased.

"Wonderful. Thank you both so much. And just so you know, serving the drinks is a great way to meet people. They have a way of making you feel right at home," Mr. Jenkins said, waving at another woman. "Got to run. Need to find someone to stay and help clean up after."

Rusty led Courtney to the table overloaded with two bowls of pink punch loaded with fresh lemons and limes, gadzooks of plastic cups and stacks of white napkins. Soon, the line was backed up with people gathered around for their share of the punch, some wanting refills.

Next to them, another table was filled with a wide array of cookies and pastries and a young man served those on tiny plates. Rusty didn't remember this part of church and figured it was something new. After all, no kid would forget free food. Innovative idea to get people to church, the way he saw things.

"Mom, I'm going to go check out the table where all those kids are gathered around. Must be something fun happening," Trevor said, using the assumptive-close technique.

Courtney nodded. "Sure thing, but don't leave the church building without checking with me first," she reminded him.

Always on duty, it would seem Courtney shouldered the solo task of raising Trevor without so much as a complaint. Trevor was a lucky boy in that respect, his mother having done everything possible to hold their family together after the tragedy that changed their lives.

"Okay," Trevor said, dodging through an opening of the grownups to make his way across the room.

Courtney watched as he disappeared in the crowd. "I'm not sure how we got roped into this, but I guess it beats mingling and talking to strangers." She grinned. "That was never my strong suit."

Finding out Courtney considered herself an introvert was mind boggling, and not something he would have guessed. "Or in my case, talking to people I know who only want to talk about the rodeo. Thanks, but no thanks. It's one of the reasons I've stayed away," he explained.

"And the other?" she prompted, curious what made this man tick.

"People are nosey." He shot her a wink. That was the most he intended to say on that subject...at least for now with said people all around him in the room.

Ten minutes later, the line for punch started to diminish. The pastor came over and picked up a cup. "Good to see you again, Rusty. Thanks for stepping in to help out," he said, reaching out to shake hands.

"Good to see you too, Pastor Phil. It wasn't a problem. We were both glad to help. This is Courtney Winters. Her truck broke down outside of town and Charlie's working on getting it fixed up," Rusty offered, making the introductions.

"*Ahhh*, young Trevor's mother. He's quite a charmer, that boy. He's been telling everyone about Destiny and Hope." The pastor glanced back at him and chuckled. "Of course, Trevor also expressed concern you might have forgotten to feed them this morning." He shook his head. "I assured him you wouldn't forget such an important task."

Rusty groaned. Destiny and Hope were supposed to be their little secret. "I fed them, so there's no worries on that account."

"Who are Destiny and Hope?" Courtney asked, her brow furrowed in a lack of understanding.

"Their kittens," the pastor chimed in. "Trevor is in his element telling everyone the story of his kitten, and how he and Rusty came up with their names."

Courtney nodded, but the frown on her face stuck. "I see. Sort of. The thing is, Trevor doesn't have a kitten, as I told him no."

"Now that's interesting. Perhaps I should talk to your son about tall tales. Or maybe I let him have his dreams a little longer." The pastor shot her a grin as he moved away when someone called out to him.

"Neither of us have a kitten," Rusty reassured her, seeing the question in her gaze.

"But you named them?" Suddenly, her expression visibly relaxed. "Which kitten is yours?" she asked, her hand falling on his arm.

Her teasing grin meant she was having far too much fun with this. "Destiny," Rusty muttered under his breath, not at all happy to have his secret shared with everyone in town. He would have to talk to Trevor about what it meant to keep shared confidences.

"Because..."

Rusty let out a deep sigh. "Because I figured her Destiny wasn't with me, but that her destiny would be revealed soon when she found a new home." He knew she wouldn't like his answer but it was the only one he would give. The truth was, when he had named the kitten he was thinking more about life and the pursuit of happiness and wondering where his life would lead. And by extension, the kitten. The thought of the kitten being taken from his home and relocated put the two of them on equal footing. *No man's land*.

Courtney frowned and shook her head. "So that's how you want to play it. Well, then, what about Hope?"

"Now that's the easy name to explain. *Hope*. Trevor *hopes* you will relent and let him have the kitten." Rusty grinned, knowing it was the absolute truth and enough of an answer he was sure it would convince Courtney to change the subject.

Instead, she surprised him by laughing. "You Mr. Devoe, are a softie. A sweet softie."

"Don't let that get around. It will ruin my reputation."

"Hey, Rusty. When did you decide to keep one of the kittens?" Rebecca asked, joining them.

"Good grief. I'm not." Rusty searched the room for Trevor. The easiest way to get the kid to stop telling folks the kittens were theirs was to get him out of the church.

And Rusty knew just how to make it happen. "I've got to go. I'll take Trevor with me back to the ranch. I promised him a roping lesson today since we ran out of time yesterday." He also intended to make him do the boring part of the lesson twice as long for breaking their secret promise about the kittens.

"Running away?" Courtney asked.

"Absolutely." Rusty grinned. He walked away, leaving his sister and Courtney to prattle on about the kittens. He'd heard enough for one day.

Maybe even a lifetime.

Chapter Sixteen

♥

STANDING AT THE WINDOW, Courtney watched for Rusty to arrive. She glanced at her watch. There was still plenty of time to run errands, but he was later than expected and normally quite punctual. And of course, Trevor didn't mind since it meant more time playing with the kitten.

Ten minutes later, Rusty pulled into the driveway. Her pulse quickened as he walked up the path. She waved when he noticed her standing in the window, hoping to conceal the awkwardness she felt at being caught watching. "Trevor, Rusty's here and you need to grab your backpack," she called out, raising her voice slightly to make sure she captured his attention.

"Okay." Trevor gave the kitten a kiss goodbye on the head. "You be a good kitty today."

Satisfied, Courtney moved to the door and pulled it open. "Hey there," she said, stepping back to let Rusty inside.

He pulled off his hat as he entered. "Good morning. Sorry I'm a little late. The bank was busier than I expected and my meeting with the loan officer ran long."

"So what did the guy say? Are you going to get approved?" she asked, hoping everything worked out for Rusty and his plan for the school. Loving what you did day in and day out was half the battle in the search for happiness.

Rusty shrugged. "I didn't really get a read off of Jarod. He was all banker if you know what I mean. Said it would take a few days to go over my application and the business prospectus, and then he'd get back to me. He asked a lot of questions, but luckily, I had done my homework."

"At least it's only a few days. I've been waiting for the insurance company for almost a year." *And she was still getting the runaround.* Maybe she should do some research of her own and figure out if what they were doing was even legal. Something worth thinking more about later. Right now, there was work to be done.

"There is that. So is Trevor ready? And do you think you can handle everything at the community center without me this morning?" Rusty asked.

The thoughtfulness of his question was endearing, but he need not have worried. "He just ran upstairs to get his backpack. And absolutely, I'll be just fine. Now that I know where everything is, and what we have and don't have, it's fairly straight forward. And Italian night is going to be a big hit—I'm sure of it. Lots of pasta, salad, and bread." After finding the perfect combination of both recipes that would be easy and ones that had reviews that promised delicious, her menu was locked into place. All that was left was shopping and preparation.

"*Mmmm*. You're making my mouth water just thinking of it," Rusty said, rubbing his belly in an exaggerated move.

"Wait 'til you taste it." Even though she hadn't made the main recipe as of yet, she had a sense of what worked and what didn't, trusting her palette to guide the way. Even if it wasn't perfect, she would know exactly what to add for the touch of excellence.

"Nothing like a show of confidence and a positive way of thinking. Sounds like a recipe for success."

"Right back at you, mister." Courtney grinned. "And here's your star pupil now," she added as Trevor came running down the stairs.

"Good morning, young man," Laura said, coming into the room from the kitchen. "Another riding lesson?"

"Rusty said I'm gonna learn to rope. Maybe even a bull. Right, Rusty?" Her son looked up at him with adoration in his eyes.

Laura's mouth dropped in a wide o. "Surely not?" she asked, looking to Rusty for confirmation.

Courtney had the same question, but the older woman saved her from having to ask.

"Not quite. What I said was that he would have a roping lesson today and that he needed to learn the basics. The basics don't come anywhere close to a bull."

"Thank goodness. If only I was twenty years younger, I might sign up for a class or two. For riding lessons, that is," Laura corrected. "An old lady like me up on a horse, now that would stir up the Crossroads Creek gossip chain plenty." She grinned.

"Hey, you're plenty young enough to learn to ride...on the right horse," Rusty offered.

Always kind and considerate and wanting others to feel good; Rusty was a down-home cowboy to the core and had a heart of gold to prove it. "Even I've taken two lessons," Courtney chimed in.

"No. That's quite all right. You run along and have fun. And these are for you," Laura said, holding out a set of keys to Courtney.

"Thank you. I'll take good care of the car, I promise."

Laura nodded. "You'll be fine. It's not like it's Grand Central Station in this part of Texas," she added, laughing at her own joke.

Good point. "True. I should be back by lunch. And Trevor, you be good for Rusty and mind him." Courtney hugged her son, dropping a kiss on his forehead.

"Yes, ma'am." Judging by his level of excitement, he would promise her the moon right about now.

They all walked outside and Rusty stopped to hold the driver-side door of the car open. "Thank you," she said, appreciative of the gesture. Greg used to do the same thing and it was one of his many endearing qualities. There was nothing wrong with a little chivalry no matter that they were in the twenty-first century.

"My pleasure. Any idea when we should expect you at the ranch?" Rusty asked.

His nearness intensified the emotional roller coaster she felt around him, and if anything the connection had grown stronger since she had drawn the proverbial line in the sand between them. "Probably late afternoon. I want to pick up what I need at the store, have lunch with Laura, and then head back to the community center to get organized."

Rusty nodded. "Works for me. Call if you need anything. Oh, and here's your check for Wednesday night," he added, reaching into the pocket of his jacket to pull out an envelope and hand it to her.

"Thank you. This will certainly come in handy with Christmas just around the corner. Talk about small blessings. First the truck money and now Christmas money."

"It's you that has been a life saver by helping out at the community center. Which is why I keep trying to convince you to stick around town," he teased, shooting her a wink.

She enjoyed the easy camaraderie between them, even if she tried to deny it meant anything.

Rusty walked to the truck and it wasn't long before the two guys left and Courtney backed out of the driveway. Alone, she had plenty of time to think about the man giving lessons to her son. And to her, for that matter. Someone who was also her boss—and a friend.

Courtney parked the car at the Kroger and went inside, her list in hand. Aisle after aisle, she loaded up cart after cart, parking them at the front of the store when each one was filled to the brim. Hopefully, one of the employees could give her a hand loading everything into the car. It would take every inch of space there was, if not two trips to the community center; something she preferred to avoid.

"Good morning. Courtney isn't it?" The man's voice caught her off guard, especially as she realized the guy was talking to her since no one else was around.

She spun around. "Yes. And good morning, Pastor Phil." The kindly man she'd met Sunday stood there dressed in a suit, his warm smile always welcoming.

"That's a lot of food, young lady." He chuckled, glancing at her cart. "I take it you're working at the community center again?"

Courtney nodded. "I am. And there are four more carts just like this up front. It's positively overwhelming doing this on my own, but I'm determined to get it right." More validation she could handle a deli business, this time doing everything on her own except the final food preparation Wednesday evening.

"You did such a good job with the event last week. Fate must have brought you here because Rusty sure needed you after Alfred left town. A volunteer job of this size and nature is not an easy one to fill, especially on short notice. But you have managed to fill in with such grace and beauty, it's almost as if you're already a part of the community. Perhaps you should consider staying on. The town needs more helpful and kind folks living here, whereas most of the younger folk keep moving to the big cities. They always think they are missing out on something, when all they need can be found right here."

Courtney only half heard what the pastor was saying, her brain stuck on one word and unable to move forward.

Volunteer.

Except she was paid for the job. Both times.

Inside, she was fuming. Outside, she forced herself to play it cool. "Are all the event positions volunteer, or just the lead organizer and cook? she asked, rephrasing what she had heard in a way to confirm without being obvious she hadn't known.

"The whole event is volunteer. People donate to the cause and that's what funds the food and extra expenses associated with it. Rusty's idea to bring this program to Crossroads Creek was a grand one that has grown in leaps and bounds over the past six months."

"I see." *Seeing red was more like it.* Rusty was paying her as if she were a charity case. A very large sum of money at that. "Well, hopefully he finds someone for next week, seeing as Charlie thinks my truck will be ready this Saturday and then I'm leaving for Lafayette."

"I guess we will count our blessings while you're in town then. There's still time for the good Lord to change your mind." He grinned. "I reckon I should get a move on. My wife is waiting on a roast she needs to get in the crock-pot."

"Thank you. I'll see you on Wednesday." Everyone in town was so nice, but it didn't change the fact that Rusty had overstepped his bounds. Ever since Greg had passed away, she had been trying to become more independent and take care of her son. She didn't want to be someone's charity case.

Courtney withdrew the envelope from her purse that Rusty had given her this morning and pulled out the check. Seeing it written out to her name only intensified her negativity towards what he had done. Without giving it a second thought, she ripped the check in two. And then shredded it over and over, before dropping the tiny pieces back into the envelope.

First chance she got, Courtney planned to give Rusty a piece of her mind, and the pieces of the check. But she wouldn't walk away from doing what was right. A promise was a promise, and she would still cook and serve Wednesday evening. After that, she just wanted her truck fixed and to leave town.

But until Saturday, Courtney would need to bide her time. Rusty had lied to her and trust was a two-way street. She didn't need him to fix her life, and his deceit made her feel like a fool for not realizing what he was doing.

By the time she had checked out and taken the groceries to the community center, it was later than she expected. Courtney had no stomach for lunch or small talk. She called Laura to cancel out on their plans. The only thing she wanted to do was confront Rusty and then get her son and leave, preferring to put this whole mess behind her.

Courtney pulled into the long driveway that led to the ranch house. Off to the side of the barn she spotted Rusty and her son in the horse pen, Angel tied off to the side. With each step, her anger took root and any calming effects she had used prior to her arrival, vanished.

Letting out a deep sigh, she dug her hands in her pockets, refusing to return Rusty's wave when he noticed her and headed in her direction. Trevor was practicing throwing a rope toward a wooden saw horse in the middle of the pen. Intent on what he was doing, he wasn't aware of her arrival.

Rusty leaned against the fence, his pose relaxed as he kept an eye on her son. "You're earlier than I expected, but this is great so you can see Trevor in action. He's doing pretty good on the roping lessons, even if he's a bit put out about not getting to train from the back of a horse." Rusty chuckled.

Courtney tried to channel her focus and find the right words. The last thing she wanted was to involve Trevor in her dispute with Rusty. "We need to talk."

He turned to face her, his easy smile gone. "What's wrong?"

"Keep your voice down. I don't want Trevor to overhear what I have to say," she fumed.

"*Ummm*, okay." Rusty frowned, glancing back at Trevor. "Hey Trev, how about we take a short break and you can ride Angel around the pen while I talk to your mom. You've earned some free time. Use the mounting stool by the gate and you'll be fine."

"Yes, sir," her son answered, his smile lighting his face like he had received an early Christmas present. "Hi, Mom. Wait till I show you what I learned. Rusty said I'm doing really good."

"I'm sure you are." Unfortunately, her son's exuberant mood wouldn't last past this visit. Courtney had no intention of coming back to the ranch, or letting her son continue lessons. She hated it for Trevor, but what was done, was done. Rusty had lied and broken the trust between them, succinctly putting an end to anything that resembled charity in Courtney's mind.

Trevor untied the reins, climbed up on the wooden box, and then pulled himself into the saddle. "Watch me, Mom."

"I'm watching," Courtney said, trying not to let him see how upset she was.

Rusty moved closer to her as Trevor started to make the rounds in the ring. "So what's going on?"

"This," she said, slapping the envelope against his arm. "Take it," Courtney ground out in a low voice.

The lines across Rusty's forehead deepened like ravines mapping out his frustration. "I don't understand."

"It's charity money. I don't need your hand-outs, *or* your lies. Imagine my surprise when I found out from the pastor that the job I'm doing at the community center is a volunteer one, just like all the others who help out. You've made a fool of me, leading me to believe I was earning money. It was all a lie." She struggled to hold back the emotions ripping through her. Emotions that caused her eyes to tear, threatening to spill over.

Rusty had the good graces to look guilty. "I'm sorry. I just figured with your truck breaking down, you could use the help. I didn't mean to hurt you. It can't be easy raising Trevor on your own and all the changes you're having to deal with," he said, shoving his hands in his front pockets as if uncomfortable.

His platitudes were too late, the damage done. She had spent some of the money he'd given her last week and couldn't pay it back right away. *But she would.* "Except my financial affairs are none of your business. I'm handling my life. And no, it hasn't been easy, but I have my pride and my independence. I'm tired of people managing things for me." *Especially because then they thought they had a right to offer their opinions and tell you what to do. Her in-laws a case in point.*

"Please believe me, I didn't mean to upset you."

His sincerity was hard to resist, but she needed to stay strong. "Well you did. You can keep your money...I don't want it. And when I get a job in Lafayette, I intend to pay you back every cent from last week's check. I'm not a charity case."

A scream sounded from the pen.

Trevor.

Courtney whipped her head around as her son landed on the ground. "Trevor," she called out, racing toward him as he lay curled up in a ball. "Oh my gosh. What happened? Are you okay?" she asked, dropping to her knees beside him.

Rusty knelt next to her, his hands running over Trevor's limbs. "Does anything hurt? Did you hit your head?" he asked, brushing her son's hair from side-to-side checking for injuries.

"I'm okay. I didn't hit my head. It just scared me," Trevor said.

Courtney let out a heavy sigh of relief. "What happened?" she asked. "Did the horse throw you?" She shot Rusty an accusatory glare. "I thought you said the horse was safe and gentle?"

"Angel *is* safe and gentle. Trevor, can you tell me what happened?"

Something in Rusty's voice caught her attention, but when her son looked away, the truth was staring her right in the face. It wasn't the horse's fault. Call it mother's intuition, or whatever, but there was more to Trevor's fall than he wanted to share.

Rusty let out a deep breath and glanced around. His lips formed a tight, thin line as he looked back at Trevor. "You tried to throw the rope from the back of the horse, didn't you?" he asked, his voice firm and determined to figure out what happened.

Trevor looked away. "Yes. I'm sorry. I just wanted to show my mom," he whined.

Rusty's hardened expression grew more tense. "But I told you not to. That you weren't ready. My rules are to be followed. And I told you there are consequences if you don't follow the rules. I'm glad you're okay, but there will be no riding or roping lessons tomorrow. And since you're not hurt, it's time we groomed the horses and put them back in the barn."

Clearly the man wasn't moved by her son's excuse. *Nor should he be.*

Trevor shifted his gaze back and forth from her to Rusty, his lower lip in heavy pout. "That's not fair. I just wanted to show my mom." Crocodile tears welled up in his eyes.

Rusty shook his head. "It is fair. More than fair. The rules are to keep you safe. My decision stands—take it or leave it."

As he issued the ultimatum, it suddenly occurred to Courtney that none of the rules or conditions applied to the situation. *Not anymore.* "It doesn't matter. Trevor's lessons are over anyway. We're leaving Saturday and there's no use risking him getting hurt over learning something he'll never get to do again. It's not like my mom has a horse. And you," she said, leveling Rusty with a glare, "you were supposed to keep him safe." It wasn't a fair accusation as they had both been distracted during the argument, but it was a convenient way to put an end to the lessons and their association.

Rusty removed his hat and ran a hand through his hair, tension vibrating from every inch of his body. "You're right, it is my fault. I let myself get distracted. Something I won't let happen again. And don't worry about Angel, I'll take care of her for Trevor." He stood, giving her son a hand to his feet.

"Fine," Courtney snapped. They both knew she was the one who distracted him. And even if she did have cause, her timing was terrible.

Trevor looked back and forth between them. "But I don't want to leave. I'm sorry, Rusty."

"It's your mom's call, buddy. But if you ever ride again, please promise me you'll follow the rules. It's for your own safety."

"Yes, sir. I promise," Trevor mumbled as he headed for the car, his gait slow as he kicked the ground in defiance with each step.

"Thanks for all you've done for him," she said, her voice stilted. "I'll finish out working at the community center, but perhaps you could find someone else to serve with me at the table. It wouldn't do for the whole town to witness our falling out, and I certainly don't want to have to explain it to anyone. I do have my pride, whether you understand it or not."

Courtney turned and walked away, her parting comment giving her a sense of satisfaction. If only the rest of her could agree. But judging by the heaviness in her heart, she was a long way from being happy about the situation.

By Wednesday, Trevor's mood hadn't improved. For that matter, neither had Courtneys. Not even finding a couple of jobs posted online working at restaurants in Lafayette could brighten her spirits. Between prepping for the Wednesday evening meal and searching for a job, she had kept busy, not wanting time to think over what had happened.

At first, the job availability had been like a blessing. It was as if God was reminding her of the goals she'd set for herself, and all roads kept pointing her in the right direction. But if it was true, then why was she upset? And why did it feel like she was losing a new best friend? *Someone important to her.*

"You know, this thing between you and Rusty isn't doing you any good. Maybe you should forgive him. It's easier to forgive than harbor a grudge," Laura said, looking up from her needlework.

"But he lied." Courtney had told Laura the whole truth, needing someone to talk to, but not wanting to involve her mother.

"*Aww*, but you're forgetting one very important point. His motives were pure. Rusty was trying to do a good thing, even if he didn't understand at the time how it might be perceived by the recipient of such a generous gift. Perhaps he too has his reasons for the generosity. Something you would do well to consider." The older woman continued to knit, not missing a stitch as she delivered the gentle rebuke.

It was surprising how much Laura had been pushing her toward forgiveness, but this was a novel concept. "Like what kind of reasons?" Courtney asked, suddenly interested, and wondering if Laura knew more than she was letting on.

"That's for him to tell you. He's a good man, and you shouldn't turn away help from people who give without strings attached. Look at me, for instance. I don't see you mad at me for letting you stay here." Faith uncurled from her sleeping position and stretched before rubbing up against the scarf Laura was knitting.

It was a valid point, but one Courtney could justify. "That's different. You offered me a place to stay. Whereas he gave me money, and then lied about it. Acted like I was earning the wages." They had come full circle and it was all back to the lie. *And monetary charity.*

Laura shook her head, putting the scarf aside to pet Faith. "Generosity comes in many forms, my dear. Perhaps you should focus more on understanding and forgiveness, knowing he meant well."

"Perhaps you're right." Courtney said, letting out a deep sigh. "It would be a lot easier to forgive and move forward. I promised to pay him back, so maybe that needs to be the end of it. I shall think it over. Thank you." Maybe forgiveness would also help Courtney move forward, because right now, she was dwelling on the negative and it was affecting her mood. Her mother had once said, forgiveness is more for yourself and the ability to move on, than for the person who wronged you.

"See that you do, my dear. See that you do." Laura set Faith on the floor and headed for the kitchen, the door swinging closed behind her, effectively ending the discussion.

Courtney wanted to forgive Rusty because he had given her the money with a proper heart. Just like the free riding and roping lessons he'd given Trevor. Rusty was generous to a fault, something he'd proven over and over.

Trevor's fall wasn't Rusty's fault. Her son had a rebellious streak at times and trying to rope from a horse after being specifically told not to, well that was certainly one of those times. And the truth was, they both should have been watching him, not fussing over her offense at Rusty's generosity.

Chapter Seventeen

♥

RUSTY RUBBED THE SLEEP out of his eyes and stretched, recalling the previous evening. The night had gone well, everyone loving Courtney's Italian-themed dining experience. That is, other than the odd looks and questioning gazes people shot between him and Courtney. The town gossips curiosity had been in high gear all night long, although no one asked him a single question.

He had honored Courtney's request and served as a greeter last night, staying out of her way. It wasn't easy, and he missed their camaraderie, but then, all he had to do was think of the mistakes he'd made and his resolve was instantly strengthened. The desire to help her had been a good one, but perhaps Courtney was more than a little right—it was not a well-thought-out plan.

Rusty knew what it felt like to be treated differently, the product of charity, and should have been more aware—or at the least, more sensitive in his approach. Instead, he'd barreled into the situation with the grace of a bull.

And then there was the issue with Trevor. The kid fell off Angel on Rusty's watch, the gut-wrenching moment of fear when he spotted Trevor on the ground still having the power to haunt him. It was a blessing Trevor wasn't hurt, but it didn't absolve Rusty of his part in the fiasco.

His job had been to keep the boy safe and allowing himself to be distracted was a problem. It didn't matter he had told Trevor not to try roping from the horse yet, because if he had been paying attention to his student, Rusty could have stopped the colossal mistake before it happened.

And there-in lay another huge problem. *What if he wasn't cut out to teach kids?*

Shoving his doubts aside, he got dressed and headed into town. One thing he didn't doubt in the slightest was that he needed to apologize to Courtney...*if* she would let him. *The other possibility was that she might close the door in his face.*

Flowers were always a good choice. Rusty made a U-turn, pulled into the florist shop parking lot, and headed inside. "Good morning, Frank," he called out as the bell above his head jingled, announcing his arrival.

The old man poked his head out from behind the counter. "Morning, Rusty. Funny thing you coming in today, as the most interesting thing happened this morning."

Rusty grinned, not at all sure what the old man was talking about, but then he did like to talk so chances were, it meant nothing at all. "Not sure I'm here on a funny cause, more like an apology cause. I was wondering if you would deliver some flowers to Courtney Winters from me. She's staying at Laura's place."

"Delivering flowers is what a florist shop does." Frank chuckled. He pushed his wire-rim spectacles back on his nose and then rubbed his chin as if deep in thought. "Apology flowers...let me think. I know. A mixed bouquet with some yellow and orange roses and lots of greenery says I'm sorry to someone special. It will brighten her day for sure."

The florist could have said black and Rusty wouldn't have known any better. Okay...so that was a bit of a stretch. Even he knew black represented death. "Sounds perfect. I'll write a note you can attach," Rusty said, picking up one of the little cards next to the register. He suddenly remembered the old man's comment when he arrived and had to admit his curiosity was piqued. "You said something about it being funny I showed up today. Why is that?"

Frank took Rusty's credit card and swiped it through the machine. "Oh, that. Yes, *ummm*, well that whole thing just got more interesting if you ask me, seeing as you're sending flowers to that Courtney woman. You see, *she* was just in *here* this morning," he said, adding the last part as if it were the latest hot gossip.

"She was?" Perhaps ordering flowers to apologize to him. *Not a chance.* "Who did she want flowers for?" he asked, unable to resist.

"She didn't want flowers. Ms. Winters wanted information." The old man stopped what he was doing and drilled Rusty with an assessing gaze. "More specifically, information about a W.D. who might live in Crossroads Creek. Know anyone by those initials?" Frank grinned.

Rusty pulled back, frowning. "I don't understand." It wasn't that he didn't know anyone in town who fit the description, considering he was one of them. It was the same reason Frank was enjoying every second of this conversation. The bigger issue at the moment, was to figure out why Courtney was asking Frank about a man named W.D. "What did she say?"

"She was real careful with her words, if you ask me. Didn't say right much, just that she was curious because she once had communication with the person. Seems she stopped at several businesses this morning with the same inquiry but didn't have any luck. This town can be better than Fort Knox when it comes to protecting one of our own."

Which wasn't something Rusty had ever witnessed firsthand, seeing as he left town when he graduated high school and never looked back. *Until now.*

Frank handed him back the credit card and scooped up the personalized note Rusty had written.

"What did you tell her?" Rusty asked.

"We do have several W.D.'s in town. And I'm not Edna. That woman would have grilled Courtney for more information, but not me. Reckon I got enough on my plate without bringing trouble to my doorstep." He chuckled. "Courtney is a beautiful and kind woman, inside and out to all appearances, but she is still a stranger—just passing through town."

Passing through town.

Except Crossroads Creek wasn't a passing-through town. Not by any stretch of the imagination. As Rusty tried to figure out why Courtney might be interested in finding W.D., the answers that popped into his head weren't ones he liked. In fact, they were mind-boggling and stomach twisting all in one swift kick to the gut. Too many coincidences for his liking. "I'll look into it. Thanks for letting me know. And why don't we keep this between us for good measure. At least for the time being."

"Will do, but there's no telling about the others," Frank said, nodding. "They may not tell Courtney about you, but they will talk to each other. Be prepared."

"Will do. And thanks." Rusty headed outside into the bright sunlight just as a cloud slipped over to block it. Mother Nature was mocking his own internal conflict. He prayed his suspicion would prove unfounded, but he was holding out little hope.

Crossroads Creek.

W.D.

Courtney's husband died last year.

Too many coincidences for sure.

He headed back to the ranch and made a beeline for the desk in his room, not wanting to be disturbed. Flicking the switch on his laptop, the screen lit up a few seconds later and he typed Courtney Winters into the search bar. With only the barest hint of a pause, he hit enter. There were several entries that populated the screen and he scrolled down, not interested in all the gimmicky resources trying to capture your information and sell reports as you searched for a person. After two pages of useless results, he clicked on the news tab, hoping it would cut through the bull. And then he saw it.

Greg Winters obituary. Died November 11th. Last year. The same day as Rusty's operation. Another coincidence, this almost enough to convince him of the truth staring him in the face. He read on, needing to know for sure. The man was survived by Courtney, Trevor, and his parents. Was it possible? He scrolled on down the page, seeking more entries.

And then wished he hadn't.

Deadly Accident in Crossroads Creek, TX. One man left dead after losing control of his vehicle at Farrier Overlook. Greg Winters. November 11th.

Why else would Courtney be in Crossroads Creek? Adrenaline shot through Rusty's veins, the truth undeniable. Perhaps not a hundred percent positive, but at the very least, 99.9 %. Neither the hospital nor the organ donor agency would confirm what he knew, but at this point, he didn't need them to.

The information was all there in black and white. The room began to spin and he lowered his head into his hands, trying to stabilize the dizzying effect of the news as it settled into his brain.

Greg Winter's was the heart donor who gave Rusty life.

Courtney.

No. He ran his hands through his hair and gave a gentle pull, needing to feel something. *Anything.*

Rusty would have to tell Courtney of his suspicions—but how? This wouldn't end well and he knew it. He slid his fingers to his temples and rubbed in a circular motion, trying to ease the tension. And then he started to pray. Only God could give him the guidance and strength he needed to deal with this situation head on. For so long, he had been wanting to help the donor's widow, and now, it would seem he had been given the chance.

Except for the fact he had already helped Courtney once and it backfired. *But this was different.* She was the widow of the man whose heart beat in his chest. He couldn't *not* help her. There would be no lies involved—only an anonymous gift. And Rusty would make sure Charlie never revealed his identity as the donor. Much the same as the organ donor program—only this was the organ-donor-thank-you program.

Not that it was enough...as it would never be enough. But it was a start.

His heart.

Her love for another man.

Totally hopeless.

Nothing is hopeless when you trust in the Lord. The message came to him, filling him with the barest hint of peace. Rusty needed more where that came from, but it would take time.

All day he waited on tenterhooks for Courtney to call, letting him know she received the flowers. And all day he had gone over in his head what to say when they got together to talk. All day, he failed to come up with the right words.

His phone beeped, indicating a message had come in. Rusty held his breath as he read the text.

Thank you for the beautiful flowers. And yes, you're forgiven. Someone recently reminded me about well-meaning intentions and graciously receiving help. I didn't do that very well. Hope you will forgive me also. Call and let's talk.

She had forgiven him, which was more than he deserved considering how close Trevor came to getting hurt. He started to press the call button, but then hesitated. What would he say? This was a conversation that needed to take place face to face. Rusty shoved the phone in his back pocket.

It was going to be a long night, but at least it would give him time to figure out what to say.

Rusty had gotten very little sleep throughout the night, which did nothing for his mood this morning.

"What's with the long face?" his mother asked when he entered the kitchen. "You skipped dinner and now this. What's going on?"

His mother was good at reading her kid's moods as youngsters, and even as adults, she still managed to keep her finger on the pulse of everything going on around the ranch. "Rough day." He shrugged. "I heard some information in town and I'm not quite sure what to do with it." It was the closest he planned on admitting any of the details, but he valued her opinion and any words of wisdom she might have to guide him in the right direction would be welcome. *Generally speaking, of course.*

"Gossip?" she questioned, quirking one eyebrow up in surprise.

"No. The information came straight from one of the two people in a conversation." His mother was one of those people who stayed far, far away from gossip, only dealing in facts.

"Hurtful information?" she pressed, trying to get to the root of what she needed to know to offer advice.

Rusty still remembered one of her common lessons...or lectures depending how you looked at them. *Idle hands make idle minds and will bring you nothing but trouble.*

"In a roundabout way," he hedged, filling his cup with coffee. Taking a sip, the hot liquid scalded his tongue, giving him a reprieve from having to expand on his answer.

"Then stay out of it. Mind your ABCs. A and B conversation, C your way out." She grinned, reciting the saying every parent muttered at least once to their children.

The lesson had taught him a great way to stay out of the mix of trouble that always seemed to hover around kids trying to grow up. Too bad it wasn't the same thing now. "Except C is directly involved," he admitted.

His mother came to stand next to him, laying her hand on his shoulder. "And you're certain you can't sit tight on the information? Sometimes, if you let time pass by, how it plays out in the short run might affect your choices. It's a delicate balance for sure."

"Not this information. It's not so much a question of whether to say anything, but *what* to say." Rusty ran a hand through his hair. This kind of conversation wasn't something anyone could prepare for.

"I'm sure you'll figure it out. You normally do. And if you want a sounding board and are prepared to help me understand more than the generalities you've provided, I'm right here." She squeezed his shoulder and walked back to the stove.

"Thanks, Mom. But I need to talk to her...*ummm*...I mean the person first," he corrected, knowing his slip up just eliminated half the population in town.

His mother frowned. "Her? So this involves Courtney."

Nothing he could say would change her opinion judging by the matter-of-fact tone of her voice. He let out a sigh, knowing he wouldn't lie. "Yes."

"Well then, whatever it is…fix it. You two are good together and it's a shame that she and Trevor stopped visiting." His mother placed a plate of ham and eggs in front of him. "Eat up, plenty more where that came from."

Normally, he could put away a heaping portion of breakfast his mother had prepared, but at the moment, the thought of food churned his stomach knowing what the day held. A revelation so big it would surely upset Courtney and drive her out of his life. "We were never together—just friends." Although, if that were true, then why did the truth of where his new heart came from bother him so much?

"If you say so. Except that's not what I saw between the two of you, but then, what do I know? I'm just your mother," she huffed. "Don't you let those two leave town without so much as a goodbye."

"Yes, ma'am." Rusty pushed his plate away. "Sorry, I'm not sure breakfast is what I need. Give this to Clay when he comes in." He carried the untouched plate back to the stove.

"Fine. You need to eat, the doctor warned you—"

"Mother...you promised."

"Fine. Go. I'll take care of this. Just don't do anything rash or that you will regret. Courtney is a special person whether you recognize it or not just yet."

Rusty did recognize it, which was the problem. He strode out the door and headed for the bank. He'd be early for his eight-thirty appointment, but then the balance of his future hung on this meeting, so who could blame him?

Tamping down the knot of apprehension that settled in the pit of his stomach, he pulled open the door of the bank for another customer, letting the woman pass ahead of him. Making his way to the plush cushioned chairs, he picked up a copy of Western Life magazine, thinking it would help pass the gut-wrenching moments as he waited for Jarod to call him into his office.

"Hey there, Rusty. Good to see you again," Jarod said, coming to stand next to him.

Rusty stood and the two friends shook hands. "I'm a little early, but I was anxious to talk with you. I hope you have good news," Rusty said, preferring to get right down to the business of why he was there. There were other pressing issues he needed to attend.

An unreadable expression crossed over Jarod's face. "Why don't you come in my office and we can talk."

Rusty followed Jarod, but the tone of his friend's voice gave him an uneasy feeling. "What's up? Is everything in order with the loan?" he asked, preferring to get this over with and sensing the answer wasn't favorable.

Jarod picked up a file on his desk and leaned back in his oversized leather chair. "Unfortunately no. I really wanted to make you the loan, and I tried to push it past my district manager, but he's sticking hard on this one. The ability to repay is a huge risk given that you've never done this type of program before and you are currently only working at the family ranch. To be honest, your ability to repay the loan is in question."

Not only a no, but a big, fat no. Not even a breath of hope crossed the man's lips. "But I have money saved up and I'll earn more as I go."

Jarod shook his head. "I'm sorry, but it's a risk the bank isn't willing to take. You were in the rodeo, not teaching at equestrian schools over the past ten years. The numbers simply don't add up as a good business model."

Rusty stiffened. There was more to this and it didn't take a rocket scientist to figure it out. "What you really mean is that I'm a risk because of my heart. I didn't think you could use that information against me," Rusty said, frustration surging through his veins. Life was stacking up against him, reinforcing his need to understand why he was chosen for the heart transplant.

For the first time, a new idea hit him. What if it wasn't God who picked him, and it was simply a matter of logistics? *Dumb luck.* He'd never thought to ask, and no one ever brought it up. How was his name picked from the list? He had only been on the waiting list five months, which was a pretty quick turnaround by all standards. Although having Type A blood had certainly helped his cause. But what about the other candidates ahead of him?

Jarod flipped the pages of his file. "This has nothing to do with your health. It's not on the application and therefore has no bearing," Jarod said unconvincingly.

"That's a load of hogwash and you know it. You already know the information so it's not like you're in the discovery phase. Roping and riding has been my life. Who better to teach kids than a professional cowboy?" There was also bull riding to add to his resume, but that wasn't something he had planned on adding to the program.

"I'm sorry. There's nothing I can do," Jarod said. He stood, signaling the meeting was over.

"Thanks for nothing," Rusty mumbled before he left the office. So everything he started to think would be possible was all for naught. He was still just a washed-up rodeo cowboy.

Rusty pushed through the front door, anger and frustration ripping through him like a wildfire. After the incident with Trevor, Rusty had begun to question if opening a school was the right path for him. Being turned down for the loan, now he had answers. God was sending him a clear signal this was not the path intended for him. And if the school wasn't the answer, and working at the ranch wasn't the answer, there was only one thing left for him to do.

Leave town. The same thing he planned on doing before he came up with the grandiose idea of operating a roping and riding school and settling down.

Once a cowboy, always a cowboy. But where that left him, he didn't have a clue.

Chapter Eighteen

♥

AFTER COURTNEY HAD SENT Rusty a text message to thank him for the flowers and apologize, she fully expected to hear from him. But that was Thursday evening and this was Saturday morning, and she hadn't heard a word.

Saturday...the day she was leaving town.

Laura had clearly been wrong in her appraisal of the situation, and her apology to Rusty had meant nothing at all. Trevor, of course, had been a handful the past couple of days, not at all understanding why his lessons ended. He broke Rusty's rules, and although Courtney had tried to explain why it wasn't a good choice, she was also quick to make sure he understood the end of his lessons had nothing to do with his actions. Her explanation about adults and disagreements hadn't made him feel any better. Rightly so, considering he was the one caught in the middle.

But none of this would matter in a few hours, as she and Trevor would be well on their way to Lafayette. Charlie had let her know the part arrived, and he would be finished installing the radiator by noon. Courtney had packed their belongings, notified her mother of their impending arrival time, and now, she was more than ready to leave.

Rusty's absence had given her plenty of time to put in a few job applications, and she had said more than a couple of prayers hoping to get one of them. She needed the money to live on, but also, more importantly, to pay Rusty back. His change in attitude even with an apology, was proof she was right not to let her emotions get involved.

Love didn't come around but once in a lifetime—and hers had been with Greg.

The default ring tone filled the room with sing-song bells. Courtney grabbed her phone off the bed. "Hey, Charlie," she said, recognizing the number.

"Got your truck all fixed up. Runs like a champ," he said, getting straight to the point.

Courtney let out a heavy sigh. Whether with relief or disappointment, she wasn't sure. "Wonderful news. Thank you. I'll have Laura run me over as soon as she gets back from the store."

"Sounds good. See you then." Charlie hung up before she had a chance to reply. It wasn't like him to be so abrupt. Courtney shrugged. The guy was the epitome of a good-old country boy who liked to chat...with everyone. So perhaps, he was simply busy.

Twenty minutes later, Laura arrived back at the house. "Here, let me help carry in the groceries," Courtney said, grabbing the one closest to the outside.

"Thank you, dear. You are always such a big help to me."

"That's sweet of you to say, but I'm afraid my time here is over. Charlie called and my truck is ready. You have been such a blessing to Trevor and I. Thank you so much." Her generosity and warm welcome had made their stay in Crossroads Creek easy. Of course, Rusty was also a big factor, but that wasn't something Courtney needed to dwell on.

"I sure wish you didn't have to leave," Laura said, her normally animated face now in quiet repose.

It was the wistful tone of her voice that took hold and stuck. Laura was a lonely woman and it was more than a little sad. "I'm sorry. Unfortunately, I do need to get on with my regular life. This has been just the respite I needed to renew my strength, but now I need to figure out the next steps to starting over. It will be easier for me to do at my mother's."

"Just promise me you'll keep in touch," Laura said, laying one wrinkled and bony hand on Courtney's arm.

"I will. I promise." They carried in the rest of the groceries, Trevor still sulking on the stairs. Courtney wasn't about to push her luck and force her son to help, not wanting to end their visit on a sour note. It wouldn't be the right thing to do for Laura. *Not after all her kindness.*

When they were done, Courtney loaded their suitcases and bags into the car. The tearful goodbye took longer than the five-minute ride to the garage. She hugged Laura and watched as the woman drove away, brushing away the tears that slid down her cheeks. It was like losing a new-found friend, even though she had promised to keep in touch.

All that was left to do was pay Charlie and be on her way. It seemed strange to leave without saying goodbye to Rusty and his family, but she had to respect his choice to keep his distance.

Trevor followed her inside, leaving their bags by the front door. In terms of personal security, Courtney had come a long way from when she first arrived. Leaving her bags outside the garage wasn't anything she would have dreamed of doing before this. Small-town living was growing on her in more ways than she could have planned.

Charlie wasn't in the front office and she went through the side door into the garage section.

A heavy smell of grease permeated the air. She made her way to the desk in the corner where she could hear a Hank Williams tune playing on the radio. An eccentric, wiry-haired man sat rocking in his chair, his gaze distant. With only a few gray hairs scattered on his head and his weathered skin, Courtney figured the guy to be in his nineties. *Charlie's father perhaps.*

"Excuse me," she said, trying not to startle him.

He glanced up at her and smiled. "Sorry. I didn't hear you come in. Hearing aids are turned down," he added, fumbling with the device in his ear.

So he had the hearing aids turned down and the music turned up. *An oddity for sure.* She grinned. "It's okay. That's a great song."

The man nodded, shifting in his rocker to get more comfortable. "Hank is one of the golden oldies. Never get tired of his songs."

"I'm looking for Charlie. Do you know where he is?" she asked, glancing around.

"Not here. Said something about getting lunch. At least I think that's what he said.

Memory ain't so spot on anymore if you know what I mean."

Another delay would put their arrival time well after dark. "I do, but I was sure he would be here. I was supposed to pick up my truck and he told me to come on over."

"That yours?" the old man asked, jerking his thumb toward her Ford.

"Yes, it is."

The man leaned forward, grabbing a set of keys off the wall at the back of the desk. "These are yours then, I reckon." He held them out to her.

"Yes. Thank you. How much do I owe?" Courtney asked, fumbling in her purse to find her credit card. She hadn't intended to pay this way, but the money in her checking account belonged to Rusty. And she had no intentions of using any more of the balance at this point unless it was a dire emergency.

The man shook his head. "Nothing. All paid for already," he said, his tone nonchalant, as if it were a common occurrence.

A sense of deja vu hit her. "What do you mean? I haven't paid for the repairs yet. There must be some mistake." The last thing she wanted to do was leave town, only to find out later when creditors started calling that he had been wrong and collection hounds were hot on her heels.

The man shook his head again. "No mistake. That Wade boy was in here and paid it earlier this morning. Saw it myself and heard him and Charlie talking about it."

Courtney was thoroughly confused. "Wade boy?"

"Yup, Mary Devoe's boy...good looking cowboy," the old man grinned. "Shame about his heart condition and having to leave the rodeo. But he's doing good stuff in town, so I reckon Crossroads Creek is better off having him around."

Courtney sucked in a deep breath, adrenaline surging through her.

Wade boy. Mary Devoe. Wade Devoe. W.D. Rodeo Cowboy.

Rusty.

No way. The coincidences were all there. How many Mary Devoe's could there be in Crossroads Creek? And Courtney knew Rusty had a medical condition he didn't like to talk about. Could it be a heart condition?

It didn't seem possible, but all signs pointed to Rusty being the recipient of Greg's heart. Her hands shook, the odds astronomical. Except maybe not as much as she first suspected. Greg's accident had been here in Crossroads Creek, but Greg had been airlifted to a hospital in Dallas. And if Rusty had a heart condition, Dallas would have been where the specialists team were located. But the odds of the recipient living in the town where Greg died...that was insanely unlikely.

Images of doctors and planes flying organs around the country came to mind. But apparently, made for TV drama wasn't reality. At least based on what she suspected in this situation.

It was all too much to take in. The question was, did Rusty know? Had he somehow known all along and that's why he paid her the money to work at the community center? And now he had gone ahead and paid the truck after she specifically told him she didn't want his charity.

Courtney didn't want to believe Rusty would know and not tell her. And to think they had almost kissed. *No. No. No.* Her chest felt constricted, her throat closing as she struggled for composure. "Thank you," she squeaked out. "Trevor, get in the truck."

Her son looked at her strangely, but luckily, didn't question her and did as he was told.

Courtney had to get out of there. "Tell Charlie I said thanks for everything," she said, forcing the words from her mouth.

"Is everything okay, miss? You seem a bit out of sorts," the old man asked, a concerned look on his face.

Courtney gripped the keys tight, the edges digging into the palm of her hand. "Everything will be okay. I just need to get a move on to get to my mother's place by dark. See you later," she said, forcing the words to come out when all she wanted to do was scream.

Not that she'd have that luxury with Trevor sitting in the front seat. The truck started right up, and with a quick wave, she backed out of the garage.

Destination—Lafayette.

With one stop before she left town. *The Devoe ranch.* It would have been easier to turn tail and run, or drive, in the opposite direction—but this was something she had to do. She had to know the truth. And it was the only thing that had the power to change her mind with regards to getting out of Dodge.

Please, Lord. Just in case Rusty doesn't know, I pray you'll give me the right words to say because it will come as a huge shock to him, as much as it was to me. Not that she believed for a minute he didn't know, but she wouldn't jump to conclusions and charge in with accusations. Thank goodness she was leaving Crossroads Creek because anything else sounded complicated with a capital C.

She pulled onto the dirt driveway that led to the ranch house.

"Why are we stopping here, Mom?" Trevor asked, his face brightening with pleasure.

"I needed to talk with Rusty and we should say our goodbyes to the Devoe family and thank them for all they have done for us." Her reasoning was a bit of a fudge to the truth, but deep down, it was no less than she should have done anyway given the family's kindness.

She spotted Rusty's Chevy in front of the house. They got out of the truck just as Rusty came down the front steps, drawing up short when they all came face to face. His uneasy gaze was her first clue something wasn't right.

"Hey, Rusty. I've missed coming here, but Mom said no. And now we have to leave," Trevor said, throwing her under the bus without so much as a second thought. He was trying to be tough, but Courtney knew her son too well.

Rusty kneeled down next to him. "Your mom's a smart lady and you should always trust her judgement," he said, man to man style.

"Yes, sir," Trevor mumbled.

"Why don't you run inside so I can talk with your mom? You'll find my mother in the kitchen and she's baking cookies. I bet you could sweet talk her into a few." Rusty winked.

"Sounds good to me. Grown up talk is boring." Her son turned and ran in the house.

Rusty stood, giving her his full attention. "I see you got your truck fixed," he said, darting a glance at the Ford.

"As if you didn't know that already, considering it would seem you paid for the repairs. Why would you do that?" she asked, wanting to get the conversation out in the open.

Rusty winced. "I know what you said, but this was different. I swear I had to pay the bill. Please try to understand—"

"But we just went—"

"This was different. Trust me," Rusty said, no backing down.

They were both bent on getting their point across, but real answers were in short supply. "Different how?" she relented, giving him a chance to explain.

Rusty frowned, but Courtney caught the uncomfortable look that settled in his eyes before he gazed toward the pasture. "I've been trying to talk to you since Thursday night about something I found out. Finding the right words hasn't been easy. I'm sorry if I didn't return your text, but I simply couldn't. Not then. And preferably not now, but your arrival changes that a bit." He shifted his stance, glancing down at his boots.

It would seem looking anywhere other than at her was his goal. This Rusty wasn't the confident cowboy she knew and cared about. *Past tense.* That is if she could convince her heart to agree.

Clearly, finding the right words was a problem they shared. "Go on," she said, letting him talk first as a means to buy herself more time. *So much for taking the bull by the horns.*

"I get that you were upset with me about the money I paid you for the community center event. I honestly didn't think it through before I made the offer. I needed help, and you seemed down on your luck. It was a win/win situation. As to your truck, it is completely different. I had to pay for those repairs." Rusty's warm, chocolatey eyes landed on her with an intensity she hadn't expected. "You know I have a medical condition, but the truth is so much more than that. It's my—"

"Heart," she finished for him.

Rusty drew back sharply. "How did you know? Who told you?" he asked, his brow lines deepening.

Courtney heaved a deep sigh. There was no evading the subject any longer. "Charlie's father. Why didn't you want me to know?" she said, voicing the million-dollar question.

"Because I'm tired of all the sympathetic looks and questions from well-meaning people. I just want to get on with my life. I want to be me again, not heart-patient extraordinaire."

The last part was spoken with such a volume of frustration, she couldn't help but feel sorry for what he might have gone through this past year...because she knew the truth, and it all made sense. *Now.* "So what changed? Why tell me today?" she asked, still wanting to verify what he knew before she blurted out the unconceivable truth. It was far too delicate of a situation not to be patient.

Rusty shook his head. "Because there's more to my story. And by more, I mean a part that involves you."

Courtney closed her eyes to the truth. She wouldn't have to tell him because he already knew. "I'm listening." She opened her eyes back up, and crossed her arms in front of her chest, trying to form a wall to protect herself from the emotions threatening to consume her and spill over in a moment of weakness.

"I had a heart transplant," Rusty said in a rush, as if wanting to get the moment over with. "I'm a washed-up cowboy with the gift of a heart. Someone who didn't deserve the gift. When I tried to help you the first time, it was my way to assuage some of my guilt over a situation I have no control over. I've always worried about the widow of the man who died, the man whose heart I have beating in my chest. The agency doesn't reveal identities to donor's families or recipients, so I couldn't help the woman, which is why I helped you instead. You were a widow, so by transference, it was a roundabout way to do something right...sort of like an atonement for the gift."

Courtney couldn't breathe. This wasn't at all what she expected to hear. Maybe some of it, but now she felt like a heel for her ungracious reception of his generosity. Was it possible he still didn't know the whole truth? "I understand. On that note, there's something I need to tell you also."

Rusty held up his hand. "Let me finish. The hardest part is yet to come and I need to tell you everything. You deserve that and so much more."

"Go on."

Rusty closed his eyes, his hands going to his temples. Reopening his eyes, he let out a heavy sigh. "When I paid for the truck repair it was different. Different because I was helping the donor's widow, and as it turns out, her son."

His words sunk in, as did the intensity of his gaze. "Me?" she squeaked. Even already knowing the truth, didn't make this moment any easier. Especially since this confirmed Rusty had known the truth. The question was...for how long?

Rusty reached for her hand. "Yes, you. My real name is Wade Devoe. Rusty has been my nickname since I was five years old and stepped on a rusty nail. I'm the W. D. who sent you a note. The recipient of Greg's heart. I'm so sorry, Courtney."

Her head was spinning with an intensity she couldn't control. She reached for the railing on the front steps for support, pulling her other hand from his and covering her heart as if it would ward off the inevitable ache. Courtney needed to tell him the truth...the same as he had done for her. "I know," the words came out in a hushed whisper.

"You do?" he asked. "I don't understand. Why didn't you say something?"

"I only just figured it out when I picked up the truck." Unable to check her emotions any longer, tears trickled down her face, but no matter how much she brushed them away, others soon took their place. An overwhelming urge took hold. Courtney reached out toward his chest, hesitating midway. "May I?" she asked, swallowing hard as she struggled to breathe.

Tears glistened in Rusty's eyes as he gazed down at her. Taking her outstretched hand, he drew her close, laying her open palm over his heart. It was as though the world cease to exist around them.

The dizzying realization of the moment was almost more than she could bear. Courtney closed her eyes, absorbing the connection that superseded all understanding. The steady beat of his heart pulsed under her hand. "Thank you," she said, stepping back.

"I'm so sorry about all this, Courtney. I know it can't be easy for you."

"This is just sort of...surreal."

"I wish I knew what to say, but I don't. I didn't intend for you to find out like this. Charlie wasn't supposed to say anything.

"It wasn't Charlie. It was an older man at the garage. Charlie's father, I presume. I mean, that's how I found out about your heart condition and your real name. Then I put two and two together on my own."

"I see. I wanted to tell you myself, but finding the right words wasn't easy. It didn't help because I care about you...a lot. And I was having a hard time trying to reconcile the information. And then I got rejected for the loan, and it felt like my life was falling apart all over again."

Courtney could feel his pain all the way down to her toes. "You were rejected? I'm so sorry, as I know what the school meant to you. I should have never come to Crossroads Creek. I swear it wasn't what I planned. I thought if I visited the accident site, I might find closure to the past. But I never expected this. Or us. It's good that we parted ways a few days ago, as it makes this easier." The closure she'd found was on a future she never considered, but not on the past.

"Makes what easier?" he asked.

"Leaving. Trevor and I are on our way out of town," she said the words that would finalize the ending of whatever it was they had shared while she was in town.

Rusty let out a deep breath. "I see."

"Don't give up on your dreams of the school. Try again. Believe in yourself. And you're wrong about not deserving Greg's heart. You are worthy. God is in control, even if you or I don't understand." It was the same thought that had stood her in good stead throughout the entire past year. Understanding may never come to those hurting and left behind. But making the best of the new life she never wanted, now that was a way to honor Greg and the life they had shared.

Rusty shrugged. "I hear you. I just wish the message would come through loud and clear because right now, I don't get it."

"You will when the time is right. Just have faith." She glanced at her watch. "It's time Trevor and I left. This is really hard for me. I'm just not sure I'm ready for anyone special in my life, or if I'll ever be ready. But all this other stuff, between us, makes it impossible even if I thought I could move forward and venture into another relationship." The lump in her throat made it impossible to continue.

Rusty pulled her in for a hug and kissed the top of her head. "I understand. I'm so sorry to cause you such pain. I'll get Trevor for you. I wish things were different, but life sometimes throws us curveballs we can't catch. You and Trevor deserve the very best and I hope everything works out for you." Rusty gazed at her as if there was more he wanted to say, but suddenly he was gone...disappearing inside the house.

It gave Courtney just enough time to pull herself together before Trevor showed up, Mary Devoe right behind him. More hugs were exchanged and a fresh wave of tears flowed.

"Take care, Courtney. And you're always welcome here," Mary said, handing her a bag. "Lots of treats for the ride."

"Thank you. And thank you for the goody bag. I'm sure the treats will come in handy and save me from a few *are-we-there-yet* questions." She hugged the older woman again.

"Why is everyone crying? We can come back. I mean everything is good now between you and Rusty. Right?" her son asked, looking from one adult to another.

"It's always sad when you leave new friends behind." It was the best excuse she could give Trevor, but it was only the beginning.

They climbed in the Ford, waved goodbye, and Courtney backed the truck up. As she headed down the driveway she glanced in the rearview mirror, but suddenly wishing she hadn't. Rusty stood there watching her drive away.

Courtney clenched the steering wheel. The urge to visit Greg's accident site was stronger than ever. It would seem she needed to make one more stop—the very reason she arrived in Crossroads Creek to begin with. A chance to say goodbye to her husband, and now, also the chance to ask for his forgiveness. It felt wrong to have developed feelings for Rusty, but whether she wanted them or not, they were there.

She pulled off the side of the road at Farrier Overlook. It was an incredible view, the valley laid out below for as far as the eye could see.

"Why are we stopping here?" Trevor asked, looking up from his video game.

"I just want to make a memory of this place. I'll only be a minute." She didn't want her son to know the truth and upset him. This was for her. For closure.

"Fine. I'll stay here and play my game. It's cold outside."

Courtney edged closer to the cliff and looked over. There was no evidence of the accident, other than a shiny, new guardrail. The accident was now only a blip in time—but with never ending results. She hugged herself and uttered a prayer for peace.

Except for some reason, the closure she wanted wouldn't come. The sense of peace was non-existent. Instead, the feeling was more one that she was leaving something behind. The sun came out from behind the clouds and shone brightly. A sense of hope and wonder filled Courtney, reminding her nothing was impossible for God.

Chapter Nineteen

♥

THE TUG IN RUSTY'S heart as Courtney drove away wasn't one he could ignore. And he knew it had everything to do with caring about someone who was destined to be forever wrong. Aside from the obvious issue of Courtney being unable to deal with the fact Greg's heart beat in his chest, there was also the issue of not wanting to put Courtney through the possibility of a painful loss a second time.

Knowing he had a medical condition of this magnitude, it would be devastating if something happened to him and they were in a relationship. Rusty's hold on life was tenuous at best, each day waiting for something to go wrong that would land him back in the hospital.

It was no life for Courtney and Trevor.

Which is exactly the reason why he didn't try to stop her from leaving or try to change her mind. At one point, he thought the reason Courtney had landed in his life might mean more to his future and he had dared to hope. But once again, thinking turned out to be more a case of dreaming.

And then there was the riding school. Another case of dreaming gone wrong. But if not Courtney and not the school, then what? Surely God had a plan for his life, considering he saved him with a matching heart when he needed one. But the plan itself was as elusive as finding a needle in a haystack.

Another reason to start looking in a different haystack. The big city draw of Dallas wasn't calling his name, but perhaps nearby Austin. Close enough to visit family. Far enough to live his own life—whatever that life turned out to be.

Two days later, and far too many curious but thankfully quiet looks, Rusty knew he couldn't evade the inevitable any longer. It was time to come clean to his family—about everything. He had sent out messages for a meeting time and they were all currently downstairs waiting on him. Over and over he'd gone over what to say, but each version spun a new tale, each one more elaborate than the other. It didn't take long for him to admit only the truth would suffice.

He headed down the stairs, his boots heavy on the wooden steps. His mother, brother, and sister all looked up upon his arrival, their conversation brought to a screeching halt. "Thanks for showing up. I know you're wondering why I've called this family meeting...something I've always avoided in the past," he added, smiling to ease his own building tension.

"Our curiosity has certainly been piqued little brother," Rebecca said, coming straight to the point. "Wouldn't miss this for anything. And the kids are at a friend's house, so talk away."

"Go on, Rusty," his mother said, urging him to continue, her tone tense as if she were more than a little worried.

Perhaps she could sense he would rather be anywhere other than here, or her concern was for his health. The fear of losing him would have made a rough year on her, something he should have been far more considerate about in his daily dealings around the ranch.

Rusty nodded, moving to stand next to the fireplace, his hands shoved deep in his pockets. "Let me start by saying thank you. You all have been here for me since I returned home. More so since the operation. I know I haven't made it easy and won't make excuses, but I did promise to move forward and that's what this is all about. And because you all have been so patient, you deserve the truth about what's going on. With me. With Courtney...with everything."

His mother rose and came to stand beside him, laying a hand on his arm. "You haven't been that bad," she said, a soft smile on her face.

"Yes, he has," Rebecca said. "Don't sugarcoat the situation, Mother. Rusty, I know I've been tough on you, but you need to know that as my little brother, I only wanted your happiness."

Rusty nodded. "I know...and thanks, Sis."

"I'm all ears, too. But I've got a date tonight so we need to move this family gathering along. Sorry," his brother added as an afterthought.

"Who's the lucky lady?" Rusty asked, not against delaying the inevitable.

"This isn't the time for a change in subject," his mother said, moving to sit back down.

Rusty drew in a deep breath and exhaled. "Fine. Let's start from the beginning. Or should I say, pick up from when I came home and then after the operation. At first it was the anger at my change in circumstances that brought me home. Not allowed to do anything, I wallowed in my own self-pity as I waited for the call.

After the call came and I had the surgery, it was over and done with in the blink of an eye. Afterward, a feeling of guilt settled in. I didn't feel worthy of the gift I received. A washed-up cowboy with nothing to offer shouldn't have been a candidate at the top of the list for a transplant."

"Rusty—" his mother said, coming to her feet.

Mama bear to his defense.

He held up his hand. "Please. This is difficult enough as it is without everyone challenging what I'm saying. This is how I feel. I'm not saying it's right, just telling it the way I see it. When I finish, if you still have something to say, I'll listen. Besides, Clay is on a timetable." *Thankfully.* It would keep this meeting short.

"Okay. Go on," his mother said, sitting back down. "But mark my words, I will have a rebuttal."

"I wasn't expecting anything less," he teased, trying to ease his tension, and therefore, the throbbing in his head. "To continue...I talked to the donor agency about the man's heart I received. They don't give out the information on the donor, but they did let it slip there was a widow involved. With that in mind, I penned a thank you note knowing they would forward it to the woman." Rusty's gaze landed on the Christmas tree, but the tiny white lights glistening were only a blur as he tried to explain.

"None of this helped me accept my new lot in life considering I didn't know what direction my life should take. That about covers this past year and a half. Fast forward to the day Courtney's truck broke down. She's a sweet, generous, and beautiful widow, so I chose to help her in my own way, hoping it would make up for what I couldn't do for the donor's widow. Courtney was a substitute of sorts. I paid her for the volunteer work she was doing at the community center. The whole thing backfired when she found out and became furious, feeling like a charity case. Something I can relate to having lived here at home this past year without a true sense of worth."

Rebecca frowned, and Clay shook his head. His mother, on the other hand, reached for a tissue.

He wasn't trying to hurt his family. It wasn't their fault, but what happened here on the ranch was part of the truth, and something they needed to hear and understand. "I'm sorry. Trust me it's nothing you all did. It was my reaction to it. As to Courtney, I really admire her, and yes, you all were right on that score—she's a unique woman and more than a little special. And Trevor is a great kid. But Courtney was always leaving town, something no one wanted to accept. Turns out, it's a good thing because I'm not sure Crossroads Creek could ever bring her true happiness."

Rebecca stood, hands on her hips, glaring at him. "Sorry to interrupt, but this is making no sense. Are you telling us that you love the woman and you let her leave?" She crossed her arms and huffed, clearly thinking he was daft.

"I didn't say love. The word I used was admired—but none of this matters. Courtney was furious and I decided to apologize by sending her flowers and a note. It was at the florist that everything started to change. Frank told me Courtney had been in that morning asking about a W.D in town."

His mother's indrawn breath and Rebecca's choking cough were proof they understood the importance of his words.

"I don't understand. There are only a handful of W.D.'s that I know of, but the *why* would seem more relevant—especially given you are one of them. What aren't you telling us?" his mother asked.

"Nothing like you're thinking. I didn't do anything to her. The truth is, she was looking for the man who sent her a thank you note." No dawning comprehension light glittered on any of their faces. "A donor recipient thank you note," Rusty clarified.

"No way." His sister jumped to her feet and started to pace. Clay sat back and shook his head, catching up to the others in understanding.

His mother's pale expression struck him the hardest. "I don't believe it. Does she know?"

Rusty shrugged. "She does now. But I knew days before she did, but I couldn't find a way to tell her. I paid her repair bill at Charlie's when her truck was fixed. It was my way of taking care of the donor's widow the way I always wanted to. It was Charlie's dad who slipped up and spilled the beans, and Courtney was able to put it all together. She came here to rip me to shreds for paying the bill, I reckon. But in the end, she understood." *And left*. It was the only thing she could do given the circumstances.

His sister stopped pacing. "So what's the problem? Why did she leave? Or should I be asking, why are you still here? Seems to me if you love her, you go after her."

"Seriously? You seem stuck on the love thing. The problem you seem to be missing is that Courtney loved her husband with all of her heart. And now, I have his heart beating in my chest. There is no way to get past that hurdle. I mean, what are the odds?" He shook his head, the familiar gut-wrenching ache ripping through him. In time, he could only hope it would subside.

"But if you love each other..." his mother said.

"We like each other, but neither one of us is ripe for love, or so it would seem." For his part, it was a lie—but admitting the truth to his family would only make it worse. "Anyway, she's gone. This leads me to the rest of the story. As promised, I did try to put my life together. I put in for a loan to start up a roping and riding school, but I was turned down. So my dream of sharing what I love with kids died, just like my own rodeo career." He wasn't looking for sympathy but understanding with regards to his decision to leave.

"That would have been awesome, Rusty. Is there anything I can do to help you?" Clay asked. Big brother to the rescue. *Charity*. Something he was all too familiar with and something he should have understood better when it came to Courtney and her feelings.

"Thanks, but no. It would take a lot of capital and I know things aren't rolling in the green here at the ranch. I want to do something on my own. Actually, I've decided to head to Austin and see what I can find for a job there," he said, delivering the final bomb and then waiting for the fallout.

"No, please don't go," his mother pleaded. "I've loved having you around."

"Not always," Rusty teased, trying to lighten the mood. "But it's for the best, trust me. You want me to get back on my feet and that's what I'm doing." Surely that was something they could understand.

"But what about Christmas?" Rebecca asked. "The kids were looking forward to having you here and playing with their Uncle Rusty. It's a big deal having you home...and healthy."

Another reminder that last year he was home but recovering from surgery. "What about Christmas?"

"Will you stay through Christmas? Please," his mother added, tugging at his sentimental side.

They had all done so much for him. It was the least he could do to make them happy. "Fine. I'll stay through Christmas. Then I won't miss your fruitcake." Rusty chuckled. The stuff was a tradition, but a tiny piece was enough to go along way, not to mention, add ten pounds to the scale. *With one serving.*

"I'm sorry you feel the need to leave but thank you for agreeing to stay for the holidays. And

Rusty, I'm sorry about Courtney. I could tell how much you liked her. I may be old, but my eyes see as good as ever."

Rusty kissed his mother on the top of the head. "Thank you. Everything will be okay." He might not know what everything entailed, but the commitment to figure it out was genuine.

"I still can't believe it. Of all the rotten luck. You two were good together," his sister said, coming to hug him.

"We were, weren't we? Guess it wasn't meant to be. Besides, the last thing Courtney needs is someone who might put her through another devastating loss. Not going to be me." He regretted the words that foretold of his deepest secrets the minute they left his mouth.

"Rusty...life is for living. Losses come whether planned or otherwise, and it's how many memories you made while you had the chance that's important," his mother said.

Clay nodded. "That's where the real devastation would come from...not dancing while you could have," his brother added, the comment more profound than usual from Clay.

In fact, downright odd. Was it possible his date tonight was more serious than he made it out to be? And the problem was...Clay was right. "I hear you, brother, but unfortunately, it changes nothing for Courtney. And I can't say as I blame her. Even if she could accept this," he said, tapping his chest, "I still have nothing to offer her and Trevor. It's best to leave this one alone."

His brother stood and reached out to shake his hand. "I believe in you, and I'm there for you if you need me, but I do understand. I've got to run."

"So this date...pretty serious, huh?" Rusty asked.

"Maybe...maybe not. I'm not one to kiss and tell." Clay chuckled and moved off toward the front door.

"Hey, why haven't I heard anything about this woman? May I remind you, I'm your mother."

"You'll know when it's important to know. I see the way you and Rebecca meddle. Thanks but no thanks," he said, walking out of the house, his laughter loud enough to be heard by all.

"I've got to go too and pick up the kids," his sister said, giving Rusty a hug. "Sorry, little brother. That's a tough break, but I'm sure you'll figure this out. I've left you and Mom a casserole in the oven. Your favorite...spicy chicken enchiladas."

"Thank you. I knew I smelled something good cooking, especially since my stomach started growling the minute I got downstairs."

After the others left, he and his mother headed for the kitchen. They set the table just as the buzzer rang, indicating the casserole was done. "I'll get it out of the oven," he said, grabbing the pot holder next to the stove.

"Thank you. Do you want a glass of milk with this?"

"Milk and enchiladas?" he asked, one eyebrow raised, the very idea enough to make him ill. "*Ummm*, no thanks. I'll have a lime sparkling water. Lime and Mexican food always go together." He winked.

They sat down to eat and an awkward silence fell between them.

His mother reached out to touch his arm. "I'm sorry if I've been heavy-handed in my interference of your life since the surgery. I truly just wanted you to be happy and I knew that meant finding yourself again. The new you, that is. This can't have been easy and I hate that I made it worse."

Rusty covered her hand in his. "It's all good, Mother. You were offering support for all the right reasons and I wasn't listening."

Her eyes filled with tears. "No. Better than good. You are here...and alive. You got a second chance and for that I will always be grateful to God. I love you so much and couldn't bear to lose you."

Rusty fought back against the emotional surge that settled in the pit of his stomach. "I love you, too, Mom," he said, giving her hand a squeeze. "I'll ask the blessing and then we can eat before it gets cold," Rusty added, with a wink, trying to move past the subject.

Conversation flowed easily, mostly centered on the ranch. When they were finished eating, Rusty cleaned up the kitchen, working side by side with his mother. He couldn't help but notice how much she had aged over the years. Still beautiful, but her skin was weathered and lined. Perhaps he should have come home more often. After all, with his father gone, there was no reason to avoid the ranch, other than not wanting the successes of his siblings constantly rubbed in his face.

But he had missed his family. *More than they would ever know.*

"I'm going to grab some firewood and we can watch a movie. I'll even let you pick what we watch," he offered. It wouldn't bring back the years, but it could close the distance between them.

"Really? Even knowing I'll pick a romance?" she asked, a teasing glint in her eyes.

"Absolutely. I'm sure if anyone knows how to pick a romance, it would be you, the romance queen of America." He chuckled.

"Stop. I'm not that bad."

"Yes, you are." He slipped out the back door just as an odd pain ripped across his chest. Rusty stopped short and frowned, trying to see if it would happen again. It was something he was always on alert for, the never-ending fear of another heart attack always looming in his head. Nothing happened, and he breathed a sigh of relief.

He made his way to the woodpile, picking up several sticks until he had an armload, pulling a balancing act as he headed for the house.

Another pain gripped his chest, causing him to stumble. It was more intense and lasted longer than the first. Sweat beaded on his forehead even though it was cold outside. His brain tried to process what he should do, but fear paralyzed him. Another pain ripped across his chest, dropping him to his knees, the firewood crashing to the ground.

"Rusty, what is it?" his mother hollered, rushing toward him.

"My chest. It's hard to breathe," he said, forcing the words from his mouth, his hands going to his chest as he tried to stop the pain.

"Oh my goodness. Not again. No. No. No," she cried out, anguish in her voice as she pulled out her phone. "Operator, I need an ambulance. My son is having a heart attack."

The blood rushed in his head, pounding loudly. The pressure in his chest was crippling. He hated to put his mother through this again. This was precisely why he shouldn't have stayed at the ranch. It was more than his mother should have to bear. For that matter, more than any woman should have to deal with, the image of Courtney flashing in his head. "I'm sorry," he said through pursed lips as another spasm rifled through his body.

The intense pain was worse than being thrown off a bull.

Sirens filled the air and Rusty knew they were coming for him.

The question was...would he be lucky enough to live through another heart attack?

Chapter Twenty

♥

IT HAD BEEN A week since Courtney left Cross-roads Creek. A long, but somewhat satisfying week. That is, it would be if she didn't miss Rusty. Her mother, of course, was happy to have her and Trevor both living at home. The re-minder that the situation wouldn't be for long, did little to dampen her mother's joy.

As for Trevor, he wasn't quite himself, mostly quiet and withdrawn despite her attempts to draw him out. He also had a case of the *missing-Rusty blues*, but add to that the horses, the kittens, and all the wonderful people they had met at Crossroads Creek, and his mood was easily explained.

The day after Courtney moved home, the insurance company had made good on the life-insurance payment and three days later the money was sitting in her bank account. A tremendous weight had been lifted off her shoulders, and the past few days she was flat-out busy inspecting properties for a deli. And this morning, had been her lucky day. She found the perfect place.

Space for the deli downstairs, complete with a recently remodeled kitchen. And upstairs, a two-bedroom apartment. Courtney was more than ready to sign, but unfortunately, it would have to wait a few days. The realtor informed her the owner was on vacation in the Caribbean soaking up the sun and wouldn't be available to sign documents until the Monday after Christmas.

The building had been a pizza place that went out of business. The realtor claimed it had been from a bad business model, and Courtney was inclined to agree. The location was ideal for local traffic and tourists alike. It was as if God was smiling down on her and paving the road clear for everything she needed to happen to get her life back in order.

She would soon have her independence and answer to no one but herself for her decisions. But even knowing it was everything she wanted, the joy she expected wasn't living up to its potential. And the worse part was, she knew why. *Rusty*. It was unreasonable to expect she could have another great love in her life, although people did manage to do exactly that sometimes. And maybe, just maybe, she could have...if it weren't for...the rest of the story.

She shoved the thought aside, unwilling to dwell on the things she couldn't change.

Trevor sat on the couch playing his video game, lost in his own little world. The slump of his shoulders was more than enough to tell her he was in a blue mood. *Again*. She didn't have it in her to tell him to sit up straight. What she needed to do was act—find a way to draw him out.

Christmas was days away and now that she had money in her account, she needed to buy some presents. *Something special*. What her son had wanted most for Christmas was a kitten. Courtney had said no so many times, it hadn't crossed her mind things had changed now and it was finally a possibility. They were getting their own place, and a promise was a promise.

And it had nothing to do with calling the Devoe ranch and checking up on Rusty. *Nothing at all.* Or at least that's what she tried to convince herself, but she couldn't keep the bubble of excitement at bay at the prospect of making a connection—even if it was with Rusty's mother.

Courtney poked her head into the living room. "Hey, Mom, can you keep an eye on Trevor for a couple of hours? I've got some Christmas shopping to do," she said, more excited than she had been in a while. I've got a great idea what to get Trevor and I need to make some arrangements." She dangled the carrot in front of her son, hoping to get him excited for the holidays.

Nothing. No response.

Her mother nodded. "Sure thing. But I hope it's not more games...he needs to play with something more than his tablet for a change. Or make some friends. Such a shame."

"I agree. And I'm going to try and fix it for him. Trust me, I think it will work wonders as an attitude adjustment."

"I hope so. Run along, dear."

Courtney kissed her son on the top of his head. "I'll be back soon."

Still no response. He simply continued to play his game. Courtney would do anything to see Trevor smiling again. The way he did when he played with the kitten. Or riding a horse. Or spending time with Rusty.

Once in the car, she pulled out her phone. Her first choice for a kitten, of course, was Hope. Barring her availability, Courtney would have to scramble to find another if the rest of the litter had already found new homes. Christmas was a popular time for new pets.

"Hello?" Mary said, answering the house phone.

"Hi there. This is Courtney. Courtney Winters," she offered, fearing Mary didn't recognize the name when the woman didn't immediately respond.

"I know who you are, dear. I was just taken by surprise that you were calling. A lovely surprise indeed," Mary added.

Courtney relaxed. She could almost feel the warmth of Mary's smile radiating through the telephone line. "Thank you. A lot has happened since I've been in Lafayette and some big changes are just around the corner for Trevor and me. I'm calling to find out if you still have the kitten Trevor fell in love with—the one he and Rusty named Hope."

"You're in luck because she's still here. It's been so hectic these past few days and with the holidays fast approaching, I haven't had time to find the last two kittens new homes. The others are gone, but knowing Rusty formed an attachment to Destiny, and Trevor with Hope, I sort of felt the two belonged here in a way. I couldn't get rid of the dears, not just yet. Maybe I'm hoping for a miracle."

Mary's remarks seemed to go in all directions, but one thing was clear—Rusty's secret wasn't a secret from anyone. "You know about his kitten?" Trevor had leaked the news to everyone and it hadn't gone unnoticed.

"Of course, dear. I know a great many things that go on around here, especially anything concerning Rusty. Someone's got to keep an eye on him," Mary said, her voice growing quite serious.

It was something in the way she said the last comment that took Courtney off guard. "How is he? Rusty, I mean," she clarified.

"Better than yesterday, for sure. That was a rough day for us all." Mary was being vague and the tone of the woman's voice set off warning bells.

"What happened?" Courtney asked, gripping the steering wheel, her knuckles turning white.

"We don't know. I probably shouldn't say anything, but seeing as the whole town knows, it's not like it's a giant secret. He had some severe chest pains. I found him on the ground, the wood he was carrying scattered everywhere, and he was clutching his chest. I called 911 and he's in the hospital."

Courtney sucked in a deep breath. This wasn't at all what she expected to hear. "Is he going to be okay?" she asked, closing her eyes, and fighting back the wave of nausea threatening to overtake her. It reminded her all too well of the call she got from the police when they let her know about Greg.

"He's stable and they are running some tests. I understand that you are aware of his heart transplant now, so I'm sure you understand they are being extra cautious and keeping him for further observation. Just to be safe. So far they haven't found anything. That's the good news I'm focusing on at the moment. But even if everything is okay, Rusty will need to make some changes if he plans to stay out of the hospital. It was a long night, to say the least. For all of us, but mostly for him."

"Thank goodness, he's okay," Courtney said in a rush, letting out the breath she'd been holding. She rocked back and forth, trying to calm her nerves. It suddenly dawned on Courtney, the intensity of reaction to the news about Rusty left her in no doubt of her feelings for the man, making it even more difficult to accept the hands of fate life dealt them.

"The good Lord took care of him, the same way he did before. God's not done with my son yet. Now, what did you call about again? Oh, yeah, the kitten. What did you have in mind?"

"I want to get Hope as Trevor's Christmas present. He's been down in the dumps since we left Crossroads Creek and I want to make it up to him." The truth hit her like a brick, but it wasn't until she said the words out loud that they sank in. Trevor had been happy in Crossroads Creek. It wasn't just when he was spending time with Rusty or playing with the kitten...it was his entire attitude about life in general. Her son had found a place of peace after the loss of his father.

And now, it was as though he'd returned to the way he was before they'd arrived there in the first place. *If only she could change things.* "I'm just trying to figure out how to make it happen because my mom is working and I can't leave Trevor alone for that long. If I bring him with me, it won't be much of a surprise."

"Oh, don't you worry about that, my dear. You just get me the address and I'll make sure Hope is delivered in time for Christmas," Mary said, her tone back to singsong and happy.

The Mary she knew was up to something again, but far be it for Courtney to say no to the offer. "Really? You'd do that? Thank you so much. I'll pay for someone's time and gas to make it worth their while." Money in the bank paved the way to be generous.

"That won't be necessary but thank you for offering. I know how much it would mean to Trevor to have the kitten, and I know how much it would mean for me for the kitten to have a wonderful home. It's a double blessing."

Courtney couldn't believe her luck. She rattled off the address and then repeated it, not wanting there to be any mistakes.

"Got it. You know, I told you once, you can visit us anytime. The offer still stands. I think

Rusty was missing you before all this happened, and now he's talking of leaving Crossroads Creek. Might be nice if you two got together again before that happened."

Rusty was leaving Crossroads Creek? The idea didn't set well with her at all. It was his home and where he belonged, even if he didn't see it yet. "I appreciate the invite. It's just been so busy here trying to get settled in. And as to Rusty, I miss him too. He's a good friend. I hate that he wants to leave town. The people there love him and it's incredible what he's done to bring hope and healing to others."

"*Hmmph.* It's not just the people in town who love him if you ask me. The two of you belong together, no matter what the circumstances if you get my drift." His mother had lifted the veil of implied matchmaking, zeroing in on what she was after.

It also occurred to Courtney that Rusty must have told his mother everything about their situation. "It's complicated, I'm sorry. Rusty and I agree things are best this way. We would have never worked out."

"Don't be too sure of that, my dear." Mary chuckled.

It was easier to let the subject drop. "I've got to run to the pet store to get some supplies while my mom is watching Trevor. Please keep me posted about Rusty."

"I certainly will. Take care, Courtney. I'll text you when I know what time the kitten will be delivered."

After they hung up, she realized Mary hadn't said who would do the delivering. An image of Rusty delivering Hope came to mind, followed closely by a rush of adrenaline.

Mary wouldn't.

Mary would.

Except Rusty was in the hospital. Any momentary rush of exhilaration whooshed out of her.

Courtney wished she had been there for him. She knew his fears of the future and was certain this would not have played out well. And it was a close call by the sounds of things.

Please, Lord, let Rusty be okay. And if Mary wants to send him here to deliver the kitten, I'm all in. Especially since seeing him would help to reassure Courtney that he was okay.

It was nothing more than that.

Chapter Twenty-One

♥

THE DOCTOR WALKED OUT of the room, leaving Rusty alone to ponder his words. After days of being picked and prodded, listening to the whirring and beeping of machines, and the endless stream of well-wishers from town, he was exhausted. Hour after hour had passed with little to no information forthcoming and Rusty had gone over everything in his head yet again, waiting for the doctor to deliver the verdict. It had been a year since the surgery, and suddenly, it seemed as though he was right back where he started from—or so he thought.

Heartburn. The doctor's diagnosis reverberated in his head like a bongo drum on repeat.

The incident had been nothing more than his sister's spicy enchiladas combined with sparkling water. It had felt so real...and he'd been positive it was another heart attack. The news was a Christmas miracle...one day early.

Rusty let out a deep sigh just as the door pushed open and his family filed into the room.

So much for quiet time.

"We just talked to the doctor. Such good news," his mother exclaimed, coming to stand by the side of the bed and leaning down to drop a kiss on his forehead, reminding him of the way she did when he was a child. She was unusually chipper, but then her son had just been given news that would make any mother rejoice.

"Yes, good news for sure. I thought I was a goner. I should have known Rebecca would try to kill me," he said, shooting his sister a teasing glance as she moved closer, knowing she would hear.

"Hey, it's not my fault you're a lightweight when it comes to spicy. Cowboys are known for having cast-iron stomachs. You must have gone soft while out on the rodeo circuit," she shot back, giving his shoulder a playful slap.

"I'm with Rusty. I've eaten your cooking far too many times and know that one has to build a tolerance to the heat you toss in," Clay added, defending him.

"Either way, I'll stick to Mom's cooking from now on, thank you very much." He was just teasing, but the playful banter felt good.

"It wasn't that bad," she insisted, defending herself.

Just one last shot, and then he'd give it a rest. "Hotter than Hades is the expression I think."

"That's enough, you three," his mother admonished, always one for keeping the peace amongst her children.

"You wouldn't believe all the help I've had at the ranch the past couple of days from folks in town. Even as I speak, they are out checking fences, feeding the cows and horses, and doing whatever they think needs getting done. Even the vet stopped by to check on the animals free of charge and catch us up on vaccinations.

Maybe they should keep you here in the hospital longer," Clay teased.

Rusty ignored the dig, trying to make sense of the rest of his brother's comment. "Why would everyone do that? Did you put out a call for help...or something?"

His mother's smile softened, her eyes full of love. "No calls went out. This town takes care of its own and you are one of us. Doesn't matter if you left and came back, you still belong."

"Just like the prodigal son?" Rusty tossed out, still trying to wrap his head around what they were telling him. If his mother was to be believed, the townsfolks' interest wasn't just for gossip—it was sincere. The same thing had happened here in the hospital. There had been an endless stream of people who visited offering prayers and support, and none seemed inclined to offer him the poor, pitiful-you attitude he had expected.

"Sounds about right," his brother said, grinning from ear-to-ear.

"Knock it off, Clay. The last thing Rusty needs is someone to condone his wrong way of thinking." His mother turned back to him. "And in case you didn't know, lots of folks volunteered to cover for you Wednesday night at the community center. They've been singing your praises about the program and they want to show their appreciation."

Rusty was more than a little shocked. Maybe his mother was right and he did belong in Crossroads Creek. And maybe there was something else he could do to find a way to stick around town and make a life for himself, even if it wasn't the school. It was certainly worth thinking about when he got home. "That's incredible. Except by the sound of things, I can handle Wednesday evening. Well, maybe everything except the cooking. For that, maybe I can get Rebecca to lend a hand. No...on second thought..." He chuckled, his comment earning him a glare from his sister, but otherwise she didn't rise to the bait.

"I'll be sure to give my thanks to everyone for their kind offer and generosity. I'll be out of here as soon as they finish working up the discharge papers, and then I can get started on the planning. Hopefully I learned something from Courtney along the way." Things were looking up, and Rusty couldn't help but be affected by the love he was being shown.

"Maybe for once, you should step back and actually let others help you. Not something you've done much of since you came home. Jarod, from over at the bank, is spearheading the entire event and you need to trust him and the others volunteering. It's their way to show you how much they appreciate it. Enjoy their Christmas gift—*with them*. Be their guest for a change, Rusty," his mother said, her tone not brooking any opposition.

Rusty was surprised to hear Jarod's name. Perhaps he'd been too quick to judge his friend, thinking his loan rejection was personal. Except personal took on a new meaning when the man was offering to pitch in and take the lead role in Rusty's absence for a program that meant a great deal to the community.

The nurse came in the room. "I'm sorry to break up the party, but I've got to go over the discharge papers with Rusty so he can get out of here."

"I'll be out in the lobby, waiting to take you home," his mother said, gathering up her belongings.

"Sounds good. I know this couldn't have been easy on any of you, what with everything you have to handle on a daily basis. Give the kids a hug for me, Rebecca. Just know, all of you being here, meant something to me," he said, shooting his brother and sister a smile as they filed out of the room.

In less than ten minutes, the nurse had gone over the instructions and he signed the release forms. He quickly dressed and sat back to wait for someone on the staff to arrive with a wheelchair. It was hospital protocol, and for once, Rusty wouldn't object to the help. People had many reasons for lending a hand to others, something he needed to consider more going forward.

The silence of the room echoed loudly. No machines beeping. No voices. No medical personnel going in and out of the room.

So much had happened but the message was abundantly clear. It was time to stop running, and time to grab life by the horns. *And not the bull horns.* Life was on God's timing and not his own, and not living each day to the fullest was short changing himself and everyone around him.

Rusty vowed to change that...starting today. There was a reason God had brought him home to Crossroads Creek and he intended to find out what it was.

And until then, he would practice patience, and preferably not as a patient.

The ranch was a welcome sight as his mother parked in front of the house.

Home. The word had a different ring to it...his new appreciation of life having a most profound effect on him. Colors looked brighter, laughter more joyful, and even the smells of a ranch that wafted toward him as he exited the truck were stronger. *In a good way.*

"Welcome, home," his mother said, as she leaned into the truck and started to reach for his overnight bag.

"Thanks. It's good to be home. And I've got the bag, Mother."

His mother only paused a second before releasing her hold on the straps. "While you're at it, there's a new heater in the back seat for the spare room. Once you get settled, can you bring it in for me?"

"Absolutely. And thanks." His mother was making good on her word not to pamper him and he appreciated her effort. There was so much more he could do to help out at the ranch and it was time he started pulling his weight. Yes, he would still have to be careful given his condition, but careful didn't include not working hard. And by the sounds of things, Clay needed more help with some of the heavy lifting that went on at a ranch.

Rusty headed upstairs to drop off his bag, and then returned to the truck to get the heater. He carried it inside and to the spare room. In the kitchen, his mother was already fixing lunch. Rusty's stomach rumbled, the aromas more than a little appealing after hospital food for the past three days.

"I've got some homemade turkey soup heating, and I'm fixing you a grilled ham and cheese sandwich. I figure you were more than ready for some home cooking," his mother said, flipping the sandwich in the cast iron skillet.

"You can say that again. Hospital food is like cardboard. Although, apparently better than Rebecca's," he teased, unable to resist.

His mother shook her head. "I know your sister feels awful about what happened. You should probably ease up on her," she admonished.

It was no less than he had already decided for himself. "Oh, I don't know. It's so much fun."

"Rusty..." It was her you're-going-to-find yourself-in-the-corner tone, one he heard often enough as a young boy.

"I'm kidding, Mom. I've already forgiven her, but I'll make sure she knows it as well."

"Thank you, that would be wonderful." She scooped up a bowl of soup and set it in front of him. "Speaking of wonderful, I hope I'm not overstepping my bounds, you know, considering our agreement and all."

It would seem their truce was already ending. "What is it, this time?" he asked, not sure he wanted to hear, but good graces demanded he listen to the request.

"I need a very special favor. There's a new owner waiting on delivery for one of the kittens, and they want her before Christmas. It's been so busy with you in the hospital and I plum forgot until now. It would be terrible if Hope wasn't delivered by tomorrow."

"Hope? But that's Tre…" Rusty stopped, realizing the error of his thinking. The kitten didn't belong to Trevor.

His mother nodded. "Actually, the kitten is for Trevor. You told me you and Courtney are still friends, and seeing as she needs the kitten, and seeing as—"

"Yes." His mother didn't need to sell him on the idea. It was the perfect reason to see Courtney again. Not that he needed another reason other than he wanted to, but on such short notice, delivering the kitten would be ideal.

"Yes, as in you'll do it?" She beamed.

Almost too much.

But then what was too much? "Yes. I would love to see both of them again." Rusty's new way of looking at life changed more than the decision of whether to stay or go in Crossroads Creek.

"Well then, that's settled. When will you go? If you leave soon, you might make it there by dark," his mother said, suddenly animated as if Santa had visited *her* early.

Rusty shook his head. There was much to be done before he could leave and showing up late and unannounced on Christmas Eve might not be well received. "No. I'll go tomorrow. I need to get a few things in town first."

His mother frowned. "But that's Christmas. What about our family dinner here at the ranch?"

"If I leave early in the morning. It should get me back here by dinner. It's not like I'm looking for Santa to leave me any gifts under the tree. I haven't exactly been good this year." He chuckled, suddenly feeling happier than he had in days. Truth was, it was the happiest he had been since Courtney and Trevor left.

"Well, okay then. Christmas is all about friends and family. And I think Santa will understand. I'll even pack you a goody bag for Trevor. He loves my cooking."

"Doesn't everyone? But that is a good point," he said, frowning when he realized one very important detail he might have forgotten. "Is the kitten courtesy of Santa?"

"*Hmmm.* I don't think so. At least, Courtney didn't say when we talked about it. She did mention she was buying all the cat accessories, which tells me the kitten is from her."

"How do you figure that?" he asked, her line of thinking unclear.

"Common sense. There's no way she would know Santa was bringing a kitten, at least from Trevor's perspective. Therefore, Courtney wouldn't have known to buy cat accessories for his gifts."

Rusty laughed. "I see. That's good to know because that way, the kitten doesn't have to be there when Trevor wakes up and opens his gifts from Santa."

"I have a feeling you will arrive just in time." There was that smile of hers again. She was up to something, but for once Rusty didn't care.

A few days in the hospital shed some light on a lot of things, one of them Courtney and Trevor. He was done fighting his feelings for her. Love had struck when he least expected it, and he wasn't going to run away. Instead, he would face his feelings head on and give Courtney the same opportunity.

There was no guarantee she would feel the same, or allow herself to love again, but Rusty intended to find out. She was right when she called the friendship complicated, but it was about to get more complicated. But first he had to convince her that he wasn't trying to take anything away from the love she had for Greg, but perhaps asking her to make room for both of them in her heart.

Rusty devoured his lunch, anxious to get into town before the shops closed for the holiday evening. He knew the perfect gift for Trevor, and Courtney's...well that was another story entirely. Before she had even left town, Rusty had consigned a piece of jewelry to be made special for her. He simply never got around to picking it up, not wanting the reminder of all he had lost when she moved on.

Except now, things had changed.

Tomorrow, Rusty would make a special Christmas delivery.

Chapter Twenty-Two

♥

CHRISTMAS MORNING DAWNED, AND the glow of sunrise filtered through Courtney's bedroom window. A smile lit her face in anticipation of Trevor's joy as the day unfolded. She wasn't going to let the fact her main Christmas gift to her son hadn't materialized. *Yet*. Mary's text yesterday and the promise it held had captured her attention and excitement. Even though it wasn't entirely clear as to who would be delivering the kitten, she was more than a little convinced it was Rusty. She pulled up the text on her phone and read it again, just to be certain.

Mary: So sorry for the delay, but Hope will be delivered Christmas morning. Rusty was released from the hospital today and it's been a little hectic. Please forgive me.

Of course she would forgive Mary. Not only was she ensuring the kitten's delivery, but between her generosity and the warm welcome she'd given Courtney, there was more than enough to forever place Mary in a special category of friends.

Knowing Rusty was out of the hospital lifted her spirits and she said a prayer of thanks for the tenth time since she'd read the message. She couldn't control the past, and she could no more change the way she felt about Rusty, than she could control day and night. What to do about her feelings she wasn't certain, but the fact he was healthy and more than likely on his way to Lafayette was more than enough to put an extra beat of excitement racing through her veins.

The only problem for this morning's Christmas time festivities was that almost all of her gifts to Trevor revolved around the kitten. She couldn't very well give him any of the cat-related gifts without ruining the secret surprise.

Luckily, Santa came last night and her son would be busy opening presents and playing with his new toys. Most likely, he would not even notice all the remaining unopened packages until much later in the day.

As if on cue, Trevor burst through the open doorway, jumping on her bed. "Merry Christmas, Mom," he said, a brighter smile on his face than she'd seen in a week.

The celebration of Jesus's birth was great cause for joy, love, and peace around the world, and today...it would fill the corners of her mother's home. "Merry Christmas," she said, planting a kiss on his forehead and giving him a big hug. "Did you stop and peek to see if Santa came last night?"

"I did. I didn't open any presents, but one, wasn't even wrapped. It just had a great big bow on it. Santa brought me a new bike. Isn't that cool?" he asked, his eyes wide with wonder. "If you get up, maybe I can go outside and ride."

"Not so fast." Courtney laughed. "You will get to go outside and ride soon enough, I promise. But we have lots more to do this morning."

With the move, there had been no room for the rusty bike he'd outgrown and she was forced to leave it behind. "We need to make sure Grandma is up, get the cinnamon rolls in the oven, and then open gifts. You did say Santa brought you other presents, right?" She added the last, enjoying the fact her son still believed in Santa, an innocence she preferred to keep alive for as long as possible.

"Yup. I must have been a good boy this year." Trevor grinned, except the smile faded as fast as it appeared. "Well, *umm*, other than when I disobeyed Rusty. Do you think that's why he doesn't call us? I thought he was our friend." It was as if a switch had flipped in her son.

Rusty had been a light in their life, and even a boy of eight had figured it out. "He is still our friend, honey. Rusty's been sick, but he's all better now," she added quickly, to reassure him.

"Are you sure he's okay?" Trevor asked, his expression one of concern. Losing his father had hurt him deeply and losing someone else he cared about would be a fear he would carry for some time.

"He's fine. I spoke with his mother and she kept me updated. And I'm sure Rusty has forgiven you for not listening to him. You made a mistake...and as long as you learned from it and make better choices in the future, then all will be well. So don't let it worry you anymore." She ruffled his hair. "Besides, today we are celebrating Jesus's birth and with Jesus on our side, all is forgiven."

"I like the sound of that," he said with a nod, his smile resurfacing.

"Good. Let's go find Grandma," she said, climbing out of bed, pulling on her fluffy green robe, and sliding into her red-nosed Rudolph slippers. All in the spirit of Christmas, of course.

"She's already in the kitchen."

Courtney laughed. "That must be why I have cinnamon rolls on the brain. I can smell them baking." The tradition of Cinnamon Grand rolls with cream cheese frosting had been an annual Christmas favorite for as long as she could remember. The sweet, delectable pastries dripped with gooey icing and made a mess, but they sure came under the category of finger-licking good.

Trevor bounded off the bed. "Race you to the kitchen." He shot out of the room before she could even answer.

Making her way down the hall, the scent of cinnamon rolls grew stronger. The Christmas tree lights were twinkling, and Trevor's bike had been moved into the center of the living room. She wondered if he had tried riding the bike in the house. Something that could prove disastrous given her mother's penchant for knickknacks. "Good morning, Mother. Merry Christmas."

"Good morning, dear. Merry Christmas to you also. Trevor has been anxiously waiting for you to wake up and join us."

"I'm sure. The rolls smell wonderful and I'm so glad you remembered them."

"Remembered them? The year I forget, you have my permission to take over planning the festivities." Her mother chuckled.

Many Christmas moons would pass before her mother would be ready to hand over the reins. Which was all well and good for Courtney. Sometimes, it was fun to take the back seat and simply enjoy the festivities.

The timer went off and her mother pulled the rolls from the oven.

"Can I put the icing on?" Trevor asked, hovering nearby.

"Sure thing, young man," her mother said, handing him the butter knife. "Make sure you only do a little on each one and then whatever is left, you add more to each as needed. The goal is to make sure they have about the same amount of icing."

Easier said than done for an eight-year-old boy. A lot of the icing did make it on top of the rolls, but some landed on the tin foil, some down the side of the icing container, and lastly, some on his fingers. Of course, he lost no time in licking the sticky mess away. "*Mmmm,* this is so good."

"Try to get it on the rolls," Courtney teased, bumping his shoulder playfully. "One would almost think you are making a mess on purpose." She laughed, reaching over to make a swipe at the icing on the tin foil, joining in the fun.

Her mother cut the rolls apart from one another, putting one on each plate, handing a napkin out with each delivery. "Courtney, if you'll take mine into the living room, I'll bring a tray with coffee and some hot chocolate for Trevor."

"Sure thing," Courtney said, grabbing the other plate and making her way into the other room, Trevor hot on her heels.

They were soon settled in front of the tree, the soft Christmas music and cinnamon-pine candles adding to the ambiance. Courtney sat back and listened as her mother read the traditional Christmas story, making sure Trevor was reminded of the reason for the season. Of course, he was more than a little excited to open his gifts from Santa, and he fidgeted in his seat through the entire story.

"Thank you, Mom. That story never fails to set the tone for the true meaning of Christmas." She turned to Trevor. "Go ahead, dear.

Find the gifts from Santa and pick which one you want to open first.

"Yes!" he exclaimed, jumping out of his seat, and grabbing the square one in front of the tree. Trevor ripped the paper away and held up his gift. "Look, Mom. Santa brought me a cool helmet for when I ride my bike. And it's blue...my favorite color."

"That is pretty cool," she said, smiling at him and then at her mother.

An hour and a half later, the last of the gifts that could be opened had been unwrapped. It took a lot of time because each gift had to come out of its box, be admired, and then, of course, played with if it was a toy.

"What about the others?" Trevor asked eyeing the remaining gifts under the tree.

She should have known her son would be curious and not miss the fact several packages remained unopened. "Those are from me to you, but I feel like we need a break. Why don't you play with what you have already for a little bit? Grandma needs to put the ham in the oven, and

I'd like to get dressed. Then we can reconvene and finish the tree."

Trevor glanced at the presents and then back at her. And then at his new toys. "Okay. I want to play with my new firetruck. And after lunch, can I ride my bike?"

"Technically, it's called dinner because it's the largest meal of the day. Or at least, some people refer to it that way, depending on where you grew up. And yes, after dinner, you can ride your bike." She glanced at her watch, wondering how much longer she would need to hold him off. At least for now, he appeared more than a little satisfied as he sat on the floor, totally absorbed in play time.

"I'll be in to help with dinner as soon as I get dressed," Courtney said, walking out of the room with her mother.

"Take your time. I kept it simple. Ham. Squash. Potatoes. Rolls. And, of course, Pistachio Pudding salad because it's green and sweet, and Trevor's favorite," her mother said, grinning.

"Sounds delicious." Courtney headed down the hall and to her room. Choosing her favorite Christmas sweater, the one with Rudolph and the other reindeer dancing around a tree, she pulled it over her head. A pair of comfortable blue jeans and black flats completed the outfit. A small touch of makeup, her normal amount, and she was ready to join the others. And for the kitten to be delivered. *AKA hopefully Rusty's arrival.* Which was also the reason Courtney made sure she wasn't caught in her fluffy robe and Rudolph slippers.

Courtney checked her phone in case she had missed a call or text. *Nothing.*

No news was good news though. And Mary had promised the kitten would be delivered today. Back in the kitchen, she helped set the table and fix the meal. Courtney could tell her mother was enjoying having them home, and she was glad to be here. It just couldn't stay this way. Little things, but things none the less. Staying up later than normal. Or picking up his room for him. Or letting Trevor have a third cinnamon grand roll and a candy cane before his dinner.

It was Christmas, so she didn't contradict her mother. As the morning wore on, Courtney also realized that despite their differences, her mother truly loved them and everything she did was with the best of intentions. Even after they moved out, Courtney would make a point of visiting and spending time with her mother.

Family was a precious gift, and not one to be taken lightly. Greg's sudden death was more than enough proof of just how precious time could be with someone.

"Have you heard anything from Mary?" her mother asked, dropping her voice to a low whisper.

She shook her head. "No. It's only eleven, but I'm worried how to explain to Trevor why he can't open his gifts from me. Maybe I shouldn't have centered all of his Christmas presents from me on the one I didn't have in hand."

"From what you told me, I'm sure your friend will honor her promise." Her mother patted her hand. "Be patient."

"Tell that to—"

The doorbell rang, sending a rush of adrenaline racing through Courtney's body. Would it be Rusty or was it just a dream on her part?

There was only one way to find out.

Chapter Twenty-Three

♥

"RUSTY!" TREVOR YELLED, FLINGING himself against the imposing man who stood in the doorway.

Courtney's question regarding the identity of the delivery person quickly ended, but it was only the beginning of the butterflies and nervous anticipation of seeing him again now that he was here. He looked good, and not at all like a man who had a close call and spent the last few days in a hospital.

Rusty knelt to give Trevor a hug. "Merry Christmas, Trevor."

"Merry Christmas. What are you doing here? Are you a present from Santa? I asked Santa to bring you back to us," Trevor beamed, as if Rusty showing up was all his doing.

"I'm here because I needed to see my favorite people on Christmas Day. And I come bearing gifts." His gaze sought Courtney out, his smile widening when he spotted her.

It was the same smile that always made her feel warm and fuzzy inside. As if—as if she were special. "Hi there. Merry Christmas," she said, stepping into his arms to give him a Christmas hug, a move almost as natural as breathing.

He held her close for a second before releasing her. "Merry Christmas. I've got gifts in the truck and you'll need to tell me what to do with them," he said, shooting a meaningful gaze at Trevor and then back at her.

Courtney knew what one gift was,...but gifts? She hadn't gotten Rusty anything and the thought made her somewhat uncomfortable. Maybe his gifts were strictly for Trevor, considering how things were left between them. "I'll help you unload, but first, let me introduce my mother. Mom, this is Rusty Devoe, the man who helped me when my truck broke down in Crossroads Creek."

Her mother stepped forward to hug him, ignoring his outstretched hand. "It's nice to meet you. And thank you for taking such good care of Courtney and Trevor. I've heard nothing but good things about you and your family."

"Thank you. It's nice to meet you, ma'am," Rusty said returning the hug, but not before he shot Courtney a surprised glance.

Her mother shook her head and frowned. "I'll have none of that ma'am business. I'll take Andrea any day. Ma'am makes me sound old," she teased.

"Yes, ma'am. I mean, Andrea," Rusty said, quickly correcting himself. "Trevor, you wait here, and your mom and I will be right back. Deal, partner?"

"Deal. I can't believe you are here. This is so cool." Her son was beaming, his Christmas wish had come true.

A Christmas wish Courtney hadn't known about, but one that reinforced all she suspected about her son's happiness. *He idolized Rusty.*

"Believe it," Rusty said, with a nod, ruffling her son's hair in a show of affection.

She stepped outside, right behind Rusty, unable to ignore his broad set of shoulders. A man's man. "I wondered if your mother would send you on this delivery errand," she said, getting straight to the point to quell her nerves.

"She did. But the question is...are you okay with me being here? I can just drop off the kitten and leave if I'm making you uncomfortable." He stopped and turned to face her as they stood by the truck.

"I..."

He held up his hand. "Before you answer, let me just add this. When my mother asked me, I was all in for helping, mainly because I had already made the decision to visit you. As far as I'm concerned, we need to talk. There's a lot I need to tell you...about so many things. If you'll let me."

Courtney laughed. It was the easiest way to stop her brain from running away in fifteen different tangents. "I was going to say it would be lovely if you stayed for Christmas dinner.

Lunch to some people, but to us...it's Christmas dinner...at noon." Her pulse raced in triple time as she tried to vocalize her request.

Rusty nodded, his warm smile reaching his eyes. "I'd love to stay. My mother's expecting me for dinner. Actual dinner," he added with a grin.

His teasing comment helped settle her nerves. "What did you want to talk about?" she asked, curiosity getting the better of her. Now who was acting like a kid at Christmas?

"You'll know soon enough." Rusty shot her a wink. "Right now, we need to get this little girl inside." He picked up the carrier and handed it to her. "I just put Hope in the carrier when I got here. Mom put the bow on it since she didn't know if you would have one. I'm thinking Trevor is going to be over the moon."

"That's an understatement."

Rusty picked up a box from the back of the truck. "All set. I've also got a special gift for Trevor."

She'd been right to think the extra gift was for her son. "That's an awfully big box."

"It's a big gift," he teased. "But a well-deserved one. Sort of my way to reward Trevor and apologize to him. I'm hoping you'll approve. Maybe I should have asked you first," he paused on the sidewalk, as if the idea had suddenly occurred to him. "I'm not used to the whole parenting thing, and I never thought how it would impact Trevor if you said no."

Courtney shook her head and grinned. "It's a little late for approval considering he's about to open it anyway." She couldn't imagine anything Rusty would pick out for Trevor would be considered wrong. "What is it?" It's not like it was a horse or a car.

Rusty shifted the box in his arms and then set it on the ground. "It's a saddle. I thought maybe we could revisit his ability to come to Crossroads Creek every now and then for lessons. The kid is a natural and I would love to continue to work with him."

"He didn't get it from me or his father," she teased. It was a generous gift and not one she'd stand in the way of. Not by a long shot. "I know he misses you and the ranch. I've done some thinking about everything, and if you still want to give him lessons, perhaps I could drive Trevor to Crossroads Creek once a month. But I insist on paying for his lessons."

Rusty's left eyebrow shot up, the lines across his forehead deepening. "Oh? Did something happen to change your circumstances?"

Total understatement. "Yes. The insurance money came in. I've found a place in town and I'm hoping to sign documents to buy the place next week. It will serve as a deli and home combo and couldn't have been more perfect for us." It was in that moment, Courtney began to see a light of hope shining down on their future. Everything was coming together exactly as it needed to happen.

Rusty frowned. "I see."

Courtney thought he would be happy for her, but his reaction...wasn't even close. "What's wrong?"

"Nothing. That's great news," he said, forcing a smile to his face.

The man was a terrible liar.

Meow. The little furball reminded her Trevor was waiting inside for his special gift. She couldn't let Rusty's attitude dampen her enthusiasm and joy to give her son a magical gift he would love for years to come. "The saddle is fine, and it's quite generous of you. We should go in," she said, moving toward the house and leaving Rusty to follow.

He set the box down behind the sofa. "I've got one more gift out in the truck. Be right back."

"Trevor," she called out, "it's time for you to open the rest of your gifts." She stood in the doorway to the living room, careful to keep the carrier hidden as her son came into the room from the kitchen. "Take a seat by the tree."

Trevor nodded. "Okay. I love presents."

What kid didn't? But in this case, Rusty was right in suspecting it would be the highlight of Trevor's Christmas. Although Rusty's presence, his gift, and what his gift would mean for Trevor, might hit the Richter scale at the same high level. *Or higher.*

When Rusty came back into the room, she picked up the carrier. "Close your eyes."

"Hold out your hands," Courtney said, as her mom and Rusty moved closer. Placing the carrier in her son's lap, she stepped back. "You can—"

Meow. Meow.

Trevor's eyes flew open.

The kitten had done the announcing for her.

"Hope," he squealed, peering through the mesh fabric. He unzipped the carrier, reached inside, and pulled out the feline furball, hugging Hope to his chest. "I can't believe you got me a kitten. My kitten. Thank you, Mom."

Courtney snapped off pictures and looked to see Rusty equally doing the same. The man was a softie when it came to her son.

"Grandma, this is Hope." Trevor held the kitten up for her mother's inspection. "This is the kitten I kept hoping to get, but Mom wouldn't let me have, cause' you don't like cats. But I reckon since we are moving to our own place soon, she changed her mind. Isn't Hope the prettiest kitten you've ever seen?"

"She's adorable, but I never said I don't like cats. I've simply never had a pet. Not growing up, and then not when I was married." Her mother stood and moved closer to Trevor, kneeling on the floor next to him. "Your grand-father was allergic to cats and dogs because of the fur." She reached out to stroke the kitten's head. "She's so soft. You're a lucky boy, Trevor."

This was all news to Courtney. "I didn't know that's why I couldn't have a pet. But then I stopped asking after the third time I begged and pleaded."

Her mother's smile softened. "Dear, you were six by the third time you begged us and I didn't want you to blame your father."

"Well then. Guess I should have been more persistent," Courtney said, joining the kitten party on the floor.

The kitten jumped off Trevor's lap and move to explore under the tree. Which was a great reminder they needed to open the rest of the presents. Hope needed a cat box. *Stat.*

Courtney handed Trevor the rest of his gifts from under the tree, her son thrilled to have every "cat essential" at his disposal, especially the catnip toys.

Rusty hadn't said much, letting Trevor bask in the moment. But now he stepped forward, moving the large box into view from behind the sofa.

"What's that?" Trevor asked, craning his neck back to look up at Rusty.

"A little something from me to you. But before you open my gift, I want to say I'm sorry for getting so upset when you disobeyed my rules. The truth is, I should have been paying closer attention and then things wouldn't have gotten out of hand. You're an excellent rider and I hope it's not something you let go of as a part of your life."

Trevor pursed his lips and heaved a heavy sigh. "I love riding, but my mom won't—"

"Your mother has changed her mind. I'm sure we can work something out for you to take lessons at least once a month, if that works for you," Rusty said, shooting her a glance for confirmation.

"Really?" her son asked.

Courtney nodded. "Really." She had been wrong when she ran away from Crossroads Creek, thinking more about her own issues, not the effect it would have on Trevor.

Rusty moved the box closer. "And on that note, I think this is something you'll find will come in handy."

Trevor stood next the box and started to remove the wrapping paper and bow. "It's not a horse." He grinned.

"No, definitely not a horse."

Rusty pulled out a jackknife and slid open the tape on the top.

Trevor pulled open the two flaps and peered inside. "A saddle? My very own saddle? This is so cool. Come look, Mom," he squealed, unable to contain his excitement.

Rusty lifted the saddle out of the box as she neared.

Trevor rubbed a hand over the leather. "Look, it's even got my name etched on the side. Thank you so much. This is awesome."

Courtney was pleased Trevor had remembered his manners and all without prompting.

It was a very special gift indeed and was extremely thoughtful.

"I'm glad you like it. I've also got a gift for your mom, and of course, a basket of sweet treats and goodies for your grandmother. Courtesy of my mom," Rusty added, handing the basket to her mother.

"Thank you so much. What a thoughtful present," her mother said, pouring over the contents. She always loved gift baskets, and Mary it would seem, had gone over the top. The basket piled high with cheeses, chocolates, wafers, and fruit, and of course, some homemade cookies.

But it was the part of his remark that confirmed he had also gotten her something that left Courtney feeling slightly adrift. It never occurred to her to get him something as she technically hadn't even known for sure he was coming. *Even if she had suspected as much.*

Rusty stepped toward her. "I'll admit to being more than a little nervous giving you this, but I won't be a coward and run at the first, second, or even third in this case, sign of adversity. So this is from me to you." He held out a blue fabric-covered box.

Now she was more curious than ever. "Thank you for thinking of me." Courtney pulled at one end of the delicate blue bow with silver threads to unravel it and setting it on the coffee table as a keeper. The box was its own wrapper and she gently lifted the top off. Inside was the most beautiful heart-shaped pendant she had ever seen. Diamonds bordered the edge, glistening in the light. "This is gorgeous. I don't know what to say, other than you shouldn't have. And thank you, of course," she said, lifting the breathtaking pendent from the black velvet bed.

"There was no question of whether I should or not. *No regrets* is my new motto," Rusty said, his voice almost solemn. "Turn it over. I had the jeweler add something yesterday."

She looked up at him, noting the strange glimmer in his dark, chocolaty-brown eyes before she focused on the pendant and flipped it over.

My heart. My love.

W.D.

Her brain raced with possibilities, but nothing solid stuck. Was he trying to tell her what she thought he was saying? And if so, how did she feel about it? It's not like it was a ring and he was asking her to marry him, but it certainly looked like a declaration of his feelings.

She glanced up at him, and there Courtney found her answer. *Love.*

Courtney pulled at the fasteners holding the necklace in place to hide her nervousness. Rusty had crept into her own heart in a way she would have never expected again. She held it out to him, letting Rusty have the honors of clasping it around her neck. It also gave her the time she needed to think over his lovely gift and how she felt about the engraving.

"What is it, dear?" her mother asked.

"An exquisite diamond and rose gold pendant." She intentionally left off mention of the inscription on the back, not ready to discuss the possible meaning. The soft sounds of Christmas music played in the background. Brenda Lee's "I Saw Mommy Kissing Santa Claus" reminded her of the almost kiss she and Rusty shared. It was as if his heart was speaking to her heart.

Except Rusty's heart was Greg's heart.

She closed her eyes and tried to rein in her emotions. When she reopened them, her gaze landed on the Christmas tree angel. It was then she realized the truth. *The whole truth.* Rusty's heart was hers for the taking, no matter where he got it, but the fact it was Greg's made it all the more poignant. *Special.*

And not a problem unless she herself made it one.

It was also the explanation to the odd connection she felt when they first met, even though she had tried to deny the feelings. Courtney took a deep breath and turned around to face Rusty. "I love the pendant and will always treasure it." She moved forward to kiss him on the cheek. "Thank you," she said, her voice dropping to a whisper.

Rusty's smile could have lit the state of Louisiana with its intensity, the man looking more than a little relieved. "In that case, I reckon your other gift is in order."

"Another one? This is already enough."

Rusty pulled a small box from his coat pocket. "For you, there is never enough. I've got a long way to go to make things right for us, but I'm hoping this is a step in the right direction. Although in light of what you told me today, I probably shouldn't give you this one, but I will anyway. Just in case you change your mind."

She lifted the lid from the box and pulled out a key attached to a gold-plated keychain. Courtney looked up at him, somewhat confused. She frowned, suddenly worried. "I don't understand."

His chuckle only served to confuse her more. "It's not what you think. Read it."

She picked up the key chain to read the inscription. "Courtney's Deli," she said out loud for the benefit of the others.

"A lot has changed for me in the past few weeks, and most recently, I've had a few epiphanies. Life-changing ones, in fact. I'm planning to stay in Crossroads Creek and I'm not giving up on my dream of the riding school. Clay and I have worked out some arrangements and I'm going to be a foreman at the ranch and take on more responsibilities. And if you come back to town it would give us a chance to make a relationship work and see where it leads. I know Trevor loves it there, and I thought you did also. I know you found a place here, but I'm hoping you'll reconsider. That key is to a place in Crossroads Creek that's available for rent. It would be perfect for your deli...and you did say you haven't signed anything yet, so the choice is yours."

He was right, Trevor did love Crossroads Creek. So did she, for that matter. Except here, she had her independence. But what good was independence if you left behind someone you loved to gain it? Or maybe the answer was to balance both independence and a relationship, the two not exclusive of each other.

Crossroads Creek had come into her life when she was at a crossroads. It was a town where community, family values, and faith were strong. In this case, it would seem x marked the spot where she belonged. With or without Rusty. Although Rusty was a huge bonus where things stood now between them, and she was more than willing to give their relationship a chance.

Courtney's eyes misted over and she brushed away her tears. "I've missed you so much, and so has Trevor. Perhaps all along, this has been God's plan for our lives. I don't need more time to think it over. Yes, we will move to Crossroads Creek."

"Really?" Trevor shouted, flinging himself into her arms for a hug. "This is so cool. Thanks, Mom. This is the best Christmas ever."

"I agree," Rusty said, his broad grin crinkling the corners of his eyes. He took her by the hand and pulled her close. "Thank you for giving us a chance."

Courtney laid a hand on his chest, gazing up at him. She might not have a Christmas gift under the tree for Rusty, but she knew the perfect gift to give him. Convincing him to accept would be the difficult part. "There are, however, a few conditions."

"Oh?" he asked, not daunted in the slightest.

"Yes. The first condition is that I will buy the rental place you found, or I will find another. Either way is fine, but I want to own my business and have the independence that comes with it."

Rusty nodded. "That can be arranged, I'm sure. The guy renting the place was originally looking to sell, but I convinced him otherwise. Reckon I can convince him to go back to the master plan."

"Good. I'm glad that's settled." This was going to work, positive energy bouncing off the walls from all around them.

"What's your second condition?" he asked.

This was the tough part. "That you let me fund the riding school as an investor. You said you were looking for sponsors, but I want to do more than just sponsor. I totally believe in you and you deserve this opportunity." Courtney held her breath, hoping he would agree. It wasn't a deal breaker, but she wasn't against making it seem like one.

"No." Rusty's answer was short and to the point and brooked no opposition.

Except he hadn't faced off with her before when it came to getting her way. *Until now, that is.* "Not so fast, mister. You need to consider all the facts. Put your pride away and listen up. When I first showed up in town, you doled out money to help me. And I might add, argued with me when I found out, claiming your actions were out of love and kindness—and not charity. You had a deep-seated need to help someone."

Rusty shook his head. "And you ripped up my check."

"Only the second one," she defended.

"But you planned to pay back the first. Let's not sugarcoat this," he said. "You didn't like it then any more than I do now."

"True. But then you also paid for my truck repairs, again, not out of charity, but a deep-rooted desire to help me. That's all I'm offering you here. Money I can afford to invest and give to someone I care deeply about and want to help. It's not charity. It's my Christmas gift to you, but more importantly, it's love," she added, hoping the last word would make an impact.

His expression altered, his eyes shining brightly as he ran a hand through his hair. Rusty nodded and let out a deep breath. "I see. Love," he repeated the word, testing it out loud.

"Love." Courtney wanted him to get her meaning loud and clear, hoping to get him to agree. It was important Rusty understand they were partners in any relationship they shared together moving forward.

He glanced down at Trevor and then back at her. "Okay."

One simple word with a wealth of meaning. "Really? You mean it?" she asked, unable to believe he agreed. There were no certainties in the future, but this was a relationship she was willing to surrender her heart to for a second time, trusting in God's plan for her life. How else would any of this had been possible?

"I mean it," he said, lowering his head to kiss her. "Because I love you, too."

Soft, sweet, and gentle. In other words, the perfect Christmas kiss in front of her son and her mother. *And one Courtney would remember forever.*

Epilogue

♥

COURTNEY WAS RACING AROUND the place, little last-minute fixes on her must-do list. Moving a vase on a table. Straightening the artwork on the wall. Cleaning the glass on the deli case for the hundredth time making sure no fingerprints marred the surface. "I am. Just nervous. This is a dream come true."***

Rusty grinned and moved to stand next to her. "I had total faith you would make it happen. The place looks great," he said, dropping a kiss on her lips.

"Well, it happened in no small part to you. I can't thank you enough for your countless hours of help. You and your family have been an incredible blessing as Trevor and I settled into Crossroads Creek."

The months had flown by, the two of them spending most of their time working on their futures, all while juggling the demands of current life. *Their life together.* Courtney had found a house to rent not far from Laura Goodman's place, and Trevor loved the attention of a third "grandmother" figure in his life. "Of course, I helped. Just like you believed in me and made it possible for me to buy a ranch and get the riding school program up and running, I believed in you."

"It's called love," she said, her eyes shining bright with the emotion.

"I like the sound of that. A lot." Their life together had settled into a family routine. *Almost anyway.* Now Rusty was more than ready to make the "almost" a reality.

"It's time," she said, glancing up at the clock on the wall.

"It certainly is. You have a fantastic crowd outside waiting to check out the new deli in town. You'll have more than enough to keep busy for hours, so just let me say this while I have the chance. Congratulations." He moved a curtain aside next to the sink and pulled out a bouquet of bright and colorful summer flowers, handing them to her and dropping another kiss on her mouth.

Courtney smiled up at him and placed her hand in his. "Thank you. These are lovely." She leaned forward and inhaled the sweet fragrance that filled the air.

"Not as lovely as you, but they were the best I could find in town." Rusty chuckled. "Now let's get this deli officially opened."

"Yes, boss," she quipped, an extra bounce in her step as she made her way to the front door.

"I like the sound of that, but I also know it will never happen. Equals...yes. But I reckon that's how any good relationship should be."

"So true," she said, turning the key in the lock.

The two of them stepped outside. Trevor stood nearby with Rusty's family. Everyone was in for a big surprise, all except Trevor, that is. There was no way Rusty would take this next step he had planned without the kid's permission. He needn't have worried though, as

Trevor was all for his mother getting remarried.

Now the only question that remained was...did she?

He was positive he knew the answer, but until she said yes, he wouldn't bank on it as a done deal. The crowd quieted when he held up his hands. "Welcome to the grand opening of Courtney's Deli. We appreciate you showing up for the occasion, and hope you brought your appetites." He chuckled. "Before Courtney officially cuts the ribbon, there's some other official business I need to attend to as well."

He turned to Courtney and dropped to one knee, adrenaline kicking in. Partly excitement. Partly nerves. This was his big moment. A moment that hopefully for years to come, they would remember with joy. "Courtney Winters, I love you with all of my heart and I want nothing more than for me, you, and Trevor to become a real family. The past six months have brought me the greatest happiness in my life. The ranch. The riding school. But mostly you and Trevor. Would you do me the great honor of becoming my wife?"

Tears coursed down Courtney's face, but clearly tears of joy judging by the smile that wreathed her face. Rusty let out a deep sigh of relief, more confident now of the ending even though she had yet to speak.

Courtney brushed her tears away and nodded. He stood as she flung herself into his arms, almost knocking them both over.

"Say yes, Mom," Trevor yelled as he moved forward. "You gotta make it official and say yes."

Courtney looked at her son and laughed. She turned back to Rusty, love shining in her eyes. "Yes. Yes, I'll marry you, and yes, we'll be a family. I love you so much."

Rusty swung Trevor up into his arms and the three shared a group hug for all to witness, the crowd clapping and cheering in excitement. Unable to resist, he kissed his beautiful fiancé again, and another wave of cheers erupted.

Turning to face the crowd, Rusty knew it was time for Courtney to shine in another moment of glory. *Her own moment*. He held Courtney's hand up in the air. "And now, the love of my life would like to share her dream with you." He pulled a pair of scissors from his back pocket and handed them to her.

Courtney stepped closer to the yellow ribbon. "Thank you all for coming today, and for the well-wishes. Courtney's Deli started out as a crazy idea, but it was one that started right here in Crossroads Creek at the community center. It's only fitting that now, as a reality, that the deli open here in town. Thank you for all the encouragement and support. And yes, I'll still make time to cook for Wednesday nights, so never fear that Rusty will take over," she teased.

A ripple of laughter echoed through the crowd. Courtney cut the ribbon, everyone clapping, cheering, and calling out their congratulations.

She waved and stepped back, turning toward Rusty. "Time for me to get to work. I'll see you both later tonight, and then we can have a double celebration."

"Sounds perfect," Rusty said, kissing her again. It was something he would never grow tired of, not in forever. "Trevor and I need to practice some more for the rodeo. I think he's going to do awesome in the goat roping event."

"I couldn't agree more, especially with you as his coach," Courtney said, before heading inside, the customers already filing in.

Six months ago when he stopped by the side of the road to help a stranded woman, he had no idea how much his life would change. From lost and lonely, Rusty's heart was now full of life ...and love.

Proof that anything was possible if you keep faith in God and let him guide your destiny.

What to Read Next?

The Help of a Cowboy
The Return of a Cowboy

***

If you enjoyed this sweet and charming romance, be sure to check out the
ALSO BY ELSIE DAVIS section on the next page for more clean and wholesome romance.

BONUS READ

Want to keep in touch with new releases and what's happening in the world of Elsie Davis? Sign up for the monthly newsletter at Elsie Davis HEA (Happily-Ever-After) and enjoy DIGGING THE DRIVER (A Celebrity Corgi Romance) as a FREE BOOK!

The greatest compliment you could give an author is to leave a review in order to help other readers discover the same great stories you enjoyed. Amazon/Bookbub/Goodreads are all great places. Many thanks!!!
Another great way to keep in touch - *Follow Elsie Davis on FaceBook*

Also By Elsie Davis

♥

Sweet, Clean and Wholesome Stories...with a Happily-Ever-After Guarantee!

Holidays in Hallbrook
(Sweet Romance Series for Holidays Throughout the Year)
Welcome to Hallbrook, New Hampshire. A small-town filled with the unexpected, lots of love, and of course, a beloved dog to ramp up the excitement.
Love & Order (Labor Day)
Love & Family (Thanksgiving)
Love & Peace (Christmas)
Love & Chocolate (Valentine's Day)

Love & Hope (Mother's Day)
Love & Liberty (Independence Day)
Love & Honor (Veteran's Day)
Love & Joy (Easter)
Love & Adventure (Father's Day)

Great Smoky Mountain Getaways
(Christian Inspirational – Women's Fiction Romances)
Juliet's Journey to Love
Poppy's Path to Love
Rachel's Road to Love

Crossroads Creek Cowboys
(Christian Inspirational Romances)
The Heart of a Cowboy
The Help of a Cowboy
The Return of a Cowboy
Coming Soon – The Care of a Cowboy

Crestfield Inn Romances

If you like special kinds of soulmates, a splash of the supernatural, and wholesome relationships, you'll adore this sweet bit of fun filled with romance and mystery.
Turning Back Time
Turning Up Roses
Turning Down Pie

Celebrity Corgi Romance
(Standalone Sweet Romance)
If you like light mystery mixed in with your happily-ever-after, you'll enjoy this second-chance romance and the race to save an adorable Corgi.
Digging the Driver

Gold Coast Retrievers
(Sweet Romance)
Special Golden Retrievers help their humans solve mysteries, save lives, and even find love...
Defending Dakota

Trinity River
(Sweet Western Romance)
Ranchers and farmers depend on the Trinity River for water, but when a secret conglomerate starts buying up property by fair means or foul, it's time for the landowners of Tumble County to fight back—Texas style. But what they don't count on, is finding love in the process.
Back in the Rancher's Arms
Small Town, Big Secrets

Coming Soon! (2023-2024)

Sundancer's Legacy – 9 Book series

Sundancer's Star
Sundancer's Joy
Sundancer's Heart
Sundancer's Majesty
Sundancer's Miracle

Sundancer's Glory
Sundancer's Kiss
Sundancer's Moon
Sundancer's Splendor

About The Author

♥

Elsie Davis is a *USA Today and International Bestselling Author* of over 25 sweet, clean, and wholesome romances. She discovered the world of Happily-Ever-After romance at the age of twelve when she began avidly reading Barbara Cartland, the Queen of Romance, and has been hooked ever since. After building her dream log home on top of a small mountain, she turned her attention to do what she loves most, writing. Elsie writes Contemporary Romance and Contemporary Christian Romance from her heart, hoping to share a little love in a big world.

When she's not writing, she can be found birding, kayaking, camping, fishing, playing disc golf, and taking nature walks—hoping to spot wildlife. Basically, she loves all things out-doors, EXCEPT cold weather. She and her husband are avid Caribbean cruisers, but Elsie's favorite vacation was their cruise to Alaska. (In spite of the cold!) Indoors, she enjoys a toasty fire, and of course, a great romance with a guaranteed Happily-Ever-After.

https://www.elsiedavishea.com